A Garden of Bones

About the author

Andy Done-Johnson was born and grew up in Derbyshire and studied at The University of Hull. After a stint as a largely out-of-work actor and barman in London, he returned to Derbyshire where he stumbled into journalism, got married and had a son, who is now a grown-up. Aside from writing, he loves books, walking, exercise, travel, history, art and dogs. He has worked as a print and online journalist for 20 years, largely in the Midlands. In 2013 he broke the Wycherley Murders. This is his 'version of events'.

A Garden of Bones

Blood runs thicker . . .

ANDY DONE-JOHNSON

A true crime novel

Cover Design - Liam Relph
Book Design - Andrew Tennant

ISBN 978-1-9163765-1-9 (print)
ISBN 978-1-9163765-0-2 (e-book)

andydonejohnson.com

To Paddy, who sat at my side while I wrote the bugger.
You are missed, my friend.

Chapter 1

The remains of two people, who have yet to be formally identified, were unearthed by police in the back garden of a house in Blenheim Close, Forest Town – unattributed article *Mansfield Chad, Friday October 11, 2013.*

Midges buzz in the glare of the spotlights as the night rolls in. The bulbs fizz, exposing the sombre drizzle that is coming down, almost forgotten in the gloomy, autumn darkness.

A domestic murder.

It makes a change.

For once it's not some kid on a corner, taking a pop at another kid riding past on a BMX with a few hundred quid's worth of heroin wraps in his pocket.

It's not some lowlife holding up an off-license to pay off a drugs debt to a crew in another part of town.

It's not an innocent shop-keeper taking one in the chest, or some big-time crack dealer, plugged in the back of the head by a rival . . . or more likely plugged on his command.

No.

But this is murder.

This is old-school murder.

This is twitching kitchen curtains, whispers in the pension queue, and shifty looks from the locals.

This isn't Agatha Christie in a 1960s suburb of brick boxes.

There are no fictional detectives here . . . only Rawlins.

Detective Inspector Tony Rawlins.

No laboured Belgian accent, no second rate Oxford degree and a drink problem, no morbid Scandinavian with a troubled love-life.

Just a copper.

Just a case.

This case.

His case.

They work in silence, Rawlin's crew.

The only sounds are the scraping of the digger's blade on the unyielding earth, the heavy thud of the engine, and the occasional order barked by the archaeologist, a stork-like figure in a white forensic suit, who is directing its work.

He motions it backwards again, then steps forward and painstakingly smooths away another half-inch of top soil, as if he's restoring a Renaissance masterpiece. Then the digger goes back in, and the process repeats, and repeats.

It had started with a couple of burly probationers with a shovel apiece, but the earth wouldn't give and the archaeologist said they may damage the site. So they'd gone and got a digger, the woeful drizzle not heavy enough to soften the ground.

Another layer comes away, and another. They are maybe a foot down now, and they've been here forever.

Rawlins stands away by the fence, listening to the faint tap, tap, tapping on the gazebo roof he is standing under.

It's been mild, but it's getting dark now and the cold is coming in. He shivers a little. He's been here a while.

His gov'nor, Detective Chief Inspector Rob Griffin, stands further into the darkness of the tent, fielding an almost endless stream of calls to his mobile, saying little in between.

Rawlins is a career copper – law graduate with a passion for criminal law. He went in with the rank and file, and he was still an inspector by the time he was thirty. He has spent a lot of time waiting at crime scenes. He has learnt to be patient.

The historical ones are the worst, like a jigsaw of missing pieces.

James Brodie, dead under a field in Lincolnshire or fed to the pigs. Chief suspect in the murder of Nottingham jeweler Marian Bates.

He had entered the Time Centre in the outlying suburb of Arnold along with two accomplices.

He had been working for the Gunn brothers – Colin and David – who had ordered the raid to recoup on some drugs bust losses, it is believed.

They had ordered no shooting, no violence . . . just in and out, softly softly.

Only Brodie had panicked when he saw Marian's daughter talking on the phone, and Mrs Bates had stepped into the bullet intended for her.

Brodie had fled on a moped, and was never seen again.

Everyone knew the Gunns were behind both the murder and Brodie's disappearance. Only they'd never proved it. Never found Brodie's body.

And years after Colin Gunn was sentenced to a 30-year stretch for another murder and his cartel had collapsed, Rawlins was still looking for Brodie . . . digging for bones in the dark.

Historical cases.

You could keep them.

As the light goes, there is a fizz and a clunk as more spot-lights are turned on, instantly transforming the tiny patch of back garden into a dank summer's day. The work goes on. The digger takes away another layer, then retreats. The archaeologist goes back in, kneels down and scrapes away more earth – the knees of his white forensic suit are stained green and brown.

Rawlins looks beyond the lights, into the blackness through the glare and the heavy mist, at the sickly yellow street lamps just flickering to life and the banks of box semi's standing proud on the high ground beyond, set way back on the other side of the road.

Blenheim Close, Forest Town, Mansfield.

Number Two.

It's about a mile outside the town centre – one of those estates they threw up in the late 1960s to deal with the housing shortage, back in the days when they still built cheap houses to deal with the housing shortage.

Square boxes – thin walls with pocket handkerchief gardens, enough for a table and a couple of deck chairs.

There's a high wooden fence to one side – six feet maybe, with the main road on the other side, beyond a pavement and an untended patch of grass. Blenheim Close is a

cul-de-sac, and Number Two is right on the corner –
Number Two, where they are now.

The main road and the high fence hide the garden on
one side – the houses beyond are a good eighty metres
away – higher, separate.

There is a house opposite on the cul-de-sac, some deaf
and grumpy old dear living there.

Number Two is joined by a dividing wall on the other
side to an identical box. At the back it is separated by
another fence, only lower, with an identical square of grass
on the other side.

At the bottom stands a scrawny hedge, and beyond that
you can see three properties, all identical to Number Two.
They overlook the garden, but they are a long way back,
further than the ones across the main road.

A community that doesn't speak, thinks Rawlins. A
community that twitches at curtains in the daylight, and
yet sees nothing, hears nothing.

The digger draws back again and falls silent. The archaeologist goes in once more, kneels down and scrapes away at
the ground; the earth he removes is bagged up and filtered
by a scene-of-crime team, thus far with nothing else to do.

Rawlins watches as the archaeologist gets back to his feet,
shakes his head and waves the digger back into action, stepping away as its thick diesel engines gun back to life with a
plume of filthy black smoke, rubbing at the shit on his knees
again. It chugs back in, and delicately scrapes again.

They hadn't rushed in. They had bided their time after
the phone call – waiting for the right moment. No blue
lights. No speeding cars. No need.

It would be a long job – at least three days in the garden alone.

The cadaver dogs had gone in first, slinking low around the lawn, one cocking its leg and pissing on the grass. They'd weaved around, hunting, skulking, sniffing; then almost in unison they'd honed in on a patch of ground just outside the patio door. They'd whined and barked, scraping at the soil.

They'd done door-to-door – a neighbour at the back saying that he remembered a young man digging a big hole there over a decade ago, joked to his wife that 'he was burying the old buggers in the back garden'.

He'd laughed, without appreciating the irony.

Then they'd done ground scans – an x-ray penetrating the earth down to 30 metres in ideal conditions, a square-metre at a time.

"This looks like a grave," the archaeologist had said when they'd viewed the scans of the ground outside the patio doors.

"There's something buried down there. Could be anything. Could be a dog."

Rawlins thinks differently. Rawlins knows what's down there. Copper's hunch, perhaps.

They'd come in mob-handed. Vans, flat-foots fanning out, thumping on doors.

He'd given the speech.

Working in the area. There might be noise, There might be light. There might be 'comings and goings'. Police investigation. We're looking into a historical murder. House on the corner. You might see vans. You might see lights. You might see us in the neighbourhood.

Don't be alarmed.

Don't be concerned.

And don't call the newspapers.

Don't tell the press because we're digging up two bodies which have been in the ground for at least fifteen years, remains that will probably be skeletal at best, and we really don't want them photographed as we load them into the back of a van.

The place is quiet, the place is calm. Rawlins tips the dregs of his long-forgotten coffee onto the ground. He looks at the apathetic midges, fluttering at the glaring lights.

He yawns, folds his arms and heavily stamps his feet.

It had all started with a phone call – an old dear called Elizabeth Edwards had contacted the Met to say her stepson Chris had been in touch.

Chris had vanished a year ago. He'd borrowed ten grand from his employers and just disappeared.

But he'd called her, she'd said, out of the blue. He was in France with Susan.

But that's not all. There are bodies. Two bodies, buried in the back garden of a house in Mansfield.

So the call-handler had made a note, then made a call to Nottinghamshire Police. A divisional detective constable had made initial enquiries, passed it onto his sergeant, who'd passed it onto his inspector.

When the inspector too thought he might be out of his depth – that there quite possibly could be two bodies buried beneath a garden on his turf, right under his nose in fact, he had called Griffin.

In reality, he had called the East Midlands Major Crime Unit, and Griffin happened to be the senior officer on call. Then Rawlins had got the call.

He'd taken the full briefing and set up an initial incident room at Mansfield Police Station, where they'd started to build the necessary operation. Scene of crime had been called, dogs unit was informed, calls went in to scientists, archaeologists, the coroner. A Home Office Pathologist was put on standby, as was a histopathologist. A formal request was made to division for more resources; grudgingly approved.

The Superintendent needed briefing, who would then brief the chief super, who would then brief the assistant chief constable, who would brief the chief.

Uniforms needed to be provided for the initial door-to-door, to preserve the scene, to talk to the neighbours. Rawlins would bring his own team in, with divisional CID doing some of the donkey work.

They had run an initial proof of life check, which had come back negative. They'd spoken to the CPS, they'd got warrants in place to search.

He'd sent out a detective constable with a uniform to make the initial approach to the current occupiers – lady in her 40s called Sue Bramley and her teenage daughter. Just rented the house from the current owner. In no way connected.

Tell them the bare bones, get them to pack an overnight bag, and get them into a hotel for the night – a few nights, ideally.

Then the uniforms had gone in, secured the site and made it ready for the scene of crime teams, and the forensic archaeologist.

They'd visited the immediate neighbours first, then fanned out to the rest of the close, the houses opposite and the streets around.

Just keep it to the point.

CID would then follow-up with routine questioning as the day wore on into night and through the following day, and the day after that if necessary.

A forensic tent was erected. Not over the burial site, not yet. It would get in the way of the digger, so it's been erected closer to the main road-side of the garden – to block the view from higher ground, and to stand under if it rains.

It rains.

Later now, and the digger's tracks are tearing steady, uneven strips of moistened sod, softened and made slippery by the steady drizzle. After that it's agonisingly slow work, but an inch at a time it goes down, and down – two abandoned shovels propped up against the fence.

As the darkness comes in and the lights pop on, Rawlins relaxes a bit – confident that their work has gone largely undetected for now.

The regional press is toothless these days – just a machine for cranking out drivel about things that nobody wants to read, about people cycling to Skegness for charity, or consultations the council is doing, bought out of habit by an ever-dwindling following of snowy-haired, shuffling readers – although there are still a couple of old dinosaurs up there on the local rag that can make a bloody nuisance of themselves.

Rawlins is not from Mansfield – although he's done his time in the area on his way up the ladder – David 'Drakey'

Draycott, shot dead on his own drive over a drugs debt to the Dawes crew – north Nottinghamshire's equivalent of the Gunns.

Bride killer Terry Rodgers, from Huthwaite, in neighbouring Ashfield, who had shot dead his newlywed daughter days after she returned from honeymoon; found accidentally in woodland while the uniforms were looking for somebody else.

Rawlins had worked them – always with Griffin as his immediate superior, climbing the ranks at a similar speed, Griffin always a a step further up.

Murders didn't happen as much up here as they did in the city, although when they did you remembered them.

But since the Dawes family had been winged – after kingpin John Dawes got 24 years for drug trafficking – the Mansfield area had returned to its stable of petty crime and drunken domestic violence, most murders now were a wife-beating gone too far.

It's a town of urban decay, Mansfield.

Once prosperous, it is decrepit and down-trodden now – its town centre a mish-mash of charity shops, bookies, bargain booze stores and boarded-up windows.

It's had 150 years of getting the shit kicked out of it – first by the mine owners, then by the Tories back in the 1980s.

It's never really recovered – although it was on its way downwards by then anyway.

Its young people look to the brighter lights of Nottingham or London; it's the sort of town you grow up wanting to leave, and those with sense or ability do.

It's a town of weekend binge drinking, of idiots fighting with door staff, vomit-splattered pavements and unromantic couplings down its darker alleyways – pissed girls impregnated over wheelie bins.

It's a town with a spiraling drugs problem, and all the knock-ons a drug problem causes – dealing, shoplifting, flogging stolen meat around the pubs. Homelessness. The occasional dead addict.

It's a town that's poor. The people drink, and they drink too much. The magistrates court is full of husbands who have got too pissed, gone home and beat up on the wife, although increasingly it's the other way round as well.

Drunken idiots fighting with the police, or each other; kicked-in bus shelters; racially abused takeaway owners; family pets set on by pitbull-crosses – followed by threats and assaults if they contact the authorities.

It's a town that's really taken a hiding – a terminal beating; a place rasping its final laboured breaths, or so Rawlins thinks.

It's a town that keeps a copper very busy – at a time when resources are rapidly diminishing.

It's a town that needs hope.

Rawlins had driven up from force headquarters Sherwood Lodge, a compound masked in leafy woodland about nine miles south of Mansfield, five miles north of Nottingham. He'd been briefing Griffin, who would brief the command team, and had been itching to get away. Griffin would follow on later.

He'd driven past the gates to Newstead Abbey, where Lord Byron had grown up, and a sign that told him he was now entering Sherwood Forest.

Not that you'd have known – as the delicate and rolling hills, spotted with woodland, soon give way to sprawling estates, wind turbines and a smattering of out-of-town retail parks.

Then he'd reached the town centre, encircled by an ugly but functional ring road, the statue of a miner standing forgotten to its side.

Mansfield Police Station is just out of town, and he'd pulled in there first to get a full briefing on developments before heading to the scene, to Blenheim Close.

House has been vacated by the occupants, scene is secure, uniforms are in the process of informing neighbours. SOCOs en route. Dogs en route. Archaeologist is delayed, but on-route now. Coroner has been informed. Still waiting for confirmation for the pathologist, but should be in the post.

Then he'd driven to the scene, stopping to buy a packet sandwich, which he'd eaten in the car, brushing the crumbs from his functual suit onto the floor.

Then he'd called the girlfriend.

It's one of those. See you in a few days. Sorry.

As he'd approached there'd been a kind of bustle in the air, or was it just in his head? There were two uniforms standing at the end of the close, a solitary streamer of police tape connecting them, fluttering in the mild wind, like they were about to start skipping.

They looked bored already and it was only early afternoon.

Way to go yet, lads. Shoulders back, chests out.

He wheeled down his driver's window and flashes a warrant card.

"DI Rawlins. East Midlands Major Crime."

Then the tape had been clumsily gathered aside, and Rawlins had parked on the close a few houses down, grimacing when his tyres had whistled along the unforgiving, concrete pavement edges and his car had brushed to an undignified stop.

He'd climbed out, clicked it locked with the press of his key and a deep metallic clunk, then he'd made his way up to Number Two, shrugging on an overcoat that he didn't really need.

There'd been a lot going on and he hadn't fancied their chances of keeping it quiet. He'd spotted a dozen high-vis' jackets, neighbours standing on their front lawns, arms folded, chatting, shaking their heads.

Others had looked through windows, some blatantly, some twitching at net curtains. There were police vehicles parked at the bottom of the cul-de-sac, more pulling up on the main road as Rawlins thrust his keys into his pocket and fumbled for his phone.

No way we're keeping this quiet. No fucking way.

There'd been another uniform standing at the edge of the drive, guarding a SOCO van with its rear doors left open. People in white suits, coming and going silently, delicately carrying bundles of kit.

Another copper stood at the shabby wooden side gate, holding it open so they could come and go.

Rawlins had gone round the back to a hive of activity, although little was being done. He'd seen his DS, watching the stream of SOCOs, talking on his phone and speaking to a recently-arrived DC at the same time.

He'd seen Rawlins and raised a hand, ending the call abruptly.

"Archaeologist's on his way," he'd said, by way of a greeting. "He was giving a lecture. Sorry."

They were stuck. Too big a job to begin without the archaeologist. Nothing much for the forensics lot to do now. Crime scene manager had done his job, but without the archaeologist they were scuppered. No blood. No fingerprints to dab for. If anyone had died here, they'd done it a long time ago.

"Bloke round the back reckons he saw some chap, couldn't remember his name, digging a big bloody hole on the lawn."

"Yeah?"

"We're getting a statement. Says it was one Sunday morning, ten or fifteen years ago. Little bloke, up to his waist in a deep hole, puffing and sweating in the sunshine."

"Good memory," Rawlins had replied, stepping backwards to let a uniformed constable go past.

"Fucker's a PCSO as well. Inspector fucking Morse. Shame he didn't call it in at the time."

Rawlins laughed, despite himself.

He'd wandered into the house, carefully wiping his feet on the bedraggled mat before going inside. He'd shrugged off his unseasonably heavy coat and hung it on the back of an open door, wiping a bead of sweat from his brow.

Scene of Crime were fluttering about, although fewer in here. The house wasn't a sterile environment. But they were not scanning for recent evidence. The primary crime scene was outside.

They'd get round to it, when they knew what secrets the earth held – but there was 15 years of fresh paint and paper over anything that might have happened.

Rawlins phone had rung.

"DI Rawlins," he'd answered, almost robotically.

"They've tracked down the home-owner", a voice had told him.

"He bought it in 2005. Been empty for years. Furniture had just been left, carpets and everything – apart from the ones in the front bedroom upstairs, which had been ripped down to underlay. Said it looked like someone had been living there until the week before.

They could still have been living there, if all the drawers hadn't been empty – if all the paperwork hadn't been stripped out. There was still the odd book lying around, but not a single gas bill.

Rawlins sits back in the kitchen now, propped on a stool and drinking the dregs of another coffee he can't even taste anymore – just sipping it out of habit, or for something to do, to mark the time passing. It is late now . . . or early.

The spotlights outside are being dimmed by the faint light of the next day. Is the digger still going? He can't hear it anymore.

He's been at Blenheim for half a day, a night, a day, and most of a night now; and apart from a few hours shuteye in the car, or taking endless calls on his phone, which is currently charging on the side, he has been graveside throughout.

He sets down his mug and rubs heavily at his eyes, listening out beyond the birdsong and other sounds of a waking world, and he can hear nothing more than the buzz of a passing moped.

The engine has stopped.

He sits in frozen silence for a second or an eternity before he hears the slap of heavy boots on the concrete path outside and the kitchen door juddering open.

"Sir! You're wanted outside."

Rawlins slops out into the breaking dawn, stretching out the aches in his legs and arms, like he's been sat in a car for too long.

The drizzle has desisted, but mist sits heavy over the lawn.

"I've started to detect some give in the soil," the archaeologist tells him. "I'm going to have to proceed manually now."

"Are we close?"

"Yes," he replies, "but it's going to take a while."

The ground scan, when it came, had arrived in two parts, the top half of the burial site captured in the first, the bottom half, nearer the patio door, followed it.

The grave is about a metre deep, maybe a little more, and it's a very big hole, according to the scan – certainly no unmourned family pet.

But that had been a night and a day ago . . . a night and a day and a night . . . and now Rawlins was back on the lawn.

He'd watched for hours now, as the archaeologist endlessly reaches a gangly arm into the trench, meticulously scraping away at the soil with a small trowel – which reminded Rawlins of an oil painter's pallet knife.

Each time an inch of soil is coaxed into the bucket it is taken away, its contents carefully sieved, examined and moved aside, before the receptacle is returned again to the archaeologist's already outstretched hand.

Rawlins watches, frozen now, until the spotlights are finally clunked off with the fizzle of the dying street lamps for the second night, and the morning arrives with the blur of early autumn sunshine as it briefly peaks over the rooftops.

"How much longer?"

"Getting nearer. Half a day, if we're lucky."

Rawlins has a meeting with the local beat inspector but it's not until 9am and it's now only a little after 7.

But he suddenly needs to get away; to see something that isn't that box house, that square patch of ground, that hole, that tent.

"I'm on my phone," he shouts, aiming for the side gate and collecting it from the kitchen.

There's the stink of grease and body odor, the flickering and buzzing of electric lights and the occasional flash as the fly-killer is activated.

There are murmured conversations, steam, and the snapping of red-top newspapers as pages are lazily turned.

A greasy-spoon cafe on the outskirts of town.

Shift workers, gorging on trans-fats on their way to work, or their way home.

A decade ago the place would have stunk of fags as well.

Outside, a procession of stressed mums dragging hesitant children to school, the early morning waifs and strays, and shop workers on their way to another day of monotony and ringing tills.

Rawlins calls the comms office. No answer – he's forgotten they start at 9am these days, not 6.30.

Daily papers don't have first editions anymore; lucky if they have more than one edition full stop.

So he calls the control room and asks the inspector to get them to ring him, whoever is on call; if they *have* anyone on call anymore.

He finishes his breakfast and sits, sipping at the bottle of orange juice he wishes he'd substituted for another coffee.

Eventually his phone – left on the formica table with dirty plates, screwed up serviettes, ketchup and abandoned newspapers – begins to vibrate.

"DI Rawlins."

He goes outside, breathing in car fumes from the main road, shouting above the impatient, strumming engines and a gaggle of radio stations which blurt from partially-opened car windows.

"Just a second," he says, walking to a sodden grass verge, surrounded by a low hedge, scorched grey by carbon monoxide.

Rawlins plonks on a bench with a slat missing, initials etched into the peeling paint, and a McFlurry container abandoned in the corner.

On-call press officer getting back to him, sounding blurry and almost asleep.

They'd been briefed the day before, but told to hold back.

Possible extraction of human remains, nothing much known, still waiting for the full transcript of the tip-off. Likely historical. Not a cause of concern for the general public. Nothing to worry about.

"Forensic exhumation is probably close to completion," he says, "although SOCOs will be at the property for a number of days yet. Need to do the insides – not that we'll find anything.

"No, we don't want to say anything . . . Yes, yes I know there's a sodding great forensic tent in the back garden . . . Well, have you had any calls?"

They agree a holding statement, should anybody ask.

We are responding to intelligence that leads us to believe that there may be human remains in the back garden of a house in Mansfield. . . . No, no don't give them the bloody street name, Christ! . . . We are currently working to establish whether this is the case. No cause for concern. Don't be alarmed. Stay away, bugger off, and leave us alone to do our job.

But only if anyone asks.

Rawlins is no journalist, but he's worked on enough big murders over the years, and he's seen them descend like jackals with the scent of blood after an injured fawn, getting in the way, taking over neighbourhoods, manipulating people and speaking to witnesses before his lads have had the chance.

The local hacks are a bloody nuisance sometimes, but there's a bit of grudging respect both ways. You sort of need each other.

No, it's when the national pack descend that communities get turned over.

It's nothing to them.

They've seen it all before, coming in trampling all over an investigation, then vanishing as soon as something better comes alone.

And they'll be coming. They'll be coming soon.

Next up it's the Local Area Commander – the beat inspector who deals with all the day-to-day shit.

Good copper. Solid. Cares about the patch and the people. Likes it quiet, calm – doesn't like dead bodies being dug up under his nose. And he's in a grump because half his strength is currently in the streets around Blenheim Close – utterly buggered if anything kicks off anywhere else.

For him it's all about reassuring the community. Round here they're prone to be a bit hysterical, a bit sensationalist. He wants it made clear, if it proves accurate, when the balloon goes up, that this is a historical case.

Otherwise they'll be rioting because they'll think a serial killer's on the loose.

They agree a strategy. In the short-term they will only release statements regarding the investigation through the press office. Nobody talking to camera about what may be in the ground.

Hopefully be in and out before anyone gets wind.

The inspector will speak to the media, if and when the time comes, but his message will be one of calm.

Nothing to worry about. Historical case. No need to panic. Carry on as you were.

In reality, the inspector will eventually give that press conference about six hours later – and he'll not be saying anything the assembled hacks want to hear.

They want bodies in back gardens, black-clad figures stalking in dark alleys, slashing and gutting the ladies of the night.

The press attend as an afterthought, as an inconvenience.

Most of them are just killing time, getting a bit of colour until the next new line – so they can charge off again, invading other people's lives.

Rawlins just wants the bodies gone, out and off to the morgue before the jackals arrive.

He heads to the HOLMES room they've set up at Mansfield nick – HOLMES.

Officially it stands for Home Office Larger Major Enquiry System, although everyone knows it's called that because they couldn't think up an acronym that spelled SHERLOCK.

Rawlins sits down and reads Elizabeth Edwards' statement in full.

In reality there are two.

The first is a transcript of the full conversation between Mrs Edwards and the Met' Police call handler – along with a slender bundle of supporting documents.

The second is a longer transcript, taken from the recorded interview between the divisional DI and Mrs Edwards.

The first is initially about Chris getting in touch; how he had gone missing, how he told Mrs Edwards he was in France. Then comes a disclosure, a claim that there were bodies at a house in Mansfield.

She can't remember the address but she gives the names of the people that had lived there, Chris's parents-in-law.

It gives them enough to track down the house.

Rawlins scan-reads the second transcript – gone missing . . . all really worried . . . not like Chris . . . just happy he'd finally got in touch.

But then he started telling her things, things about the house, things about the bodies, and she'd just had to tell somebody.

She had slept on it, she admitted, or tried to sleep. But she'd lain awake all night with the worry, and in the end she'd had to call. Those poor people, she had said. Those poor, poor people.

Rawlins scans forwards, until a paragraph catches his eye.

Chris was always useless with money. I'd helped him over and over, trying to sort out his finances, helping him with repayment agreements, even acting as a guarantor on a few.

But he'd always ended up back in the red, buying rubbish, things he didn't need – things neither of them needed.

What things?

All sorts, she had replied. Old books, medals, military stuff. Paid a fortune for it. Winston Churchill they liked – him and Susan. Winston Churchill and Charles De Gaulle. After that it was film stars. Old film stars. Pictures of them, signed photographs. Dozens of them. Then they'd get sold to pay off debts, for a pittance of what they'd forked out for them.

They'd sell them all off and get sorted. Then they'd be at it again.

And what else where they interested in?

Guns, she replied. Christopher liked shooting guns – until they banned them when those kiddies got shot in Scotland. He used to go to a club.

Christopher Edwards, it appeared was a bit of a disappointment to his family. They were all academics, university types. And Chris just had no interest. He'd held down a job as a credit controller for a company called Hallmark – not the people who made cards. He'd lived in that horrible little flat in Dagenham for years, hiding himself away with that shrewish wife of his, never seeing a soul.

And did Chris tell you why he did it?

Oh no! No! Chris didn't do it. It was all some awful accident. That's what he'd said. It wasn't him. It was an accident, that's all.

Rawlin's phone vibrates, and he shifts awkwardly in his seat to retrieve it from his trouser pocket.

"DI Rawlins."

He's needed back. They've found something. Archaeologist wants him there. Quick as possible.

Fumbling for his keys now, Rawlins is on his feet and making for the door, but then he stops dead, turns around and returns to tidy the paperwork. They are dead. They aren't going anywhere. But he's meticulous like that. His colleagues take the piss.

He places the pages back in their slender manilla folder and returns it to his in-tray. He's anal about this stuff. Pain in the arse if evidence gets lost.

It's mid-morning now, past rush-hour, but it's raining again and the traffic is slow. Rawlins doesn't know the turf well enough to take the backroads, so he's back on the plodding bypass, his sat nav barking at him to take a sharp right, which he's sure is the wrong way.

He takes it anyway, goes straight on for half a mile and at the second turning, turns left.

After a few hundred yards, the road rises into a small hill and he sees a police van parked at the top of it – a couple of uniforms loitering at its rear. They straighten as he drives past, dropping fag ends into the gutter. He hooks a left and is back in Blenheim Close.

The grass is wet now, and Rawlins slips as he walks down the lawn. Scraping the shit off his leather loafers, he curses, looking around to make sure nobody has seen.

But they're all busy, or engrossed. Every face is on the archaeologist now – forced into the pit which is finally too deep for his reach.

He works meticulously at a small patch of ground, and Rawlins can make out a shape under the surface now – just bumps and curves, like a tiny mountain range.

The archaeologist sees Rawlins and beckons him nearer.

"That side please, you're blocking the light just there."

The forensic tent has been moved into place now, over the grave – as it now clearly is – one side still open into the garden.

Rawlins moves deeper in, keeping to the tent's edge, and places himself into one of its furthest corners, away from the entry.

"Almost there," adds the archaeologist, without looking up.

Rawlins stares at the pit, at the sculpture of shapes the archaeologist is brushing away at. He thinks he can see forms – human forms perhaps – two lovers wrapped together post-coitally and forever cased in soil.

Until now.

The archaeologist works with the tiniest of trowels and two brushes – one stiff-bristled to work the earth free a dozen grains at a time. The other is softer, there to clear the grains away.

"Human?" asks Rawlins.

"That's my guess, and more than one most likely."

The archaeologist carries on with his work, focusing on a small domed area, a dome that Rawlins suddenly realises is a human head – featureless still, cloaked, but human all the same.

A clump of soil comes away, matted, almost like a thin piece of ancient pottery. The archaeologist picks it up with tweezers, places it in an evidence bag and hands it to a SOCO who is stood, motionless, in the other corner of the tent. He takes it away.

The soil breaks away now, coming off in clumps until the head is visible. Rawlins is expecting all of its gory features, but it is masked by a shroud, or at least what passes for one.

It is stained almost beyond recognition – nearly black, and a stench suddenly fills the tent, a familiar stench that is overpowering all the same: the unmistakable reek of decomposition.

Rawlins stares, transfixed.

Beyond the black gunk on the shroud, he can make out tiny pastel flowers and looping vines. A blanket, he thinks, or a duvet cover.

"What's the staining," asks Rawlins, already knowing the answer.

"I'd guess at body fluids," the archaeologist replies. "Based on the colour I'd say it's largely blood. Not common in historical finds. Indicates that the blood was able to escape the body after death, before it could coagulate internally."

"Meaning?"

"Could indicate violent death."

"Shot?"

"Who knows? Can't say at this point. Any number of ways they could have ended up like this. One for the pathologist."

Rawlins steps out into the light and sucks deeply on the fresher air.

He looks again at the skyline of boxed semi's and sorrowful trees, letting the now-returned soft drizzle dampen and cool his face.

People died here, he thinks. People died violently here.

And nobody noticed. Nobody cared.

But somebody knows.

Somebody.

Two names.

Names from the statement.

Christopher Edwards.

Susan Edwards.

Prime suspects.

Only suspects.

Chapter 2

An elderly couple who lived in a Forest Town house where two bodies have been found in the garden mysteriously disappeared in the late 1990s, neighbours have claimed – Andy Done-Johnson, Mansfield Chad, Friday October 11, 2013.

The room smells of sleep, although it's already late morning and she's still sitting in her slippers and a heavy, pink dressing gown.

Maybe they're late risers, I don't know. I don't ask.

All the windows are shut, the curtains partly drawn with no sun on the front yet, leaving the room – small and darkly carpeted – feeling more like dawn.

She's let me in moments earlier, unsmiling but not unfriendly. I tell her who I am, she nods, and opens the door a fraction wider – enough for me to squeeze inside and close it behind me.

I offer to take off my shoes but she says it doesn't matter, so I sit in an armchair, comfortable, old and slightly faded, with a dated floral design.

She's old too – not ancient but old enough to have seen a few comings and goings, late sixties maybe, or a little younger.

She'll talk to me, she says, but only me. She doesn't want bothering by any of the others, if they come.

Will you tell them that?

I say I will, knowing it wouldn't make a blind bit of difference. Doesn't work like that, at least not in their eyes.

"Your . . . husband," I guess. She doesn't correct me so I carry on.

"Your husband was just mentioning to me that you might have something to say. You might have something to say about the old couple who lived in the corner house."

She says nothing at first. She stares at her slippers and occasionally, reluctantly, at me.

"Is it them in the ground?" she asks.

"I don't know," I reply. "I expect so. Hard to imagine who else it's going to be. Did you know them?"

I sit forward, a grubby biro hovering over a blank page in my pad, waiting for her to speak some more. She won't give me her name. She doesn't want it going in the paper.

"What if it's just for me?" I ask.

"Just so I know who you are, just so I can write your name next to these notes I'm making, so I've got proof I spoke to you if anyone asks."

"Edna," she says, suspiciously. "Edna Dawson."

I write her name in the top left-hand corner of my note-pad, certain she's just given me a pseudonym.

She doesn't need to. If she doesn't want her name in the paper then that's up to her.

"I saw them," she tells me, "regular as clockwork. Every day I'd see them walking past. It was always about the same time. Him always ahead by a good ten paces, little and slumped and bent over. Her, tall, broad and ungainly – walked stiff and upright. We thought she might be a man. Odd couple."

My hand, which has been scribbling frantically, comes to an abrupt halt.

"What, like a cross-dresser?"

"I don't think she was. I don't want you writing that," she tells me, wagging a finger at me.

"She was just so much bigger than him, and always walking behind, like she was a decrepit old dog on a lead."

"And this happened every day, Edna?"

"Regular as clockwork. Each day they'd set off about two o'clock and come back about four, lugging shopping bags – her always carrying more, like a pack-horse."

I get it all down – my shorthand not what it was a decade ago – key points written in longhand in the margin to help me get it back later.

"And did they ever speak?"

"Sometimes he'd say hello," says Edna. "He'd speak if they passed and I was in the front garden. But it was always reluctant, you know, like he'd sooner not have. Or he'd wave if I was in the window, looking out."

"And her," I ask, watching Edna's face turn to a scowl, her mouth working silently as she thinks.

"Never, not that I can recall. She just stared straight ahead, or looked down at her shoes as she passed. Great, broad-shouldered, strapping woman she was, and she followed him round like a little mouse."

How long? Was it weeks? Months?

She thinks hard, like the old cogs in her brain are being forced to work too early in the day.

"It was years," she replies eventually. "It went on for years. Longer than a decade."

They'd turned up at some point in the mid-1980s, she thinks, when she's sat quietly and thought hard.

She can't remember the last time she saw them, not exactly, but it was a long time after they moved in – 1997, 1998 maybe.

There was a period towards the end when she only saw him, on his own every day, walking, hunched over, looking lost, abandoned.

"I remember wondering whether *she* was ill," Edna says.

"I wondered if she was alright, or if she'd gone away; only I was never out on the front when he passed by to ask him."

She sits for a minute, thinking hard – an old clock clunking heavily away in the background; her mouth working with concentration.

"Eventually he stopped walking past as well, and I didn't see either of them again," she says eventually. "Not to this day."

I don't ask her anything for a minute. I use the silence.

"We'd heard they'd moved away," she tells me then.

"Someone said they'd moved up to Morecambe, to be by the seaside."

"Morecambe?"

"Yes. Although we'd also heard they were in Australia. I don't remember who said that."

There's a clatter at the back door and her husband walks in, coaxing his ancient dog through the kitchen. It settles at my feet and rests its head on my knee, leaving a film of slobber which I pretend not to notice.

"Getting busy out," he says, hovering by the kitchen door.

"Who told us they'd moved to Morecambe?" she asks him.

"Don't know, he replies. "Can't remember.

"Might have been you told me. It was before my time."

I don't ask, and after a long moment he takes his leave back into the kitchen, where I can hear him fumbling through draws and the click of a kettle going on.

"Then the house was empty for ever such a long time. Years it was empty for – always dark, blinds closed and curtains drawn. Abandoned, almost."

"And that didn't strike you as odd?"

"No," she snaps.

"They'd moved away. Up to them if they didn't want to sell up. Thought they might have been saving it for their daughter."

They have a daughter?

My writing hand freezes again and starts to shake a little, so I pull my fingers back, pretending I've got a cramp.

"I think they had a daughter," she says.

"I think I heard that somewhere.

"After they'd gone there was the couple who came at the weekends sometimes.

"They didn't come regular, maybe a few times a year – although it was more often at the start. They'd just turn up and sort out the garden, you know, keep it tidy. Might even have been them that told me about Morecambe. I can't remember. They weren't much chattier than the old couple."

I flip over to a new page in the pad, quickly drawing a margin down its left-hand side.

"But I did think that was odd," Edna says.

"Why would they come and tend a garden in an empty house that nobody was coming back to? What's the point?"

"It does seem odd," I agree.

Odd that nobody smelt a rat, I think.

Odd that they'd all sat and stared at an empty house for half a decade – owned by an old couple who'd vanished overnight.

All talking, all gossiping; the Chinese whispers going round the estate, and nobody speaking to anyone that mattered.

But then why would they? People come and go all the time. People move on. People die. Houses sit empty, hedges grow, and life goes on.

Until the police turn up and dig up the garden.

"Then one day the house was sold," says Edna.

"It must have been ten years ago now. New people moved in. The lady in there now has been there a while. Maybe there were others before. I can't remember but I think they rent it."

She tells me about the comings and goings over the previous 24-hours. Seen police vans parked on the road outside, her wandering up to the front gate to have a nosey.

Then the officers had come to talk to her and she'd told them what she'd just told me, she says.

"Didn't say much. Only that they were looking into what might be a murder and not to be alarmed as it wasn't recent. And that I shouldn't talk to you lot."

"I don't suppose you remember their names do you – the old couple?"

Edna thinks for a minute.

"I think it was Bill and Pat," she says after a painful moment. "Yes, it was. Bill and Pat. Bill and Pat Wycherley."

It's dull. It's grey and raining lightly. It's hours earlier and I'm sat in our almost-empty new offices – out of town on an almost-empty business park, nestled between a new pub, a car showroom, a van rental firm and a mental hospital. I sit at my desk and watch the indifferent drizzle come down over the uninspiring landscape, littered with half-finished new-build houses, wind turbines and relief roads leading to nowhere.

There is still greenery on one side, but it's slowly being gnawed at by the developers, like some slowly spreading skin cancer into the neglected fields.

Planning permission has been granted years ago, before the recession bit, and the noise of the diggers has long faded away, the workmen packed off home, or to work in less financially ravaged parts of the country.

It's a little after nine on a Friday morning in mid-October. I'm on calls. I've been on calls for a week and I really can't be arsed today – I'm just sitting on autopilot for the last eight hours, until I can walk away and make it somebody else's problem.

You do the calls. That's what it means. You call the cops once an hour. The cops tell you there's been nothing

33

happening. Then you call the fire service, who might tell you about a minor accident up near Sherwood Forest, a hedge fire in Ashfield, or a stranded horse they've rescued from a flooded farmland field.

But it's boring today – it's boring already and I've not been here an hour yet.

I keep looking at my watch, listening to the conversations around the office and writing downpage – filler crap about charity fundraisers, or a diabetes awareness event at the local hospital. Soon be home time, I think, optimistically.

Calls depends very much on your perspective. If you're having a 'glass half full' day then it's the chance to break all the big stories; to get out of the office.

Someone gets stabbed, it's yours – get out there and bang on some doors. Bloke comes off a motorbike and hits a tree, it's yours. Missing teenager, house fire, armed robbery – all yours. Murder – yours . . . mine, today, as it happens.

But if you're not in the mood, it's an endless repetition of dragging your arse out to anything that might make a story, getting the door slammed in your face by people who don't want to talk to you. Car fire, cat up a tree, drunken fight outside one of the pubs, suicide. All yours. Get on it.

All the time you've got to fill the pages, fill the pages, fill the pages – like you're shoveling a huge hamster wheel that feeds on hearsay, gossip and the occasional fact.

Today my glass is much less than half-empty. It is a Friday morning. I'm bored. The weather is crap. I can't be arsed.

I'm not there totally alone, there are others, doing their thing, taking calls, bitching about the company, moaning about staffing levels, or the latest demands the shortness of staff is making on our time.

The regional press is now woefully under-resourced, and understaffed. The days of family-owned weeklies housed in some old redbrick property on the high street are a distant memory. Most are now the concerns of huge news corporations, companies that asset-strip from the bottom up to appease the shareholders, furious that their investment has taken another nosedive.

Back in the day, maybe only a decade earlier, newsrooms were bustling, lively places, with bank after bank of desks housing reporters, secretaries, features writers, news editors, sub editors, sports writers, not to mention the offices which were home to the various ranks of editors.

An army of photographers would come and go – rushing back between jobs to develop shots in the darkroom, often forming an orderly queue outside, chatting and joking, sharing stories, comparing cameras.

They were golden times, it seems.

The worst you had to worry about was the radio or telly getting hold of your story in the dark hours after the city final had been stoned, and before the presses could start grinding and rattling again, spilling out the following day's first edition; containing yesterday's news. Back then people still read newspapers. People still bought newspapers.

Then the internet happened and things started to go wrong for the print media, and it was largely their own fault. They did nothing about it, or next to nothing. They chopped back on their number of editions, from seven, down to three and finally to one, as a way of saving money, and in doing so made themselves irrelevant.

The recession didn't do us any favours either.

Newspapers became a slumbering, elderly beast, just churning out history while all the latest was suddenly available elsewhere at the click of a button.

They'd spent way too long sitting back and telling themselves that the internet wasn't a threat – that people wanted to read their news on the bus, on the train, on the bog, and you couldn't be dragging a computer everywhere you went.

And then somebody invented smartphones and the world of print took its terminal kicking.

Most had made some inroads into web journalism, but when I'd started at the Mansfield Chad newspaper around a year earlier, the web was still an afterthought – and nothing could be loaded onto it until it had first been in the paper.

They've made headway since, but it was probably too little, too late – and the reality of many regional publications is now a skeleton staff, doing the best they can, a smattering of college kids working for free, or as good as, and long banks of long-empty desks, abandoned notepads belonging to former colleagues stuffed into every drawer.

We'd moved out of our old offices six months earlier – not only because there were now more empty desks than occupied ones, but because there were more abandoned floors than space being used in the whole, slowly-collapsing building.

But the hacks cling on, getting more and more over-worked, getting more demotivated by the quality they are able to produce and the abuse they take from the readers.

It's not about loving the work. It's about addiction.

Many are looking to get out, maybe to a better-paid number in public relations or corporate comms. Old timers are just clinging in for redundancy pay-outs, when the board inevitably announces its next round.

This is us – asset-stripped down to fuck-all so the people at the top can secure their bonuses.

On a good day there are five of us now, but today it's less with people clawing hours back from the local council meetings they still make us attend, or taking one day off for the two days they'll be doing over the weekend.

Then there's social media, which is a curse but also a blessing. Today it's a blessing, at least it is if your glass isn't down to the last half-inch of sloppy dregs.

I do another lap of calls – police say it's all quiet, so do the fire service.

It's a waste of time, as they only ever tell you anything if it's in their interests.

I get up, put the kettle on and go for a slash.

Then I start digging around on Facebook and Twitter. These are changing times and you've got more chance of unearthing something on social media than on a phone. We're now too far out of town for any face-to-face tip-offs.

I check the police website, which has not been updated since the day before. The fire service Twitter feed just warns me to test my smoke alarm, and invites me to a charity car wash at a fire station in Nottingham.

I make tea and plonk myself back heavily at my desk.

The rain outside seems heavier now, the sky black, like it could really start coming down.

I dig around – look at what the district council are peddling, a few local charities, political parties and churches. Nothing. Nothing at all.

But then I see it. I click onto a community page that covers an area of the town. It's more gossip than news, but then people seem to prefer gossip these days.

I scroll down. I freeze.

- Does anyone know what the police are doing at that house in Blenheim Close?

- No, but there's a police tent up in the back garden, been there two nights.

- You could see the spotlights from our bedroom.

- They were still there when I passed just now.

Then my phone rings.

"Newsdesk," I answer, robotically, giving my name.

There's a voice, a male voice of indeterminate age.

"I don't want to give you my name," the caller says. "But I just thought you should know the police are digging up the back garden of a house in Forest Town. Told us there's been a murder. Told us there's bodies buried down there."

The phone disconnects with a click and a buzz.

Blenheim Close? I look on the map. Blenheim Close – smack in the middle of Forest Town.

I'm on my feet, grabbing a notepad and stuffing a clutch of pens into my jacket pocket, conscious that most of them won't work.

I fumble for car keys, then curse when I realise I've not brought a coat and it's properly pissing it down outside.

"I'm going to check something out," I shout as I head for the office door.

"What?"

Ash, my boss.

"Look at the Facebook feed on my screen, "I reply, still walking. "Looks like they've found some bodies."

I get out to the corridor, patting at my pockets frantically, thinking I'm missing something, then I turn around and walk back into the newsroom.

"Can someone call the plods," I say, "find out what's going on. And ask them why the fuck they didn't tell us about it."

Mansfield's a newsy patch, and murders come around way too frequently here. But that doesn't seem to diminish demand – there's nothing like a bloody good murder.

There's a feeling that comes on suddenly, a feeling that all the cynicism and apathy and reluctance can't shake – a feeling you only get when you're onto something big, something national, something that breaks the cycle of misery and decay that nobody else outside of Mansfield much cares about. Your heart begins beating like a strangled clock in your chest, and sweat breaks out in beads on your forehead, yet you feel calm, focused, alert – almost like you're floating. You feel hungry.

I bound down the stairs, jump in my car and drive, still not sure where I'm going.

I curse Fridays, I curse Nottinghamshire Police, I curse Facebook and the pissing rain.

'This will be fuck all' I tell myself as I swing a left into heavy traffic. "Wasting my fucking time."

But the hammering in my chest tells me differently, as I wipe the moisture from my face – a moisture that is more sweat than rain.

Blenheim Close. Blenheim Close. I fumble with the sat nav on my phone and struggle with the seatbelt. It points me towards town and then out again, taking me past our old offices, its windows boarded up now, its car park closed, fresh graffiti smeared over the pollution-stained bricks. A sign saying 'No Entry'.

If we'd been in there today the rain would have been coming through the ceiling by now – an uninvited water feature streaming down the back wall.

On the road just outside is a small seated area – the familiar group of derelicts huddled already, holding court, drinking strong lager or cheap cider and putting the world to rights, despite the weather.

Straight on, past an array of chemists and corner shops, takeaways, hairdressers and a boarded up newsagent with our logo still displayed on its grubby frontage; past side streets of dilapidated terraces, like something out of a DH Lawrence novel – only in his day the inhabitants didn't wander around shirtless or flog weed from their doorsteps to passing cars.

Today these streets are deserted though, apart from a solitary teenage mum pushing a pram, the rain keeping most of the occupants indoors.

I reach the junction at the end and the downpour suddenly slows back to a deep mist, and I'm directed left and then right, down a street of former council builds, then straight on at the end, over one of those confusing double roundabouts, where you're never totally sure who has right of way.

As I come round the bend I see a row of shops, raised up to my right, while to my left is a scruffy piece of waste ground that may once have been a park – it still has a bench.

The houses, no doubt once pristine and shiny-new – occupied by once-young families starting out together – are now drab and decayed. Mansfield has worse areas. This place just needs a damned good lick of paint and a bit of tender loving care, both from the now-elderly residents and the local council.

The grass verges are overgrown and forgotten, the roads potholed. There are burger boxes and chip wrappers stuffed into hedges, dog shit festering on pavements – a community, forgotten by most, but still hanging in. Just about.

As I reach the top of the brow I am told I have reached my destination and I swing a right up a side street, pull on the handbrake and turn off the engine. I clamber out of my knackered old Saab, slam the door and look around, getting my bearings.

At first I can see nothing, as I stand and scratch a couple of pens back to life on the inside of my pad.

Then I spot it – standing tall above a shabby but sturdy garden fence, in the rear garden of the corner house across the main road. A tent. A large, blue, multi-sided tent – more like a marquee. A standard police forensic tent, spacious enough to easily work inside, but made of a thick and dense plastic, completely blocking the goings-on within.

It stands out a mile and I wonder again why it's taken so long for someone to tell us about it. In Mansfield, if a cat gets stuck up a tree they're on the blower.

I cross the road and I'm met by a solitary copper who wanders to the corner. I see another now, standing on the pavement round the corner, blocking the drive.

Whatever it is, it's been scaled back, I think. I'm catching the tail end of it. I curse the police under my breath again, and the locals, and the weather – although the rain has now stopped and it looks like the sun might even break through.

"Can I help you, sir?"

The copper cuts me off on the corner. He's too polite, too hesitant to be the real deal, and I assume he's a Special.

"Press, mate," I tell him, digging my card out of my wallet. "This where they've dug up the bodies?"

He doesn't reply, so I nod at the tent to help him out.

"You'll need to speak to the press office, I'm afraid. We can't comment."

I go to walk past and he side-steps to block me.

"I need to ask you to please respect the privacy of neighbours."

Enough, I think.

"This road?" I say, pointing down Blenheim Close. "Is this a crime scene?"

He doesn't answer, so I walk past him.

"Just going to knock on a few doors mate. Just doing my job."

I wander to the house opposite and rap, deliberately hard on the front door, looking back and giving the coppers a false smile, one of whom is now talking into a radio.

An old dear comes to the door, tells me I'm a disgrace, tells me I should mind my business, tells me I should let people rest in peace. Then she tells me to piss off and slams the door.

Right place then, I think – moving further down the cul-de-sac without turning back to the coppers, who I imagine are smirking.

My phone rings.

Ash.

"Yeah, I've just got here," I tell him. "Something not right though. Fucking huge SOCO tent in the back garden and a couple of flat-foots guarding the front. What you got?"

He tells me.

Police have just come back to them, literally a couple of minutes ago. They've confirmed that, following a tip off . . ."

"Hang on, let me write this down." I pull the lid off a biro with my teeth and flip to a fresh page in my notepad. "Okay. Go on."

"Following intelligence, the human remains of two bodies have been unearthed in the rear garden of a house in Forest Town."

'Blenheim Close?"

"They won't confirm, but off the record, yes."

I look back over at the house on the other corner, where the coppers are still watching me, frozen – like they're hoping I might drop litter or kick the head off a rose.

"It's fine. This is the place."

"They say the bodies have been there for some time. Going big on how there's nothing to be alarmed about and for people not to worry."

"Some time? What's 'some time'?"

"They won't say, but it's not recent – they're keen for us to put out a line that there's not a mad axeman on the loose. This is historical."

"What, like Vikings? Have they just unearthed an ancient burial site back there?" I ask, only half sarcastically.

But it's not. More off the record – bodies are not recent but they won't be drawn on how long they've been down there. We're more than likely looking at a murder enquiry. Oh, and they're about to put out a statement to the rest of the media.

"Brilliant."

I end the call. Fucking circus is on its way. I get moving.

I go to the next house and press the bell, which doesn't work so I hammer on the door.

Nobody answers. I move on.

At the next house the upstairs curtains are closed – probably some bloke working nights who will be overjoyed when he gets to the front door.

I knock anyway, and wait. Nothing. I knock again. I move on.

I reach the far end of the cul-de-sac and eventually another old dear answers the door. She's pleasant enough, but can't tell me much.

She says she is deeply shocked, that the police went round yesterday, telling her not to worry.

"Did you know the people in the end house?"

She didn't. She's not been living here very long. But it's worrying, isn't it? All these police!

I agree that it must be, wanting to get away, conscious that the clock is ticking.

Others will be here soon. I don't know how many yet, but a lot – and I don't want to end up at the back of a media scrum.

I move to the next house, conscious that I'm heading further away from the crime scene, further away from anyone who might be of use.

Same at the next house. Police came round. Terrible. This sort of thing doesn't happen around here. This is a quiet street. Didn't know the people living in the end house.

The office calls. There's a snapper on route, but she's twenty minutes away. Can you get a shot of the scene and ping it over. Just putting out a holding piece.

Residents in shock, I tell them. Lots of police activity overnight, spotlights up, scene of crime officers etcetera. This sort of thing doesn't happen round here. That's all I've got for now.

I photograph the two coppers standing out front and ping it off before they can even think about trying to make me delete it.

Then I bang on the adjoining house, but again I'm met with closed curtains and silence from within, so I stumble to the corner of the street in despair and look around.

A car has pulled in behind mine and a guy is unloading a television camera out of the back.

"Brilliant."

45

I head in the other direction, towards the raised arcades. Shopkeepers always know what's going on, I tell myself hopefully.

But when I ask he knows nothing. He's seen the police, and the tent, and the spotlights.

"It was like broad daylight when I opened up at five," he says.

I scribble it down – desperate for any colour I can get.

I walk outside and lean heavily on the rusted iron railings. I call Ash.

"Nobody is saying fuck all. Just the same bollocks about the police going round."

He asks if I want to come back in. I'd love to but I'd be missing the party now, and there's more to it, I sense. If I come back in then somebody else will get to the bottom of it.

I hang up, frustrated, and start to wander back to Blenheim Close.

That's when I see him – over the road on the little forgotten park. He's standing roughly at its centre, near the bench, looking away while his geriatric little dog painfully pushes out a shit on the neglected earth.

Up the road another car has pulled to a stop, a head out of the window talking to one of the coppers.

Now or never, I think, and I cross the road and head onto the scrubland – long wet grass immediately clogging to my shoes and sticking to the bottom of my trousers.

Fuck's sake!

I try to creep up on him, to make as much ground between him and me before he sees me coming, and he stands upright just as get within speaking distance, tying a knot in a poop bag.

He looks weary, not that old, perhaps late fifties. but like he's spent a lifetime down the mines before they threw him out onto the slag heap.

"Do you live round here?"

He doesn't reply.

"Hello," I say, bending down to give the dog a delicate pat on the back of its neck.

"I used to have one a bit like him," I lie. "What is he? Has he got some collie in him?"

"Don't know what he is," he replies, eyeing me suspiciously.

I decide to show my hand, hope that playing the local-lad line will win him over, even though I'm not. Often they'll talk to us, but they'll tell the nationals to piss off when they come knocking.

"I'm from the Chad," I say. "Police tell me you've been having some fun and games."

My newspaper must be one of the most idiotically named in the whole regional press. It actually stands for Chronicle and Advertiser, but nobody's called it that in living memory. It's just the Chad to the locals, and a polite piss-take from any PR bods that come on the phone trying to punt their wares.

He stares at me for a moment longer, his dog sniffing at a weed before it cocks its leg up the bench.

"You here about the old couple?"

'What old couple?' I almost say, but I check myself and look around the park for inspiration.

"In the corner house," I motion vaguely at the area around Blenheim Close.

"The old couple?"

"Yes," I say, almost giddy. "The old couple. Did you know them?"

"No. No, I didn't," he replies. "But I know of them. They just vanished one day. Went away. Never seen again. Real mystery."

"And you didn't know them?"

"Never met them. Before my time."

Right!

"But my Mrs did. She's lived here most of her life. She can tell you all about them. She'll speak to you if you're from the Chad."

Then he pulls an ancient mobile phone out of his pocket and makes a call.

I feel like I have travelled in time. My mind buzzes with information – my brain swirls. At this point I've got it all to myself, but it won't last long. I look at my watch. It's a little after one now. I don't know how long I've been in their home but it seems like days and minutes, all rolling around.

I thank them both and I get to my feet, making my way to the front door, but I'm halted by a loud rap on its panel. I can see the outline of a head, distorted by the shape of the glass which it is trying to peer through.

Another tap, then another.

"I'm only talking to you," Edna whispers. "I'm not talking to any of the others. Will you tell them?"

I promise I will for the second time, and we wait in silence – listening for the sound of footsteps retreating up the path and the clunk of the front gate clattering shut.

Chapter 3

Matters came to light after the defendants received a letter from the authorities stating that they wished to see William Wycherley because he was approaching a hundred years of age. In a panic they fled to France –
Peter Joyce QC, R v Edwards and Edwards, Nottingham Crown Court, June 2014.

Hesitant footsteps on the stairs, laboured; one creak, then a pause, then another – like someone carrying a heavy load.

The shuffle of feet outside the door; a key, turning in a lock – a rasping clunk as it is pulled out.

The squeak of the handle, the hiss of wood gliding over carpet, and the sense that someone is standing behind her.

She doesn't turn.

After all, who else is it going to be?

She has stayed all day in the tiny flat, pokier even than their former home in Dagenham. The floors squeak when you walk around and the whole floor in the living room sinks into a corner. If you happened to drop a ball on the floor it would naturally roll towards it.

The attic rooms drop in the corners, bend in the walls, and have windows jutting upwards in a failed attempt to make more space, like an afterthought.

She looks out over the skyline, almost Russian in its multi-coloured and domed splendor, every now and then.

She wanders a lot. She wanders and looks at her watch. She clutches her hands, rubs them together a lot – so bad that she has to use cream to soften them – like there's blood on them, like a bashful Lady Macbeth.

She is slight – not short but slump-shouldered, which are slender and sagged.

Her hair is grey and forgotten, like she has been cutting it herself, and she wears no make-up. She has no need.

Her clothes are dour and shabby – an old green cardigan over her shoulders, plain cream trousers and a round-necked top of an indeterminable shade of white.

She wears no jewellery.

She never has.

There is no TV, and she couldn't understand it even if there was. They have a small radio – good enough to give them a crackly rendition of the World Service.

There is also no TV because there is no money – what little pot they had has now dwindled to a pocketful of coppers.

They are behind on the rent. They are behind on the bills.

She senses his hand hovering over her shoulder – not touching it, but almost.

Pull yourself together Susan.

You're a disgrace. You're a shitty, slutty disgrace. Pull yourself together. Pull yourself together Susan Edwards.

The creak and the puff as he sinks into the sofa, the sigh billowing from his lungs at the same time.

Silence, for a moment.

'You don't need to say!"

"What?"

"If it was good news, you'd have said."

An undetectable sigh . . . almost.

"You're silent, so it's not good news."

"I'm tired."

More silence – just the grumble of leather as he shifts on the sofa.

"No, it's not good news," he says. "I'm sorry."

Don't shout, Susan. Don't shout, because he's tried. You know that he's tried. You can see he's exhausted.

"Where did you try?"

No answer, not straight away – like he's thinking.

"All over. Knocked on doors, you know."

"What doors?"

There is a strain in his voice, like he is either going to cry or yawn. She can't decide.

"I went to offices, accountants, all sorts."

"And nothing?"

Susan rubs her hands frantically – part in fear, part in anger.

He doesn't reply, at least she doesn't think he does. Her mind is in overdrive, thoughts flashing around too quickly for her to latch on.

She is squeezing her fingers so tightly that her knuckles crack, and with that sound and the pain shooting through her fingers, she is back in the room.

*　　*　　*

Eventually she had settled – after he'd made himself look smart, straightened his tie and headed down the creaking stairs and out into the narrow, cobbled street; dragging the remaining strands of thinning hair over his exposed scalp.

When he goes out Susan has always wandered and paced; she has stared out of every window.

But finally she would settle, just like today.

She'd sat herself on an ancient dining chair, faded and scuffed, with once-scarlet velvet upholstery – next to a tiny dining table for two, pushed away into the corner.

There is a sofa also, but it is tiny – just two seats made of cracked leather, and wooden arms so blunt that they hurt your elbows.

It faces a rickety little corner table which should have supported a television or a record player at least.

On it sits a long-dead spider plant instead.

Next to her, on an unloved and long-forgotten dining chair, sits a shabby old suitcase, opened and explored – some of its contents poured out onto the table, stained by coffee mugs, as Susan works through its contents.

There are no clothes, no pants or socks or vests or sweaters. The case contains only paper, the most expensive paper Susan has ever seen.

She's gone for the pristine black and whites first – photographs of Gary Cooper and Henry Fonda and Cary Grant; Frank Sinatra, Montgomery Clift, Humphrey Bogart and Jimmy Stewart. They are all pristine, all autographed – showing chiseled jawlines, smart suits, slicked-back perfect hair; all holding a neglected cigarette, burning seductively between the second and third fingers and giving the sepia a faded feel.

They're an investment, Christopher had said.

They'd always be worth more, the longer you held onto them.

But he'd said that about the books as well; the first editions from Charles De Gaulle and Winston Churchill which they'd bought for thousands and poured over in the evenings, relishing every word, occasionally daring to brush a finger over the roughly-scrawled signatures on the inside, or breathing in the dust that had settled through the years.

They'd imagine that Charles and Winnie had scrawled their names just for them – for Susan and Chris Edwards.

But when the money had gone again and they'd been forced to sell the collection, and suddenly it would be a buyers' market and they'd be lucky to claw back whatever funds they needed to pay off one debt or another.

She'd pulled out another, a vintage Paramount studio shot; mid-career, just after High Noon – To Sarah from Gary Cooper, says the scrawled signature.

To Susan Edwards from Gary Cooper.

He looks away from the lens, staring perplexed yet secure at something off-camera to his right. His suit is pristine, his hair perfect – a checkered tie knotted tightly at his neck, his jaw tight, his skin faultless.

Chris had paid around five hundred pounds for this one.

She couldn't remember exactly, but she can remember the picture where he's wearing a cowboy hat had been a lot more expensive. But it was Gary, so it didn't matter.

So as the hours had slipped away, and more photographs had been pulled out, removed from their films, studied, poured over, then carefully returned and neatly stacked on the table, Susan had spent the day in the Hollywood of sixty years before – where she often lived when Chris was out, knocking on his doors.

She lounges in the passenger seat of a topless red Chevy Bel Air, cruising majestically down Sunset Strip as the sun goes down.

Gary at the wheel, his arm rested nonchalantly over the driver's door, the same forgotten cigarette held between his fingers.

They drive to dinner and are bustled to the best table, where Cary joins them and Sammy DJ comes over to say hello.

Then it's off to a show and they sit just back from the front while Frank croons out 'A Very Good Year', before it's time to go back to his for Martinis and dancing by the pool until dawn.

Susan is happy and giggly on Champagne. Her breasts are full, her hair is twisted, blonde and heavy, her voice seductive and deep, her dress crimson and low-cut.

She smokes cigarettes and drinks vodka neat, while Dean and Frank and Montgomery and Bobbie Mitchum vie for her attention, and she doesn't know who to pick.

But the footsteps on the stairs bring her back, and she is plain old Susan Edwards again – tatty cardigan, slumped shoulders, hair she has cut herself and hasn't washed in a week.

There are letters as well, letters from Gary and Frank mostly – but Chris has bought these for himself, because of the history, he says. Chris likes history. Susan likes film stars and romance more, because it's something she has never known.

And now Chris is home, failed again, taking the romance away from her once more. She is the Susan Edwards she sees in the mirror each morning now. She is a Plain Jane. She is Plain Jane Susan Edwards – unloved and forgotten, almost.

Their love is built on need, on longing, on hope, and on despair – a scribbled response to a lonely heart in a London newspaper, both hoping for more, perhaps.

When they first meet, in a bistro in Acton, she is hoping for Cary or Gary or Frank, and she gets Chris. She doesn't know what Chris is expecting, but she suspects it is not her. Somehow they click. They work. They can talk. They can smile. She is keen to escape, to make her own way, to be accepted. So is he.

And for a long time they are content, until they are away from each other and Susan returns to her silver-filled sepia Hollywood world. She doesn't know where Chris goes in his world, but she suspects he may be a military general, or a criminal mastermind, or a spy behind the Iron Curtain.

Chris likes films too, particularly French films, and Susan gets the idea of writing to him as the actor Gérard Depardieu, just as a joke really. But he never lets on that he doesn't know, so Susan takes the joke a little further and buys a franking machine, so it looks like Gérard's letters have been sent from Paris, written neatly in his pidgin English hand, franked and sent to his new friend Chris, over the channel in Blighty.

Christopher even keeps the letters in the envelopes. He never says he knows they are a joke, so Susan just carries on, unsure of how to stop it.

Chris even writes back, perfectly seriously, and she promises to post the letters, even though she never does.

Gérard never suggests a meeting in any of his letters. Neither does Chris.

She'd told him things that she'd hoped would make her sound more interesting, more blonde and confident and voluptuous, like she wouldn't look out of place on Frank or Gary's arm.

She'd told him that she'd met the former Liverpool football manager Bill Shankly, because she'd heard his name on the television. She'd written to him asking for an autograph, and he'd replied by inviting her to a hotel.

Nothing sordid. Bill was a real gent. But Chris' eyes had lit up, star-struck, like he was dating a princess, or a movie starlet.

And now they are in France – Lille to be precise – because they love France and they love Gérard Depardieu and they love Charles De Gaulle, and Charles De Gaulle had grown up in Lille. There was nowhere else for them to go, not under the circumstances.

It had seemed like an elopement at first – the romance and the spontaneity they had never known in their time together.

They'd rushed to the station; all the way from Dagenham Heathway on the Underground. Changed at Mile End onto the Central, carried on to Liverpool Street, then switched onto the Hammersmith and City – all the way to St Pancras.

They'd clutched the passports they have kept ready, kept up-to-date – even though they never went anywhere.

Next stop France.

They hadn't even taken keys – just closed the door on the tiny flat they have shared for the past 25 years. Their pokey little flat, where they'd sat at night, reading Winnie under a table lamp, or examining Gary through a magnifying glass.

Holding hands, they'd walked past boxed council homes, grey blocks, run-down concrete offices and art deco pubs. Over the crossing, under the blue strip of the Underground sign – even though half of it is overground – and bought tickets from the machine.

Chris had worn a hat, which he never had before, as far as Susan could remember.

On to the platform, they'd looked out for the mice scurrying around the grease-crusted rails.

They'd held a single suitcase – a single suitcase and the clothes they are standing in.

Out in Zone 5, the trains didn't flash past. They laboured and they chugged.

Chris and Susan had jumped on the first one heading west. Chris clutching the suitcase on his knee; Susan holding her passport.

They were leaving their lives behind. They were going away and not coming back – a bit of a family tradition, it has to be said.

Chris had always said that the day would come, no matter how cautious they were, the day would come.

The truth would always out. And he had been right, because the truth was out, and they needed to get away.

Susan had waited at home – much the same as she is doing the best part of a year later in another pokey flat in northern France.

She had paced, and sat, and paced some more, ignoring Monty and Sammy DJ who were sat on her sofa, smoking and joking, as they tried to keep her company.

But she'd not been in the mood for them – too much at stake.

So instead she'd paced, and sat, then paced some more. She'd looked out of the window too, but not as much as there'd been less to see.

Chris had a plan.

He had gone to his firm and asked for a loan – said his step-mother was in urgent needs of repairs on her home. Some emergency – a water leak at her house, a collapsed ceiling, a lorry taking out her front wall.

Susan didn't know. She had left the details to Chris.

He had headed in, unsure that they would buy it, unsure whether they would be able to help. But Chris had worked there for years, and he'd hoped they'd do the decent thing; knew they'd do the decent thing, deep down.

He was steady. He was reliable and loyal. Granted, he was a little odd, a bit quiet and uncommunicative, but he was part of the furniture and he'd never asked before.

So he'd headed off in the morning, head slumped, carrying a small case – much as he had done in Lille for the past ten months, only this time with somewhere to go. This time he'd had a purpose.

Susan had waited and paced and waited some more. It had been an agonising day. Neither of them liked using phones if they could help it and Chris hadn't rung.

Then eventually there had been the sound of his key in the Yale and the creak of the door, and Chris had come into the flat, like he'd been swept out of London in the squally rush hour exodus.

He'd sat on the sofa, pulled off his shoes and reached for his slippers – a faint smile on his face.

He'd bided his time, he told her – been distant and distracted, more so than usual, even lost his temper a few times over silly things, and eventually Jenkins his boss had pulled him into the office for a quiet word.

At first he had been reluctant to engage, he said, saying only that he had some family problems and he didn't want to burden them with it.

Then he'd feigned emotion, described how much he loved his step-mother Elizabeth, said how much she had helped him over the years, how she had been like a real mother to him, how close they were, and how devastated he felt that he couldn't help her in her hour of need.

Her ceiling had come down, it would seem, and she lacked the resources these days to get it repaired; lacked the resources to pay top whack on her house insurance, and how she'd pleaded with them but they wouldn't cover it.

Chris had sat forwards throughout, his elbows rested on his knees, his hands together, looking pathetic, staring at his shoes.

Eventually Jenkins had rested a manly hand on Chris' shoulder, sent him back to his desk, said he'd see what he could do. No promises, but he'd ask. No harm in asking, is there?

So Chris had carried on with his day, controlling his mood, which was genuinely unhinged. He didn't need to act. He didn't need to weep crocodile tears, because the tears that occasionally welled up were all his own. Tears of fear and panic more than remorse.

Eventually Jenkins had sent him home, puzzled as to why a step-mother's tumbledown house should be causing Chris so much angst, but surmising that all of us have our weak spots, all of us have our Achilles heels, don't we just.

And for Chris to have got himself in such a state – Chris who hardly ever spoke, serious Chris with no sense of humour, Chris who lived in a flat in Dagenham with a wife they'd never met – well, it must have got properly under his skin.

Susan hadn't understood why he'd not made it home until six, when he said they'd sent him packing just after three.

She guessed he'd been for a wander, down the Thames perhaps to Borough for a nosey at the Shard, or sat throwing breadcrumbs to pigeons in Soho Square. Perhaps he'd just walked, seeing the sites of his familiar surroundings for the final time, a last nip to the Imperial War Museum, or panicking about what Jenkins would have to say when Chris headed into the office the following day. Perhaps he'd just needed to be on his own.

*   *   *

A butterfly flaps its wings in the centre of the Pacific Ocean and sends out a tidal wave that engulfs the coasts of Eastern Asia; devastates the West Coast of America.

A cliche, Susan knows.

But that's how it feels to her as she sits and thinks about it now – Chris sitting silent on the sofa, her looking out at the Lille skyline from her little table.

A letter flapping downwards towards the mat, she remembers – like a leaf tumbling on a blustery autumn afternoon; announced by the slap of the letter box and retreating steps.

Susan had watched as it made its slow descent.

She'd always listened out for the post – it was part of her routine, part of her purpose. But she'd just happened to catch it as she passed; noticed the letter box snap closed, and seen the envelope gliding to the carpet, which they'd been on at the council about to get replaced.

A standard manilla envelope, Government-stamped, a window at the front showing a name that was neither her's nor Chris's.

For the attention of Mr William Wycherley, still redirected from his old address.

Her hands had trembled. Her hands trembled whenever the letter box snapped, whenever the letter was official-looking, whenever it carried the names of William Wycherley or Patricia Wycherley.

Usually Chris had opened all the post when he got home from work, but Susan had ripped this one open, knowing something was seriously wrong, somehow.

The frank showed it was from the Department of Work and Pensions, which was ridiculous because dad must have been almost a hundred now. What would he be wanting with a job?

Only it wasn't a job they wanted him for. It was about his pension, Susan had discovered as she'd read.

'Congratulations on your pending one hundredth birthday later this year,' it had said in heavy, bland text.

At first Susan had thought it was about his bloody telegram from the Queen.

Only it wasn't, it was much more official than that.

They'd wanted to meet with William, send out a representative 'to assess his needs' as he approached the big day.

William had been a burden on the state for most of his life, even when he'd been alive, and no doubt they'd been looking at ways of getting rid of him, or at least chopping back on what they paid out to him in these leaner times.

The butterfly had stopped flapping in Susan's chest, and she'd given the letter very little thought after that.

She'd left it on the table for Chris to read when he got home.

Chris would know what to do.

They'd dealt with William's correspondence on an almost-daily basis for almost fifteen years; Patricia's as well but less so. It was part of what Susan did. It was her job; after she'd asked Chris what he'd thought she should do.

But when Chris had got back and she'd shown him the letter, she could almost see confusion, the fear even, in his eyes; the disbelief.

He'd sat down heavily and put his head in his hands.

Something had been wrong; something had been seriously wrong.

It will catch us out one day. One day we'll have to flee.

Together they'd sat and composed the letter, Chris assuming William's rasping, fag-damaged voice, Susan copying down in her well-practiced hand.

They'd done it a thousand times to a thousand officials.

But Chris had said it had been serious and that they needed to be careful. This wasn't a letter back to the doctors declining a flu jab, or the council asking if he fancied the day centre round the corner.

Their letter had gone off and for a while Susan and Chris had almost forgotten about it; just a distant nag in the back of their minds, like someone occasionally agonising about whether they'd been nobbled by that speed camera on that day trip to Wales; the fear and anxiety fading to oblivion as the days had slipped into weeks.

But then the next letter had come.

Brown. Formal. Mr William Wycherley. Marked 'urgent'.

Respectfully we really do need to see Mr Wycherley at his earliest convenience. Mr Wycherley has now been claiming his state pension for almost thirty-five years, and was a regular claimant of other benefits before that. We note that we have had no face-to-face contact with Mr Wycherley for a great number of years and it will be necessary to organise a face-to-face meeting at his earliest convenience.

They'd tried again, more painstakingly this time, working on it through evenings for over a week before they'd sent off the reply, stalling for a few more to give the impression it had been passed around the houses.

Their letter had gone off again, but it had stayed with them this time – through every waking thought, penetrating into their dreams, keeping them awake into the small hours. Chris had been distracted at work. He'd made a few mistakes which Jenkins had told him was out of character.

Susan had paced more. Sometimes she'd even cursed and pulled hysterically at her hair when things had gotten too much through the long, empty days.

At night they'd sat in silence, not interested in Winnie or Gary, Frank or Charles, waiting for darkness so that sleep could take them away for a few oblivious hours . . . perhaps.

It may only have been a fortnight but it had seemed like a year – both of them lying in the endless stuffy darkness of summer nights in the box bedroom of their airless flat.

Both pretending they'd been asleep.

Both knowing the other had been pretending as well.

Then when Chris had come home one day the opened letter had been lying, menacingly, on the table once again, waiting patiently for him.

Susan had been sitting on their little sofa, scrubbing her hands together and drinking gin which she'd fetched from the shops.

We insist that Mr Wycherley presents himself, or tells us where he can be located in Ireland, so arrangements can be made to visit him. If we do not hear from him by so-and-so date, we will be forced to suspend all payments.

"Let them," is the first thing Susan had said after Chris had read the letter a hundred times, and they'd sat in silence until the sunlight had gone.

"It's only his pension. We can live without the pension."

But Chris had shaken his head and told her there was much more to it. It was the Government. The Government talked and shared things with itself.

One department would speak to another, and all of a sudden someone would start asking questions, like there was a missing part to the jigsaw of someone's life.

And if they were asked, they'd have insufficient answers to give them.

"I could write them a sharp letter," Susan had suggested. "Accuse them of bullying and intimidating him, telling them how well dad is and how ill he gets when he has to return to England's smoggy climate? How he feels scared and how he just wants to be left alone?"

Only Chris had said that would give them a new name to investigate … hers, and they might bring in Social Services if they thought they were up to no good.

"We always knew this time would come," Chris had said, taking her trembling hand. "We've planned for this, most of our lives together."

And Susan had known he'd been right; only it had felt too late now because she'd made him spend far too much money on Winnie and Charles; and then they'd gone away, so she'd made him blow a small fortune on the likes of Monty and Sammy and Gary.

It had gone wrong because part of the plan had been that they'd always have enough money to get away; to disappear to a beach on the far side of the world if the authorities had come knocking.

But they'd both always been terrible with money. Neither of them had the skill to manage it, because it was always too tempting, even though Chris worked in credit control.

And so when the authorities *had* come knocking, their pockets had been empty.

Chris had headed back to the office the following day to find out their fate, looking like a little boy, leaving for his first day at a new school.

He'd gone out early, much earlier than he needed to, but Susan hadn't argued with him. She'd just let him go and endured the longest day of her life.

She'd paced and she'd stared, she'd gone back to the shop and bought more gin, way before lunchtime as well, and she'd spent the afternoon in a haze – panic, calm and oblivion in equal measures, coming and going with the next slug of mother's ruin.

She'd cried a little and she'd thought about mum – wondering what she was up to in Ireland and whether the air was clement for dad's lungs and his forty-a-day habit.

She'd felt bad for mum – trapped in that hateful marriage for all those years.

Then she'd buried them both deep in her mind and thought instead about Chris at work, whether he'd manage to hold it together. She'd heard sirens, and panicked, until they'd faded into the swell of outer London hubbub.

She'd wanted to call him but she couldn't, so she'd had another gin and she'd had a lie down, furious with herself that she couldn't sleep, even though the room was starting to spin.

Only then she must have slept because suddenly Chris was home with the banging of their front door.

Susan had sat bolt upright, then she'd got to her feet and gone to meet him in the hall.

He'd looked at her funny, like he'd known she'd been drinking, but there had been a smile on his face that he couldn't disguise, and he'd produced a wad of notes from a pocket like a magician about to perform a card trick.

"We're moving to France," he'd said, and she'd grabbed him tight and hugged him until she thought she might be squeezing the life out of him, and it wasn't for a long while until she realised his shoulders had been shaking, and the baritone of his sobs were being drowned out by her shrieks, his tears soddening her shoulder.

Sitting there now, in a different room, a sea and a year away, she could still remember leading him through, into the sitting room, where she'd sat him heavily on the sofa.

She'd poured him a brandy, a dusted bottle they kept in a cupboard for medicinal purposes, and forced him to take a sip or two.

Chris wasn't really a drinker, but she could tell he'd needed a stiffener.

Susan wasn't good with feelings, and she'd wanted him to sort himself out, to pull his emotions back inside and deal with them on his own.

They didn't share like that; they hadn't for a long time.

They'd sat in silence for a while as Chris had sipped at his brandy and pulled a face, like a child being given medicine.

Then eventually, when he was calm, when his tears had been replaced by his reluctant smile, and his hands had stopped shaking, he'd been able to tell her about it.

Susan had sat next to him, her hand rested lightly on his knee, urging him on with a distant squeeze to his shoulder when his story had dried up or faltered, or got distracted, or become so excited that he'd gone off on a tangent; or felt guilt and wanted to cry all over again.

Susan had sat and listened, not asking questions, just letting Chris tell his story; giddy like a schoolboy who'd just passed his exams.

He'd gone to the office, he said, the memory fresh as a daisy still in Susan's mind, and it had gone quiet as he'd walked in, like everyone had been talking about him.

He'd wanted to be early but the tubes had been delayed and he'd made it through the door at a minute before nine, flustered, out of breath, harassed.

He'd gone to his desk and plonked down, he told her, logged onto his computer and checked his emails.

There'd been a couple of prints he'd been watching, hankering after, but when he'd seen the replies from sellers he'd panicked and deleted them – not wanting anyone to see, not under the circumstances.

He hadn't wanted Jenkins going for a rummage through his inbox, in case he'd become suspicious.

He knew they checked emails. People had got into trouble before.

He'd sat and worked until lunch, he told her, watching Jenkins out of the corner of his eye as he moved around, talking to colleagues – but not to Chris. He'd given Chris a wide birth and Chris had started to sink further and further into despair.

A couple of times he'd almost snapped, he said, thought about approaching Jenkins, or sending him an email asking for a quiet word, only somehow he'd held on and tried to keep his mind on his work, staring at his screen, occasionally wiping away the sweat that kept building up on his brow, running down his cheeks, down his neck and staining the collar of his shirt.

A few times he'd gone to the loo, just to splash cold tap water on his burning face. He'd looked hot, clammy, flustered; his thinning hair, usually light and flyaway, was dank and heavy. He looked like he'd come down with a fever.

Finally, just as people had started to file out for lunch, there'd been a tap on his shoulder and Jenkins had beckoned him into the office, sitting down behind his desk and folding his fingers together.

Chris had sat forwards, he told her, just like the day before; not looking him in the eye, not daring to hope.

They would loan him the money, ten thousand pounds, Jenkins had told him, but they're not a charity and it will need to be repaid, and repaid promptly.

They wanted five hundred pounds a month out of his pay.

And if his step-mother came into better fortune, if the insurance paid out, if she won the lottery, then they'd want it back sooner.

No interest. No point. Just don't leave town.

"And if you leave our employment before the money is repaid, then we'll want all outstanding funds in full," Jenkins had said.

Then he'd handed Chris a note and told him to give it to Cheryl in accounts, authorising the payment of £10,000. There had been a contract for Chris to sign, and he'd scrawled his hasty signature without hesitation; forcing himself to pause so it had looked like he'd been reading the small print.

Down the corridor, he'd tapped on the second door from the end; left a few minutes later with a stack of notes which were folded neatly into a wad and secured by a red rubber band.

Back to his desk, Chris had forced himself back to work; fighting the instinct to flee, battling the urge to bolt for the door and hail a taxi.

It had been the most agonising wait of Chris' life, he said in Susan's head, but he'd dug in until home time; even managing an appreciative wave to Jenkins as he'd headed for the elevator and the busy streets below.

Chris had held out the money to her, the wad of notes, let her clutch it, hold it; like a lifeline to a drowning man.

He'd pressed it into her hands, folded her fingers around the bundle and held her hands tightly, like their whole future had depended on what she nestled in her palms; which it did.

But it had been back in Chris's possession as they'd walked hesitantly through St Pancras, Susan terrified by the hustle and bustle.

So Chris had sat her down on a bench and gone off to buy tickets for the Eurostar. They hadn't booked, Chris had already checked the timetable and they departed for Lille at least once every hour.

Then they had sped towards the south coast, watching the grey-green fields flash by under a heavy and sunless sky, finally breathing a sigh of relief when the daylight had been taken away by the tunnel walls; taking them to a whole new life – a successful happy life, Susan had thought, a life that no longer required them to dread the clatter of the letterbox, a life where they were not forever looking over their shoulders.

They'd booked into a backstreet hotel under false names and paid in advance for a week, while Chris had checked cheap apartments for them to rent.

But that was almost a year ago now, the money was all gone, and their new lives had proved to be a false promise to each other.

Chris can't speak French, at least not beyond ordering a meal or asking for directions. He'd told himself he'd quickly pick it up; being around the locals, buying bread, chatting in cafes, that sort of thing.

Only to get a job in France you need to be able to speak like a native, or as good as, and no matter where Chris has gone, which doors he's banged on, they'd all told him the same thing.

He'd started with financial service companies, accountants and the like, but whenever he'd got through the door they'd quickly grasp his linguistic difficulties and promptly send him packing.

You can't work in credit control if you can't talk to the customers – no matter what your experience, no matter how good you are or where you've worked.

He'd spent time out, listening to the French speaking, while he'd sat alone and pretended to feed the birds, or look at the water; or he'd watched the old boys playing boule, or chatting on shaded benches through the warmer months.

But he'd shown no improvement – to learn a language you had to speak it; and he'd come home frustrated and desperate.

So he'd headed out again, blindly, knocking on his doors. He'd even offered English conversation classes for businesses, but they'd spoken much better English than Chris's feeble French.

Susan had agonised when, finally he'd been reduced to banging randomly on any door with a sign hanging above it; willing to do anything, pleading almost – wash dishes, sweep floors, clean windows, pick fruit or paint walls.

But most of the people that had answered couldn't understand what he wanted and waved him away, or slammed the door on him.

Unlike Susan, Chris slept soundly at night; not because he was content, simply because he was exhausted.

"I'm going to call Elizabeth."

She can feel Chris' hand clutching at her wrist. He may have been holding it for hours.

Is Chris back?

Then she remembers him coming in, slumping on the sofa, sighing.

Time means nothing to Susan now – her life now is an endless fear, punctuated by day and night.

There is nothing else.

They are finished.

They might as well take pills, like Hitler.

Winnie would have taken pills if the other lot had won. No question; cyanide capsule washed down with good Champagne.

"Why don't we just take pills?"

Chris doesn't reply.

"I'm going to call Elizabeth," he says. "I'm going to call Elizabeth and ask her to help us."

Susan doesn't reply, but she nods.

Chris goes to the tabac to buy a top-up for his phone, using one of their last remaining notes and she's alone in her head for what seems like hours.

Then she hears the door slam and Chris is back, shuffling off into the bedroom, shutting himself in.

The walls are like paper and she can hear every noise, every word.

She can hear him pacing around, sitting on the bed, getting up again, walking to the window.

She thinks she can hear a glass being knocked over, and a table overturned.

Instinctively she gets to her feet, walks to the bedroom door, thinking he's fallen, or worse.

But then she hears the bleep as he presses the numbers on his cut-price portable phone and she flees back to the sofa, not wanting to be on her feet if he happens to come out.

She can hear his voice, quiet at first, then angry, then pleading, and finally shouting.

Then she hears only silence.

She can't tell how long Chris has been in there for; she can't tell how long she has sat in silence waiting for the door to open.

When he finally does come out the skies outside are darkening and a moth is flapping around the unguarded bulb hanging from the cobwebbed ceiling.

As he returns to the sofa and holds the mobile phone in his shaking hands, Susan can still hear his voice from the room next door – quiet and calm at first, then becoming high-pitched and whiney, then croaky and laboured . . . then sullen and resigned. Susan hadn't quite heard the words, just the mood, and it hadn't made for easy listening.

Elizabeth has always been a bitch to Chris, she thinks. She's always criticised him, always looked down on him, always picked on him; pointed out his failings.

Even when she'd spent days sorting out their money, sorting out their mess, she'd only done it to make Chris feel and look like shit, like he was useless.

She'd always belittled him, always made him feel worthless – because he was never ambitious, because he never went to university like the rest of them.

Susan hates her – hates how Elizabeth controls Chris, hates how she rolls him around in her fingers, always making him grovel and submit.

But mostly she hates how he is afterwards, after he's been speaking to Elizabeth, when he's subdued and distant and blaming her; Susan knowing Elizabeth has been saying yet again that it's all down to that greedy wife of his, all down to Susan, and that they'd all told him what would happen before he married her.

And Chris had never defended her, never stood up for her; and Susan wonders if deep down he agrees with his stepmother. Part of her suspects he does.

He's always been controlling, Chris, in his own quiet and apologetic way.

Susan thought they'd be free of Elizabeth once they moved to France, but here she is again, ruining everything, once again.

Elizabeth is nothing but a bully. Susan hates her. Susan hates bullies.

Suddenly she imagines herself leaving Chris and just running away with the boys in the suitcase.

Leave him in Lille and head for the sunniest horizon.

She imagines she's independent, that she's making her own way in Berne or Berlin or Budapest.

She has skills, she thinks – shorthand and touch-typing. She has worked in a library, and as a clerical assistant for the police in London.

Only Chris hadn't wanted her to work. Chris had wanted her to stay at home and be looked after, and her skills had long lapsed.

That's what Susan had done through the years; that's all Susan had done – day after day after endless day.

Susan had stayed at home and paced and stared out of windows while she searched for a purpose; never really finding one.

So instead she had stayed at home and wandered from room to room, for days, then weeks, then years.

She had spent endless hours looking through glass; watching the lives of her neighbours unfold beneath and around her; a kaleidoscope or random occurrences, like watching an army of ants.

People look, she concluded, but they don't see.

They don't see what's happening right under their noses, or in the house across the street.

When they see, it is only inwardly.

She'd wanted to escape all these years, she'd wanted to run away.

But run away to what? Run back to whom?

There had been money. There had been lots of money until somebody had taken it away from her.

Then Chris would turn up with something new and fun from Winnie or Charlie, or later from Gary or Monty or Sammy or Jimmy, and that would settle her down for a while, settle her until the next time.

There was always a next time.

"I may have made a tactical error," Chris says finally, pacing, shuffling, hovering by the window; brushing back his few strands of hair with a movement that seems to make use of most of his arm, almost like he is holding himself.

"Chris?"

He sits down and takes her hand and tells her that he's sorry, over and over; only he'd rather got carried away, he says, he got pressured because she was controlling him, like she always did, and bullying him like she always did, and asking him questions about money and things that he couldn't think of answers for ... and then he'd just told her.

"Told her what? Chris? Told her what?"

77

He doesn't reply.

"What?" Susan screams. "What did you just tell her?"

She wants to hit him. She wants to reach over and slap his stupid face, slap his stupid bald head and shake his puny little shoulders.

She wants Gary to sweep her up into his arms and carry her away, putting a hole in Chris's chest and grinding his bones into the earth.

When eventually Chris does talk, he speaks for a very long time; rocking slightly, clasping his hands together.

"It started well," he says, daring a look at her for an instant. "She was ecstatic to hear from me, she was crying a bit when she realised it was me and that I was alright.

"She told me that the police had been round to see her because my employers had reported me missing after I hadn't turned up to work for a fortnight. They'd asked her if she 'd had any repairs on the house done recently."

Chris stops then and his shoulders shake, and Susan can't work out whether he's laughing or crying, or both.

"Somewhere near the start of the conversation, I don't remember when precisely, I just welled up, got really emotional, which isn't like me.

"I just felt like she missed me, like she was worried, and I honestly hadn't known that she cared. For the first time ever I didn't feel like a burden to her.

"And I told her that we were living in Lille, in France, and that we hadn't got any money left."

Susan sees the tears trickling reluctantly down his cheeks now, through the flicker of the naked bulb above and the sulphuric sprawl of street lighting.

"Only then everything had got awkward," he says. "It all came out in a rage, like she was furious at me for running away and marrying you in the first place.

"She asked me why we'd gone to Lille and why we didn't have any money left, and why I'd borrowed ten thousand pounds from my employers and told them it was for repairs to her house, and then disappeared?"

He reaches out then and touches her, pats her knee and sheepishly takes her hand.

"They want it back Susan," he says. "They want their money back, so they called the police and reported me missing.

"Then she asked me why I can't just come home and sort this out with my bosses and I can't remember whether I laughed or cried."

Chris can't remember whether he'd said it then, whether he'd just blurted it out, or whether there had been another period of heavy silence.

"Because there are bodies buried in the back garden of Susan's parents' home, and we can't come back. We can't come back because of that. But it's a secret. If you tell, you'll get Susan into serious trouble.

"That's what I said to her, Susan, I think, or something like that.

"Then it went silent for a long time and I shouted down the phone at her, I shouted 'Elizabeth' time and time again, but all I could hear was her hysterically heavy breathing down the line, and something that might have been sobbing.

"And then the line went dead, and after that I must have called her name over and over, time and time again I must have shouted her. Then I think I must have sat on the bed for a long time, like I was rocking backwards and forwards, like I was in a dream or something.

"But I definitely told her about the bodies."

After that darkness descends on Susan, even when the late summer sun pierces the shutterless windows. She remembers day and night, light and dark. She remembers fear and her dread of being caged.

She remembers being locked in a cell; a cell with nothing but Chris's voice piped through the walls, his sheepish but steady intonation telling her an endless story from long ago . . . a story that she has come to believe and needs to remember.

She is sat on the sofa.

It may be an hour or a day or a week or a month later.

Then the phone rings.

"Elizabeth?"

Chris is straight on his feet.

She sees him breathe in suddenly, like he's gasping for air, like he's just been punched in the chest.

He reaches out and rests a hand against the sofa, leaning over slightly.

"Yes, this is Christopher Edwards."

He listens for a moment, his head nodding, like he's taking a call from his boss, or the bank, or the devil.

"No! No, I really can't talk at the moment. I'm afraid it's not convenient. I'm going to have to hang up."

He holds the phone heavily in his slumped hand before collapsing back onto the sofa, clutching at his scalp again, rubbing at the shiny skin like he's trying to erase a bad dream.

Susan goes to him then, stands behind him and impulsively kneads her fingers into his shoulders and rubs his back, like a nursemaid burping a child.

"That was the police," he says. "That was the police in Nottinghamshire. They want to speak to us.

"They want to speak to us about Bill and Pat."

Chapter 4

Having carried out these ruthless killings you got rid of the
bodies. I use that phrase deliberately. This was in no sense a
burial. There was no dignity, no respect – Sentencing remarks,
Mrs Justice Thirlwall, R v Edwards and Edwards, June 2014.

They had lain, brutally entwined like the roots from a
long-felled tree which had been ripped from the earth.
Decay and the soil had forced them together, their slender
bones joined by fabric and fluid, fused by weight and time,
summer droughts and winter rains.

They were not buried, Rawlins had thought as he'd
watched the archaeologist brush away the last of the soil
from the mound. They were dumped. They were thrown
away; hidden. This had been an act of hatred, an act of
vengeance or greed . . . a family dog would have been given
more dignity and more love.

He'd been able to make out the forms through the blackened fabric; the remains entangled, undignified, asymmet-
rical. The hole had been too small for them and the upper
form was slumped over the lower, in a way that reminded
Rawlins of old black-and-white film footage of Holocaust
victims being hurled into mass graves.

Rawlins had imagined them thrown down from the patio doors. In a snapshot, they could have been unearthing an execution pit from fields near Krakow, or from woods outside Sarajevo from when Rawlins had still been young.

"Over to you chaps," the archaeologist had said, getting painfully off his knees and stretching out his gangly frame.

"Not a dog."

"No," Rawlins had replied, walking with him from the tent and waving at the scene of crime boys to carry on with the exhumation.

"Definitely not a dog."

It had been light by then, but grey and damp, miserable and wet. It would rain again. There would be no sunshine that day, only drizzle and greyness, and the light starting to go while people were still labouring at their desks.

Someone had handed him a coffee and he'd leaned against the wall of the house, sipping, letting it burn his lips to keep him awake, too tired to think.

There'd been the slap of rubber tyres on concrete and the rustle over gravel; the snap of a handbrake and then silence as an engine was turned off. An unmarked van had reversed onto the drive.

Private ambulance? Bit premature, Rawlins had thought. Still a way to go here, although it was less obvious than the forensics van it had replaced.

He'd walked to his car, shivering – more from exhaustion than the chilly mid-morning air. He'd unlocked the door and slumped into the driver's seat; briefly closing his eyes, sinking almost immediately into a light sleep, hugging himself for warmth, relishing being out of the rain, just for a moment.

He'd started to go then and had immediately jolted himself awake again, opening the window to force in the cold. Then he'd rubbed at his face, at his eyes, stretching back the skin and relishing the tingle as the blood began to run once more, slapping his cheeks lightly until he could feel them burn.

A ping on his phone. A text from Griffin. "Call the superintendent."

"It checks out," Rawlins had said as the phone was answered with a grumpy 'Yes?'

"Two bodies. Historical find. Been dead for a while."

"What are we looking at?"

"Can't say at this point. SOCO's are in now. Heavy presence of blood on the sheets they were wrapped in."

"Violent death?"

"They didn't die in their sleep."

"How long to extraction? Press will be onto it."

"Impossible to say at this point, Sir. I'll speak to the chief forensic and get back to you with a timescale."

Then he'd called the on-call press officer, given the same briefing, missing out most of the gore.

"Looking like a double homicide. Certainly not recent. Nothing to be released without my say so. Get back to me immediately if you get a call from the papers."

There would be a way to go. They'd be coming out of the ground an artefact at a time – bone by bone; bagged and logged, all evidence gathered and collated for further inspection back at the labs. Every part of them would be logged and recorded, measured and photographed.

But Rawlins had wanted them out. He didn't want them paraded before an army of photographers on their way to the morgue. He wanted them gone; feeling more like a grave robber than a copper that morning – unearthing things best left in the ground.

There had been a tap on the window then.

"Sir, you're needed. Forensics have found something."

Heavily, reluctantly, he'd climbed from the car, feeling his age, feeling his legs instantly cramp and his back crack. How had he got old? How old was 35 anyway?

He followed a young detective constable back to the house, like an absconded schoolboy following a teacher back to school.

Back up the drive, through the side gate, into the garden. Inside the tent, two SOCO's had been on their knees.

They had paused. They were waiting.

Rawlins had stepped inside.

The bones were exposed now, black and stained – their makeshift shrouds meticulously worked away.

"In there Sir, do you see?"

Rawlins had peered beyond an exposed ribcage, dark and broken, into the almost black body cavity below, squinting while his eyes adjusted.

"On the spinal column, Sir"

Then he'd seen it. A glint of silver from the darkness. A bullet. A bullet was lodged in the spine.

But that had been hours ago, or days ago now. Rawlins can't remember, although he knows he has slept since, if only for a while.

*   *   *

He's in a room now, clinical and clean-tiled; the buzz of electric lighting deep in his ears, the blanketed smell of death rising in his nose.

Before him stand two silver trolleys, full of knives and blades and saws, poised for their grim task; set aside meticulously, as they always are, to prize open chest cavities, to cut into stomachs, to remove organs, to saw away the tops of skulls.

Not needed, not today; not necessary, but there all the same.

Next door lies an army of bodies, all covered, all in various states of dissection, playthings for medical students – long forgotten people who signed away their remains to escape the grave or the furnace, only to be incinerated one piece at a time.

This is the morgue.

Rawlins has been here many times, watched many a person who has already seen too much violence cut to pieces, examined; then finally sewn back together, their once-functioning organs dumped back inside, like a macabre pie.

Usually he loathes it, watching the victims of one violent death or another further brutalised, further disfigured; their eyes closed and their faces pulled into a smile by gravity.

Blood sinks to the base points, depending on whether the victim has died on their backs, their sides, or their front – depending on whether they've bled out before they died, of course.

This leaves half the body black and bruised, half ghostly grey.

Sometimes the remains are stiff, sometimes not – depending on the length of time they have gone undetected.

Rawlins remembers a bit of a poem, tacky and sentimental, displayed in embroidery in a frame on the wall of a funeral home he went to once.

'Do not feel sad,' it had said, or something like that. 'For I am just in the next room.'

Maybe it tries to humanise death, to offer hope ... of reunion, or something. But here in the morgue, the dead that Rawlins sees have had the life ripped out of them, stolen from them.

Past rigor mortis the skin will develop a green sheen, black lines marbling the face and arms where once there had been rich blood flowing through veins.

But not today.

Today there are only bones, laid out in anatomical order – like they have been crushed flat, fingers and feet splayed outwards, ribcages sunk and bare. The skulls facing upwards, the top of the head pointed to the ceiling; the jawbones comically detached, revealing rows of crooked and blackened teeth, cheap silver fillings reflecting the overhead lighting.

Two skeletons, lying on separate slabs – a couple sleeping side-by-side from long ago. They could be long-lost, recently recovered Royals – lost for centuries and finally found under a car park in Leicester ... only they're not. Their lives were much more humble, Rawlins thinks, much more pained.

Rawlins thinks about a sarcophagus he has once seen on some family outing when he was a kid, a statue on a tomb

– a lord and lady lying hand in hand, set in stone, a small marble dog lying contentedly at their feet, them holding hands.

At the time Rawlins had imagined the bones trapped for all eternity inside the tomb – looking not unlike the scene stretched out before him now, only less ordered, more chaotic. He'd wondered whether, under the stone, they were really holding hands, whether they were really mingling with the bones of a dog?

These bones are not white. Bones are never white, only in cartoons or at halloween, when the kids come banging at your door.

These bones are stained black with blood and bile, they are decayed with age, rough with calcium; the sockets of their eyes stare out sightlessly, accusingly, their secrets taken away, stolen from them.

The first post-mortem has already taken place, for what it was; just a thorough logging of the bones, a detection of anything abnormal.

A slice of bone is missing from one of the smaller victim's ribs, a red sticker marking it as an entry point. A chunk has also been taken out of the pelvis.

The larger victim also has damage to the lower spine, not connected to the bullet.

Patricia Wycherley had suffered from mild spina bifida, according to her medical records. Most likely this is Patricia Wycherley.

The bullets now sit in separate evidence bags, their shine completely gone in the artificial light. They are grubby and tarnished, covered in rust and flecks of earth. In their place are more little red stickers, marking their points of retraction.

"I'd say they were both shot twice in the chest, but you'll have to wait for the ballistics boys with all their blood and thunder for the official line."

A voice from behind him, accompanied by the slapping of confident feet on the polished floor.

Rawlins turned, expecting the burly form of Dr Stuart Hamilton, the Home Office Pathologist appointed to the investigation. But instead he was met by a smaller figure, balding and podgy.

"I'm Adamson," the man had said, holding out a hand.

"DI Rawlins," he replied, confused. "Sorry, I'd been expecting Hamilton."

"He's otherwise engaged, I'm afraid," Adamson replied without apology. "So he's sent me. And we were expecting Griffin."

Rawlins lets it go, deciding not to get off on the wrong foot.

"Close range?" he asks, motioning to the bones.

"It's not my field really, but judging by the size of the bullets, you'd have needed to be pretty close. Effective all the same though. Look."

He motions at the smaller victim.

"See here look . . ."

Rawlins follows him to the slabs.

"That scuffing there, on the rib, that's been caused by the bullet clipping it on its way past."

"And no signs of exit damage?' asks Rawlins, peering into the smaller ribcage.

89

"No. Bullets all stayed inside them. No damage to the rear ribs. Also backs up the theory that it was a low-calibre round – not powerful enough to make it all the way through to the other side. Here, I'll show you something else . . ."

Adamson heads enthusiastically to a small office just off the morgue, surprisingly full of crap and clutter for such a sombre environment.

Rawlins follows and stands at the door, arms folded, while Adamson frantically taps at computer keys, scratching at his thinning hair.

"Here, look . . ."

On to the screen pops an emotive computer illustration of a man – perfect yet faceless, like the unclothed manikins you sometimes pass in shop windows.

Only on the chest there are two red pinpricks, matching the stickers left on the bones next door – the left-side is slightly higher, one dot either side of the sternum.

"He knew what he was doing, did our shooter."

Rawlins moves closer, peering over Adamson's shoulder.

"Based on the entry wound on the ribs, and the positioning of the bullets inside the chest, this is where we think this victim was shot."

"The smaller victim?"

"Yeah," replies Adamson, annoyed at the interruption.

"Look, let's call him Bill for now, shall we? Now this bullet here . . ."

He taps the computer screen lightly with his pen next to the higher wound.

"... that would quite probably have taken out the heart. This one here ..."

The pen tip lands on the second spot.

"... would have penetrated the lung. The shot to the heart would have been fatal within seconds; minutes at best, depending on how good a job he did of it. The shot to the lung, fatal without immediate medical attention. He might have lasted an hour. The shooter knew what he was doing."

"Or he was lucky?"

"Or she," corrects Adamson, pausing for effect. "Well, man or woman; if they were lucky, they were lucky twice."

He taps a key and the male manikin is replaced with its female counterpart, also marked with two red flecks.

"This one here, Patricia, let's say for now ..."

He glides his pen onto a dot which is this time closer to the centre of the chest.

"I'd say this bullet here is the one that we retrieved from the spine."

He taps the screen again with his pen.

"This bullet here would have gone straight through the main artery running up her body, her aorta."

Rawlins nods.

"That would have killed her very quickly."

"How long?"

Adamson smiles, despite himself.

"That's the body's main artery. Put a hole in that and it's like bursting a balloon full of water. Could have been seconds. Certainly not more than a minute – the length of time it took her to bleed out."

"So she died first?" Rawlins asks.

Adamson thinks, scratching his head again.

"At the moment we couldn't prove they weren't shot a year apart. We're working on it, although we're a way off. But look, assuming they were both shot at the same time, or shortly apart, even if Patricia was shot second, chances are she died first."

"And did she die first?"

Adamson looks uncomfortable, like he's being pushed away from his brief.

"Certainly based on other examples of double murders, there is an established trend where the stronger of the two victims is the one that is killed first. Patricia was bigger, younger and stronger than her husband. Chances are she was shot first, but really you'd need to ask the ballistics bloke, although as far as I'm aware he's not psychic."

Rawlins leans heavily into the doorframe, exhausted, grey, in no mood for academia and sarcasm.

"What do you think?" he asks, trying to hide the sleep and the frustration in his voice.

A funny look, like a boundary has been crossed.

"Not for evidence," Rawlins says quickly. "Just wondering what you think."

Adamson spins his chubby frame round in the swizzle chair that has long ago seen better days.

"Okay," he says, letting his arms collapse heavily into his lap.

"I'll throw you a bone, for what it's worth. I'd be surprised if whoever did this wasn't used to handling a gun. I'd say you're looking for some sort of marksman."

"Or woman?"

Adamson doesn't smile.

Even under normal circumstances, if there is such a thing, a body at a crime scene is a pain in the arse. Any crime scene attracts voyeurs – more so than rubber-neckers at a traffic accident; all of them appalled and upset, all of them hoping for just one glimpse of gore on their way home from work . . . something to tell the wife about.

Crime scenes in general are a nightmare, even a lonely blade of grass can be a clue, or evidence in copper-speak. It's days of firearms officers on their hands and knees, picking up and bagging every fag end, every sweet wrapper, every burnt-out matchstick and stray condom.

Then it's endless door-to-doors, a never-ending cycle of calls and conferences and press briefings. And that's if they're still warm, or something more close to warm than the grim collection of calcium that Rawlins had surveyed in the pit before him.

Was that yesterday, he thinks, or the day before?

If remains are discovered, whether someone has been shot, or stabbed, or they've jumped off a roof, or been hit by a truck, or whatever, the first thing you have to do is secure the scene.

So you tape it off and you leave a probationary copper to guard it until the specialists arrive – divisional CID, Scene of Crime, major crime potentially. That's what you did. That's what you do. That's how it goes.

Rawlins had been that copper, back in the day, a lifetime ago it seems.

You'd stand there, the blood starting to tingle in your boots, and you'd try not to stare. You'd stamp your feet, you'd look at the ground, you'd stretch out your shoulders and listen out for the crack in your back.

Only in the end you would stare – either out of boredom, or fascination or compulsion. You couldn't help it. It was human nature. You'd stare.

Sometimes they just looked like they were asleep, if they were young and healthy, or bloated and fat with a lot more blood to coagulate.

Other times less so.

Other times they'd go grey, ashen; they'd appear to shrink, to melt away before your eyes, their bones ephemeral, almost.

If you were there for long enough you'd see gravity sink in; the face slumping, setting to a place where the force of the earth took it. That's why many mourners thought their recently deceased relatives were smiling.

They weren't.

But they'd been fused together, those two, Bill and Pat, if that's who they were. They had become one because of time, the weight of the earth and the passing of the seasons. They had become one; reluctantly.

Jumpers were the worst. It wasn't like you saw in the films from when you were a kid, where some flame-haired lovely would smash theatrically through the roof of a car, spread out like Christ on the cross; shattering glass, folding metal and the shrill scream of a car alarm wailing her passing while her soulful eyes looked appealing to the skies above.

From height, a human body comes apart like you've just dropped your dinner on the floor at school. It's horrible. It's traumatic. It's like dropping a frozen apple, only less clean. When you find a jumper there is blood and guts and compound fractures everywhere ... and somehow the fuckers still manage to stare at you, right into your soul.

And you – the probationary copper; the only other one who can't complain about it, the one who has to just stand and stare, and obey the rules to get your badge.

Me, thinks Rawlins. That had been me.

I'd stood by like a reluctant sentry; stamping my feet to keep out the cold as I worked my way up the greasy ladder. This had all started, this whole journey, from my first day on the job to a boxed garden in a suburb of a north Nottinghamshire town, with me standing in a darkened field, guarding a corpse.

Me, waving away joggers as they sauntered past, directing them through a cornfield, down a tow path, over a hill; and all because they'd pulled out a fisherman who'd gone into the water – slipped probably, let his waders get full of water, swept away by the undercurrent. Who knows?

But he'd come out cold. He'd come out long-dead, the fisherman – bloated and green with leaves clogged in his throat, his skin marbled and breaking open.

Rawlins had stood guard all night; trying not to look and looking all the same, trying to avoid the accusing eyes and the now-familiar stench of decomposition.

That had been his first watch.

Years later, a decade at least, he'd stood in the garden of that house in Blenheim Close, he'd looked down at the grave again, at the mingled forms, crumpled into confusion in a clumsy hole in the ground.

Bones in the soil; and nothing more.

We were alive, they seemed to say, as he'd stared down into the unyielding earth.

We were human once. We were alive.

We breathed, we cried and we laughed.

We lived . . . and then someone took that from us.

Rawlins had tried not to stare, not at that pit in that shoebox back garden.

Only you had to stare at something, so he'd ended up staring at them, just like everybody else; just like they'd stare at the jumpers, the wrecked forms destroyed by desperation and gravity.

He'd stepped away then, checked his watch – it had been close to 10am.

He'd called the chief super, again; he'd called the press office, again. Still no calls.

The quiet word with the neighbours must have paid off, he remembers thinking.

He'd turned on the radio, listened out for the news – only there'd been no mention of two bodies being exhumed from the back garden of a house in Forest Town. There'd been nothing; a quiet news day.

Slumped back in the driver's seat of his car, oblivious to the day of the week, Rawlins had jolted awake when his phone pinged.

Message from the comms team. Holding statement for the media that needed his sign off.

Police were called . . . blah de blah . . . address in the

Forest Town area of Mansfield ... following information given by a member of the public ... the find is believed to be historical ... want to reassure the public there is nothing to worry about etc etc.

He messaged back.

All good. But not to be released unless asked, or until I say so.

There'd been a tap on the window then; the same young detective constable that Rawlins didn't know.

"Chief forensic says the first victim is clear, Sir," she said as he wound the window down. "You happy for it to be removed from the scene?"

"Is he happy?"

"Yes sir."

"Then I'm happy."

He followed her back up the road, like he'd done the hour or the day or the week before.

Then he'd watched as the first victim, the smaller of the two, had been loaded into the back of the unmarked van. It had mostly come out in separate SOCO bags, the ribcage – still intact – carried out on a stretcher under a thin plastic sheet.

The van had been backed up hard to the side gate. Nobody had seen the victim's exit, nobody but Rawlins and a handful of coppers.

They've checked for DNA but it could take weeks and Hamilton isn't hopeful of a quick result, Adamson had said. Neither is Rawlins, at least not from the skeletons, although they might fare better from the blood and body fluid on the sheets.

After that it's dental records. Facial recognition is difficult as they can find no photographs of either William or Patricia. Everything has gone. Everything. They have been wiped away, leaving just traces, ghosts; undetectable victims lost in time, it would seem.

If all else fails, Patricia's spina bifida and the damage to the lower spine on the deceased should do it for her. But these are early days.

They have requested bank records, doctors' records, letters from Government departments. They are waiting now. It is a frustratingly slow period in the investigation.

They don't know if Victim A and Victim B are Bill and Pat, even though Rawlins is certain they are the Wycherleys. They don't know when they died exactly, so they don't know how far to go back. Cross referencing is extremely problematic at this point. Proof of life is still proving negative.

But they are progressing on the basis that this is William and Patricia Wycherley. They are progressing on the basis that they were killed unlawfully. They are progressing on the basis that they were both shot twice in the chest. They are progressing on the basis that they knew their killers. They are progressing on the basis that they were killed by their daughter and son-in-law – Susan and Christopher Edwards. They are progressing on the basis that Susan and Christopher have fled to France, although at this stage they don't know why.

Rawlins is in his latest office, in the Holmes Room they have now moved to St Ann's Police Station in Nottingham.

St Ann's is quieter these days – still dodgy and dangerous, still not a place you'd want to walk through on your own at night. But it's not what it was; back in the days of the Nottingham triangle war – gangs from St Ann's against the Meadows against Radford.

A drug war between the three suburbs which had earned the city the handle Shottingham in the press back in the late 1990s.

It is hours or days later, he doesn't know. He has slept. He has been home, but it is a blur. He has spent hours speaking to Adamson on the phone, he has met the forensic radiographer and is awaiting his report. They have engaged an entomologist from the Natural History Museum – a hired-in specialist. They are awaiting a response; all the time reporting back to the chief inspector.

But he has his first report, his first glimmer of anything new in days, it seems.

Ballistics expert Khaldoun Kabbani has sent through his initial findings.

Kabbani was present through the follow-up post-mortems; brought in to explain how the bullets had caused damage to both victims' lower torsos – when they were shot in the chest. The rumour mill around the station was that Bill and Pat were shot from above, like they'd been forced onto their knees.

That would mean premeditation to an unprecedented level. That would mean an execution.

It would mean both the Wycherleys knew they were going to die. It would mean punishment. It would mean that their suffering at the end was significantly increased. It would mean real hate. It would mean revenge. But it's only gossip at the moment, it's just the mill.

Kabbani has also been brought in to identify the murder weapon, from the bullets retrieved from the victims.

Rawlins reads the report slowly. Then he reads it again, making key notes as he goes through it.

"I am Khaldoun Kabbani," it reads, "a ballistics expert in the employment of Key Forensic Services. I hold a Bachelor of Laws degree from the Universite La Sagesse, Lebanon, and an MPhil in Forensic Exploration from the University of Bradford. I am a member of the Association of Firearm and Tool Mark Examiners with over 19 years' hands-on experience with the use, functioning, dismantling, assembly, and characteristics of a variety of weapons.

"As a firearms expert, I have attended numerous post-mortems of casualties from firearms and improvised explosive devices.

"On October 14, 2013, I was engaged by officers from the East Midlands Major Crime Unit to carry out ballistic examinations into the skeletal remains of two persons in the mortuary at the Queen's Medical Centre, Nottingham. I was told at the time that the remains had been unearthed in the rear garden of a domestic dwelling in the Nottinghamshire town of Mansfield.

"From my initial investigation I was able to concur with the Home Office Pathologist Dr Stuart Hamilton that both victims had been shot twice in the chest cavity. There is clear evidence of one bullet entering the chest of the smaller victim (A) and no evidence of exit damage on either victim. These shells were retrieved at the time of the post-mortem and have now undergone more significant forensic testing by myself.

"My initial report details two key questions asked of me by Detective Chief Inspector Robert Griffin during the post-mortem examinations.

"Firstly, what weapon, in my professional opinion, is most likely to have discharged the fatal shots?

"I was quickly able to establish that all four cartridges were .38 calibre rounds – most commonly used in standard revolvers, although the round is also used in some automatic pistols.

"I then carried out extensive ballistic testing on .38 shells with a wide selection of revolvers and other handguns that use this particular calibre shell.

"By comparing the markings on my recently-fired shells with the markings on the bullets retrieved from Victims A and B, I was able to conclude that they were most likely shot with a Colt Commando Revolver. This was a standard firearm issued to American military personnel during the Second World War. It fires low-calibre .38 rounds. It is a variation of the standard US police-issue firearm and was produced principally through the war years."

Rawlins scrawls Colt Commando .38 in capitals on his notepad.

"Secondly, I was asked to explain why the shots had travelled downwards through the victims' bodies, causing damage to the spine of Victim B and the pelvic area of Victim A?

"As stated previously, the .38 is a relatively low-calibre round. It is typically fired from a revolver rather than a more powerful weapon, a rifle for example and, as such, is only effective at a relatively close range. The weapon is more than capable of inflicting fatal injuries, but due to the low calibre, once it comes into contact with resistance it will rapidly slow, forcing it to begin to spin end over end, rather than in a circular motion. This will have the effect of forcing the bullets downwards as they pass through the body. There is no evidence, in my opinion, that either victim was shot from above."

Something they can dismiss at least, thinks Rawlins; the rumour mill just doing overtime.

Your hair still grows. Your nails still grow when you're in the ground. That's what they say at least. The coffin lid they've nailed you under gives eventually, under the weight of the soil; weakened by a winter of water pouring through you – you and the soil becoming one.

And all of a sudden, whether your nails are still growing, or whether you are in need a trim cease to be relevant. Such matters become the least of your worries.

A body eats itself. That is the reality. That's what always haunts Rawlins.

If it were a planet, a dead human would have had a nuclear war, and then invited a load of aliens to come and invade it.

The human body is packed full of bacteria – even while it is still living and breathing, and walking around and making mistakes; even then a human body is a living and breathing bacteria colony. Bacteria lives on the skin, in the ears, in the eyes, in the stomach, up the arse.

They are everywhere, the germs. They are part of your eco-system; bumping along, feeding and multiplying, growing and spreading, while the human form is having dinner, working out, sleeping, having sex. All the time they are with you. You are their world.

The human form is rich pickings for a germ. It is much richer than the rocky earth that the hosts' bodies are forced to tread.

The human body is a feeding frenzy.

And as soon as the human host dies, it enters an explosive phase. If God exists he is an ecologist, and a genius; and also a monster.

Your heart has stopped beating.

Your brain has stopped functioning.

It is starved of oxygen.

The blood in your veins is now static; obeying gravity and sinking towards your lower extremes; at least if it's not escaped.

And from there the body gorges. It eats itself, or at least it invites its biological colony to tuck in.

Acid in the stomach burns through the walls and allows the bacteria that has lived there throughout your existence out and about to explore the neighbourhood; into parts of their brave new world previously held out of bounds to them.

Bacteria in the bowel breaks through and begins to feed and breed and multiply.

This phase marks the end of the nuclear war and the beginning of the alien invasion.

Rawlins had watched, all those days ago, or so it seems, stood on a mist-drenched box of lawn, as the bones had come out, one at a time – carried somberly, like each one was a miniature coffin, before they'd been bagged and labelled.

They had been through that journey long ago.

The dead human body begins to smell quite quickly if it is left out in the open. The hotter the weather, the quicker the putrefaction process, the quicker it begins to smell.

This attracts wildlife. Big wildlife and small wildlife. Foxes that might come and take a meal. Birds may have a peck.

But it's the little ones you have to watch out for.

Flies.

Through all of this, in those early days of life extinction, the body becomes stiff as its muscles contract and harden, and it moves through a rigid and inanimate state that begins soon after the final breath but is most prominent from 36 to 48 hours later.

It is a 'stiff', as the saying goes.

The face and outer extremes go first, after just a few hours.

Then the whole corpse follows, atom by atom, muscle by muscle, until the body lies completely rigid. At funeral homes, embalmers will have to massage the deceased from top to bottom in order to do their work if they come in during this time.

But then it passes and the body becomes quite flexible again.

This arch is roughly how pathologists estimate time of death – particularly in those first few hours into the great hereafter.

Only for Rawlins, for the first time in a career, all of this has become an irrelevance. Those morbid details which he tried not to think about and avoided talking about, did not apply.

Here there had been only bones. If they'd been older they could have carbon dated them, but they're not old enough. So suddenly it had all come down to confession, to excavation, to a pile of bones dumped in the ground, and old-school detective work.

Rawlins had watched as Patricia slowly made her way from the earth, her larger and still-connected bones delicately and finally hoisted from the soil. The corners of the duvet cover that enshroud her had quickly been folded over her to protect her from the daylight, to preserve her secrets. Then a plastic shroud had been quickly but meticulously wrapped around her and sealed with tape, preserving her in an almost vacuum.

Rawlins had heard the almost-apathetic rumble of saggy tyres once more, the ambulance once again reversing down the neglected, once-pebbled driveway of the home that used to belong to Bill and Pat Wycherley; the place they would leave a lasting mark on.

Then Patricia, like Bill, had been on her way; away from Blenheim Close for good, with the slamming of van doors and the gunning of an engine – away to new digs on neighbouring slabs in a mortuary some fifteen-or-so miles south.

Days become nights become days. It is a blur. Rawlins sits at his desk, looking at the walls, feeling like he himself is incarcerated, under interrogation; getting his story straight for when the coppers come back in and start on him again. He has slept again briefly, he has been home, he has showered and shaved again; he has pecked the girlfriend on the cheek and tried to watch the telly. But his mind is always at the station, always with the Wycherleys. Every time his phone pings he grabs for it instinctively. He checks his emails almost by the minute, knowing the mobile would alert him to any new arrivals.

Eventually, when he can stand no more, he heads back to the station; back to St Ann's to sit alone in an abandoned Holmes Room where there's nothing new to report.

He's slept briefly in the day and now it's dark outside, only he's wide awake. He could easily be sat in a hotel room on the other side of the world after a long-haul flight, working through the early morning hours while jet lag deprives him of his bed.

The entomologist has been in touch, he's on his way up from London to inspect the bodies and the burial site, which is still being combed through by the SOCOs.

He turns on his computer and is rewarded with an email from his sergeant, headed 'proof of life'.

"Sir, we've extended the proof of life search and discovered something strange," it reads. "It would seem that Patricia Wycherley took out several loans between 1998 and 2010, which she'd be hard pressed to do if she was under the turf at Blenheim Close. All were eventually repaid. She also acted as guarantor to several loans for her daughter and son-in-law over the same period. Financial boys are having a deeper look into it. I'll keep you posted."

Rawlins reads the email again and rubs heavily at his eyes.

Patricia Wycherley was taking out loans … when Patricia Wycherley was dead. So either Patricia Wycherley wasn't dead, and they'd unearthed somebody else from her back garden, or somebody has done a very good job of covering their tracks; of keeping her alive.

More, they've profited from her death. They've profited from killing both her and William.

But truly he'd known it was them as their remains had come out of the ground, bone by lonely bone.

He'd known that as he'd watched the second van drive away, when he'd briefed his sergeant at Blenheim Close, before getting in his car and following the private ambulance out of the estate on its way to the morgue.

He'd known it then.

It's them. It's Bill and Pat that we've just uncovered.

Bill and Pat. Shot and dumped in the ground.

'What do we have?' he thinks as he guns the engine.

'What do we have?'

We have a confession of sorts, made to a third party – although not a confession to the killings, only to the burial.

We have a daughter and a son-in-law who've skipped the country – stolen money and *then* skipped the country.

So what do we have?

We have two skeletons, in the ground. Dumped! No explanations!

So what do we have?

We have hatred and very little else.

So what do we have?

Just names and speculation; and two skeletal remains.

A car come towards Rawlins as he had those thoughts; a tarnished old silver Saab estate which had seen better days.

Rawlins had flashed his lights to let it pass, pulling into the side to let it through.

The driver had been a broad-shouldered bloke in his early 40s; blond hair too long for his years and a jawline in desperate need of a shave.

He'd waved an acknowledgment to Rawlins as he'd passed which hadn't been returned.

Rawlins knew him; knew his face at least – hazy memories of long-ago interviews about cases long forgotten.

They're blown. The hacks had arrived … at least the first of them.

He pulled his car into the side of the road then, turned off the engine and took out his phone.

"It's Rawlins," he said when they finally picked up. "You can put out the statement now. Press have just rocked up."

Chapter 5

A 'reclusive' Forest Town couple who police believe were murdered and buried in their own back garden were still registered to vote at their Mansfield home at least five years after they went 'missing' – Andy Done-Johnson, Mansfield Chad, Wednesday October 23, 2013.

A formica hotel with pristinely bland decor – pastel, flowered wallpaper, flimsy doors and meaningless paintings spread evenly down the length of the corridors. I've been sitting with the assembled hacks in the bar area, but I can't settle and I wander away.

It's more than a week later and things have moved on, big time.

We've been summoned and we're here to find out our fate – or at least what the cops have in mind.

I loiter in the corridor.

Two conference rooms have been set up – one for the camera crews, where the journalists have now been asked to wait, although few of us are, and a second room; at this point I don't know what it's for.

Estelle from the press office is in there talking to a senior copper with more stripes than sleeves, their voices hushed, their eyes suspicious and cagey.

I pretend to check my phone.

I could go and sit down but I don't want to – can't be arsed to get up again, can't be arsed to make smalltalk, can't be arsed to fend off the probing if the scrum realise I'm the man on the ground.

This time a week ago and I was hammering on doors around Blenheim Close, talking to Edna; getting ahead of the game.

I got to the gate and looked back; Edna still standing at the door, looking out, looking at me with a distrustful glare.

I gave her a forced smile which I hoped conveyed sincerity; then I swung open the gate and stepped into a street transformed, with the thud of the front door closing heavily behind me.

It was a real media scrum by then – beyond anything I'd ever seen – reporters banging on every door, peering in through lace curtains and tapping on glass; the national boys up already, flashing cheque books and waving wads of notes around, trying to buy their scoop.

On the main road there was now a line of satellite trucks, camera crews setting up, anchors speaking into lenses, looking concerned and sincere, snapping out of it the second they were off the air.

A gaggle of hacks were standing around a guy on a moped and I wandered over and tried to blend in at the back; tried to look like I was the local hack, woefully out of his depth, which wasn't difficult.

As I got closer I heard him saying how he'd first spotted the tent last night; how it had been all people were talking about in the neighbourhood. But he didn't know anything else, didn't know who used to live there, didn't know who lived there now. But he was shocked, he said, really shocked.

You just don't get this sort of thing happening round here.

Yeah, yeah, I thought. I'd already got a notebook full of this stuff and I was itching to get away. Why did people always say that? Even on the shittiest most violent and lawless estates, someone would always have to say 'that sort of thing just doesn't happen around here'. This was Mansfield; not St Ann's or the Meadows or Radford, but it was as hard as nails all the same. It was poor and forgotten. People got murdered here, people died horribly here, got robbed here, got beaten-up here, got raped here . . . all the time.

The town was poor. The town was run down. It has no remaining industry. It has no heart anymore. There was nothing for the locals to do but fight and fuck and hate; bringing up another desperate generation to do more of the same.

"You get anything in there?"

A girl from one of the national networks had moved in beside me. I'd seen her on the telly, and she looked pristine in her top-end coat, smart trouser suit and heels that looked impossible, especially on this potholed sink estate.

"No," I replied, nodding at the guy on the moped, "just much the same as this. Really shocked. Only lived here a few years, didn't know them or anything about it."

"You from the local paper?"

"Yeah, for my sins."

She took a business card out of her top pocket then, pressing it into my hand.

"If you hear anything give me a bell," she said. "We pay."

"I will," I lied.

Then my phone rang.

Ash.

"Police have just called in," he said. "There's going to be a press conference down the road in an hour."

"I'm heading in," I said. "You'll have to send Izzy."

"But she's meant to be going home; she's got time owed."

"We've all got time owed, Ash."

I stepped away from the gaggle, away from the twitching ears of the national news girl, talking lightly until I was far enough away.

"Look, I've struck gold," I whispered into the handset. "Send Izzy."

I hung up and headed back to the car, not looking back, pretending I was still talking into my phone. Then I was at the driver's door, and onto the seat with the squeak of leather and the slamming of the door.

I gunned the engine and took the car further up the cul-de-sac, finding an empty driveway where I could turn around.

Back at the junction, I'd given way to let a couple of cars go past, both crawling along, their drivers gawping at the scene.

I almost changed my mind then; pulled on the handbrake and parked up again.

What if I'd missed something? What if there was more gold to dig, what if . . . what if . . .

But I knew I'd got the gold, or at least my fair share of it. Certainly enough to stake a claim.

'No,' I told myself. 'This is yours. You're in the lead; you're way out in the lead. But the only way you are staying there is if you get back to the office now and get writing.'

They had news crews and sat' trucks, and teams of people to bang on doors.

I had a pen and a pad, and a knackered laptop in a dusty office three miles away.

So I swung a left, away from Blenheim Close and back towards my desk, the car showroom, the pub and the mental hospital.

I needed Izzy at the briefing so nobody missed me, wondered where I'd gone to, and why.

The national news girl clocked me as I drove away and gave me a quizzical look, as if to say, 'Where the fuck are you going?'

Shit!

But there was nothing to do but plough onwards. I waved to her innocently and drove away, trying to look clueless, already working the copy in my head.

Questions were bashing about in my brain, spinning in circles and fizzing into the ether, as I gripped the wheel and gazed in the mirror as the sat' trucks and the press scrum disappeared behind the brow of the receding hill. Then I focused on the road ahead.

*   *   *

At some point I'd gone home, late and buzzing for a boring Friday, which had been less than boring; when there was nothing else to turn into words, no more calls to make, no more speculation to have. I'd driven home, some 20 miles. I must have done because suddenly I was babbling to anyone who would listen; standing in the kitchen, necking a beer. Suddenly I was a giddy teenager with a big secret to share.

There were bodies under the garden of this house and they'd probably been there for 15 years. Everyone there. Sky fucking News was there. And so was I. And I beat them to it. I fucking beat them.

Later, I'd sat on the sofa, glued to the box; flipping from channel to channel, watching different reporters speaking to different cameras on different segments of the same street that I had been pounding hours earlier.

They were telling their audience about 'the mysterious couple who vanished'.

They were quoting one resident, who was asking not to be named, and she was saying a lot of things Edna had said; identical, in fact.

Maybe the old girl had ended up speaking to other people. Maybe there had been an orderly queue into her dark little sitting room in the hours after I'd left. Or maybe not.

I flipped over to the local coverage. The telly anchor was reporting live from the scene. She looked cold and windswept, even though she hadn't been there when I'd been there; there'd just been an intern from their digital offering.

"We've been here ever since this grim discovery was first revealed," she told the camera as I chuckled indignantly on the sofa.

Journalists are just magpies. They steal shiny things that are precious to other people. I'd done the same; I'd do it again, but it's still infuriating when others are passing off your work as their own.

I got drunk then and spent too much time whining about robbing bastard television hacks, until people got bored of me and told me to shut up.

Everyone knows it's yours, and it's good that it's out there. You wanted it out there. So what the fuck are you bleating about?

I'd tried to calm down, but instead I drank some more and passed out on the sofa in a swirling, indignant rage.

The next day I'd woken up with a thick head and an aching back, nursed a strong coffee then stumbled down to the shop for croissants and jam. I spent a few minutes flicking through the nationals in the newspaper aisle until I'd been flashed a filthy look from the shop assistant and reluctantly parted with a quid. The Wycherley Murders had made most of the nationals, in one form or another.

Same story, I noticed. The mysterious couple who vanished. Edna had been busy. A butterfly flapped its wings.

I walked back, smug and fuming in equal measures, trying to leave it in the office for a couple of days. Failing, I stumble through the front door, kicking it closed with my heel.

"Can you call Framey," my wife said as I'd dumped down an almost-empty shopping bag on the worktop.

What?

"Framey called. He says can you call him at the office."

So I called, my heart pounding slightly, feeling like my head was still in the office anyway.

Nick Frame was working over the weekend, which was why he hadn't been around the day before when the shit had hit the fan.

We took the weekends in turns, the few of us that were left.

"What?" I growled when I called him.

"They've named them," he said. "The old couple. At least they've said who they think they are."

"William and Patricia Wycherley?"

"Yeah!"

"Just put it up online," I said. "Nothing new really. We had the names yesterday, but it's a fresh line. Police confirm . . . etc."

I'd become very protective, I realised. I didn't even want colleagues anywhere near Bill and Pat.

"They're calling a press conference on Monday," he said. "You want me to go?"

"No," I replied, a little too hastily. "It's fine. I'll take it. Where?"

He'd told me the address and I wrote it down.

"I'll go straight there," I said. "No point driving to Mansfield for nine to be in Nottingham for ten-thirty."

It went quiet down the receiver.

"Anything else happens call me, yeah?"

He promised he would and I put the phone down.

And keep your hands off. Just keep your robbing hands off.

It was the following morning when I'd been properly knocked off my perch. I'd gone out the night before for a few more beers and got hammered again, so by the time I made it down for the Sunday papers it was slim pickings.

But just from the small range I had to choose from it was everywhere – and none of it was mine.

They'd gone to town and I'd taken my eye off the ball.

"Shocked relatives say they were getting Christmas cards from William and Patricia Wycherley as recently as 2011."

Should have seen it coming really. Once the names were out there the massive engines of national newsrooms had screeched into life, belching steam and bile.

They'd have frantically started searching for relatives.

News agencies – companies that do the nationals' dirty work in the provinces – would have been briefed and reporters dispatched to knock on doors.

Eventually, by process of elimination, three genuine relatives of William and Patricia Wycherley had been found – Hilary Rose, Christine Harford and Vivien Steenson: – all nieces of William, said the reports.

None of them lived anywhere near Mansfield and none had seen William and Patricia Wycherley face to face for a very long time.

They had, however, all received regular letters and Christmas cards from the Wycherleys.

And because the press had got to them before the police did, and because of the way they had been made aware of the deaths, it probably came as more than a bit of a shock.

What do you mean they've been dead since 1998? They still send me Christmas cards.

I had slept, but my mind worked overtime and I'd spent the first few hours of Monday morning staring at the darkness of the bedroom and praying for a few hours of oblivion as my mind churned on overdrive. There was to be no peace.

Then I'd finally dropped off as it was getting light and slept late, waking groggy and panicked, diving in the shower and cursing my own ineptitude.

Two hours later and I was loitering in the corridor when Anne, my photographer, came out to me – she'd been setting up in the conference room and finally had a moment to come out for a natter. Only I was distracted and distant; looking down the corridor endlessly, checking my phone every minute or so, listening to the hubbub of the hacks, nodding at the conversation she was trying to have without taking in a word of it.

"I'm going back in," Anne had said eventually.

I nodded, and carried on staring down the corridor.

Then I'd seen him heading towards me, walking quickly, like he was late – which he was. He was still slender, still young-looking. I'd not seen him in the flesh for half a decade, not since some function we were both invited to.

He' was texting into his phone, looking down, and walked straight past me; a younger, slightly taller man lapping at his feet. I'd met him before, but I couldn't think where.

I called after them.

"Rob!"

Griffin stopped, turned, smiled.

"Alright? How are you?"

We shook hands.

"Good," I said. "You?"

He didn't answer, just asked me how the family was.

I'd known Griffin for years – not as a friend, although he was a friend of a friend, and it always made things awkward if ever our paths crossed professionally, which they had done from time to time since I was a trainee reporter and he was a probationary plod.

I was hoping for a quiet word, but I didn't get one, and instead I'd watched as they were immediately summoned into a side room; the door slamming closed behind him.

So much for contacts.

But at least I was there, when an hour earlier I'd been screaming at backed-up traffic.

It can take an hour-and-a-half to get into Nottingham from where I live in rural Derbyshire; the roads are always rammed and busy and crap and you usually can't move for roadworks and trams. I was late. It was the Monday morning, three days after I'd broken the story of a lifetime, and I was trying to make it to the first major press conference the police had called – and I was late; stuck in a traffic jam ten miles out of the city, cursing myself and swearing at the cars in front.

I'd made it with minutes to spare, thinking I'd be standing at the back and craning to hear. But when I arrived the hotel lobby was full of hacks, photographers and camera guys; milling around, checking phones, talking shop. They were still setting up, somebody said. Running late.

119

This would just be routine – I already knew that. It would say nothing more than the press release I'd already been sent, embargoed until about five minutes after they expected it to end. This was just for the telly really – to let them get shots of the investigating officer, who will just read the script that had been pre-agreed with the comms monkeys; which had already been credited to him in the press release.

For them it was about getting the word out to as wide an audience as possible. They didn't seem fussed about the local press; it was all about keeping Sky and ITN happy – a sign perhaps they were looking far wider than Nottinghamshire for their killers. But they weren't there to write stories, they were there to catch killers.

Estelle was there, taking names – sat like the chairman in the middle of a political debate on the telly.

Then she introduced Griffin and said he would read a statement and then take questions.

"Will there be one-to-ones?" someone asked.

Estelle said no, greeted by a collective groan.

Press conferences are a really weird experience – especially when they involved a real media scrum like this one. You've all got your own questions. You've all got your own theories. You all want your own lines and your own angles.

It's Monday – three days since the discovery. This is still the only story.

I'd wanted to ask if the Wycherleys had any children, only I wasn't asking it in front of a room full of journalists, just in case none of them had wondered the same thing. Of course they had. But it was a question I needed to put in a quiet corner, discreetly, away from pricking ears.

Nobody else was showing their cards either, and in the end the whole event had ended up being a summary of what we already knew; plus a brief update on the post-mortem exams and the forensics.

They were still working with the theory that it was probably the Wycherleys. Probably; almost certainly – but we couldn't say it yet, not officially, because they had no firm proof.

There were boxes to tick.

They'd carried out 'proof of life' investigations, and they'd found no evidence that the Wycherleys were alive after 1998.

They'd failed to mention the numerous financial transactions Patricia Wycherley had taken out on her daughter's behalf since the time of her death and 2012. That would come out later.

There was also no firm evidence that they were dead either . . . aside from the bodies, which wouldn't be formally identified for weeks.

I put a couple of questions. Nothing earth-shattering. Nothing I didn't already know the answers to, just letting them know that I was awake and paying attention; letting Griffin know that I was there and on it, if he had anything in particular that he wanted to share in private; just marking out my territory for the stray cats up from Wapping.

It was a real gaggle – people from everywhere. There'd been something in the air, the feeling you got when a storm was about to break.

Griffin had got to the end of his pre-amble, which was greeted by a symphony of camera flashes and a forest of raised arms.

"Is there a suspect?"

Silence.

"Detective Chief Inspector, is there a suspect?"

Griffin looked uncomfortable.

There was a reticence in his voice to answer the question; an almost-unnoticed side glance to Estelle.

"We are pursuing a number of lines of enquiry," he managed eventually.

It crossed my mind to ask whether they'd identified the young couple who neighbours had described gardening, mowing the lawns after the property was empty.

But I kept my mouth shut.

They were relatives. Of course they were relatives. If you murder a stranger you don't keep going back and mowing his lawn. They must have been related, the gardeners. And the gardeners must have been the killers; they must have been – the young couple . . . mowing the lawn . . . covering their tracks . . . covering up . . . telling lies.

I scratched my pen back to life on the cover of my notepad, but otherwise sat quietly until the end.

I found a cafe down the road with free internet, turned on my laptop and wrote up my copy, occasionally stopping to sip on my rapidly-cooling black coffee, or to watch strangers as they dawdled past the grease-stained window.

I read it, then I read it again. Then I performed a dozen complex but routine manoeuvres on the editorial server, which sent it out into the ether; there for all to see.

It was into the afternoon now, so I called Ash and told him everything was online; that I was going home to work because it would take me a good hour to get to Mansfield from here, and there was stuff I needed to do.

Then I drove home in a haze, my eyelids sinking even with the windows down, eventually falling through the front door.

I'd set up my computer on the kitchen table, and logged back into the server. Then I clocked the sofa and decided to sit on it for just a few minutes; and that's where I'd woken up the following morning, cold and stiff and still tired once more.

I'd showered, got in my car and driven the dull duel-carriageway to Mansfield.

Tuesday was deadline day and I had to turn all of the past four days' worth of events into a story for the paper.

It was going on the front, obviously, with two full pages inside. I'd argued for four but been laughed at.

"It's not the only thing that's happened this week."

It's the only thing anyone cares about.

But I'd kept my mouth shut, for a change.

The newspaper was for the old folks; the ones who still got their breaking news from the nightly telly broadcasts.

It hadn't always been that way; fifteen years earlier, my first paper had still put out seven daily editions, and that was long after the dawn of the internet.

But the young and the middle-aged had abandoned the printed page and instead glued their eyes to tablets and smartphones.

I knew that all of my efforts today were to inform the older generations; the grey-haired majority who couldn't silver-surf, or tweet, or like or even log in.

Today was for those who were still reliant on the steady strumming of the presses; their weekly digest of local events dumped outside shops in rain-drenched bundles – telling yesterday's stories in water-stained frescos and smears of illegible ink.

And for me, because I still liked a newspaper . . .

I pulled into the car park outside the paper's offices and abandoned it over two spaces, the buzz of the press pack and Edna's story still ringing in my ears.

Every day I'd see them walking past, him always ahead by a good ten paces.

My head was still spinning with Blenheim Close, with neighbourhood whisperings, and twitching curtains. They'd all suspected for years, they must have done; the abandoned house, the vanished couple, the mysterious gardeners. Yet nobody had said a word; at least not to the police or the press.

I headed for the door, fumbling for my keys, and bolted up the stairs, amazed at my own sense of urgency, thinking it had been kicked out of me long ago.

I'd little recollection of the drive back from Blenheim Close but the story was spinning in my head; my brain churning with questions I didn't know the answers to. And I had a story to tell.

Who are these people? Where are these people? Under the lawn, probably, but if not then where? And if it's not the old couple then who the hell is it in the ground?

But how had it gone unnoticed really? How the fuck, in this day and age, do two people vanish and not a soul seems to notice for more than a decade?

I'd played over what I knew in my head.

The police had dug up two bodies. The bodies had been there for a long time. An old couple used to live there and then moved away. Or had they?

They were reclusive – odd, talked about by the neighbours. They were probably called Bill and Pat Wycherley. They were creatures of routine – they did the same thing day after day.

She may have disappeared before him. Is that part of the story? Did he know? Was he complicit in some way?

She was bigger than him, ungainly, awkward – wore a mac year round and walked like a man, always trailing behind him by ten paces. They'd moved away, or at least the neighbours were told they'd moved away. They hadn't said goodbye to anyone – they'd just left. Gone to Morecambe? Maybe.

After they left they hadn't sold the house for a long time. There had been another couple. They were younger. They used to come periodically to do the garden. They hadn't done the house – just the garden. Why would they do that?

I stopped suddenly at the top of the stairs.

The bodies were in the garden. They were protecting the bodies. They were guarding the bodies.

I walked into the newsroom to find it practically deserted. The editor away in Sheffield or somewhere at a meeting. Ash had abandoned ship, something about having to go and sort out the archive at the old offices. Funny how the management always had things to do away from their desks on a Friday afternoon.

Framey was working the weekend, so his desk was abandoned. There was just Helen, one of the other seniors, and Izzy – a freelancer straight out of university, looking pissed off because she'd been told her early finish was off for another week, or month, or year.

"Fun and games?" Helen asked.

I gave a theatrical sigh.

"You couldn't make it up," I managed.

Then I told them; told them everything I'd been told – the bodies, the old couple who vanished, the young couple who kept coming to the house. I'd briefed Izzy; told her there was a press conference … in 20 minutes, told her where to go, told her what to do.

"It'll just be routine, most likely," I said. "It's with the local community inspector, so it won't be telling you anything about the investigation."

"So why are we going?" she asked with a snarl.

"Because everybody else will be there" I snapped. "I need you to make a full note and come back as soon as it's over."

I hadn't told her that she was just buying me time – giving me the chance to get writing, while all the others were listening to some copper reassuring local residents.

She went, stamping her pissed off feet heavily on the vibrating flimsy floor.

I called the press office but they wouldn't say more than they'd already put out. The bodies had been removed, I squeezed out of them. There would be an initial post-mortem later that day.

"Who are they?"

No comment.

"Who do you think they are?"

No comment.

"Off the record? Who do you think they are?"

Not giving off the record on this.

"Who are the young couple?"

What young couple?

Jesus!

"A source has told me that a young couple were turning up for years afterwards to do the garden. Know anything about that?"

I'll ask the question.

"When are you going to name them?"

Don't know. Maybe tomorrow. Still tracing relatives.

"Bill and Pat Wycherley?"

No comment.

I slammed down the phone and started to write.

Time stopped and frustration melted away, as it tended to when I was writing.

It may have taken half an hour – maybe a little longer – but eventually the story was ready.

It didn't include everything I'd been told; just what I knew was safe. But it was enough; for now it was enough.

Back in the day I'd have been writing this surrounded by a sea of reporters, facing an army of production journalists; a six-strong newsdesk team and an editor tucked away in his private office, his feet up on his desk, smoking a fat cigar like Jonah Jameson.

But the Daily Bugle didn't exist, and that time was over anyway.

Today it was just me and a field of empty desks; no army of journalists surrounding me; no lawyers at the end of a phone.

The army of sub editors had been replaced by Helen occasionally hovering over my shoulder, and gold dust glistening on my faded computer screen.

"Will you read it?" I asked.

And she had; occasionally shaking her head in amazement; pointing out the odd spelling mistake.

"Publish it," she said, after an age. "You can't wait. If you wait then somebody else will get this.

Get it out there."

Twenty years earlier, a story like this would have been a nightmare for a weekly paper – double murder two days after deadline; the best part of a week before the next edition. Old news after the telly and the nationals had their fill. But not now. Now we had the internet and a growing following of new readers in a different landscape. Now we worked in just the same arena as Sky or the Beeb or ITN. Now we were immediate as well.

Helen checked the spelling one last time. I read it one last time. Then I send it – out into the ether, out into the world. I waited, anxious, panicked almost, for the thing to turn up on the website.

It had taken forever; the best stories always did, or seemed to.

Then I link it on social media, on Facebook and Twitter and all that, and waited for the clicks to go through the roof on the monitor we had on the wall. This had become a different world. More technology and fewer reporters to make the most of it.

The phone had been ringing for a while.

It's was Izzy.

"Just like you said," she told me. "Nothing to worry about. There's not a crazed killer on the loose. Historic investigation etc etc."

I refreshed my screen for the thousandth time and eventually it was there. My story. My name. My words.

Right at the top, above a photo of a shifty-looking special constable guarding a bland box of a house, I noticed the time and date: 2.15pm on Friday, October 11, 2013. At that precise time, at that precise moment, for the first time in a decade, I felt like I was back in the game.

Neighbours say old couple 'vanished' at body find home, the headline read.

An elderly couple who lived in a Forest Town house where two bodies have been found in the garden mysteriously disappeared in the late 1990s, neighbours have claimed.

They moved into the house on Blenheim Close, Forest Town, in around 1987 or 1988 and lived there for around eight years.

People thought they had come up from London. Neighbours had been told that they had moved to Morecambe . . . amongst other places.

One Blenheim Close resident, who asked not to be named, said she had seen the couple regularly walking past her house on their daily shopping trips to Mansfield.

She said: "Every day they would walk past at around 2pm and come back at around 4pm, regular as clockwork.

"Then for a long time it was only the man and I wondered if the lady was ill, or if something had happened. Then one day the house was empty. It was empty for quite a long time before new people moved in."

The resident said that after the couple disappeared, two younger people were coming to the property to maintain the garden for a period of time before the house was re-sold.

I don't remember writing any of it.

Police had arrived at the scene and excavated the back garden. The remains of two people, who have yet to be formally identified, were unearthed. The bodies have been there for some time and a post-mortem examination to establish cause of death will take place later.

It is not yet known whether the remains are those of the old couple who previously lived at the address.

Police scene of crime officers, who have been working at the location, have erected a tent in the back garden of the property, and officers are stationed outside the address.

Local residents have spoken of their shock at the news etc etc etc.

I sat back and smiled. For a brief while it was mine – ours; before it got picked apart and stolen and recycled.

It was the first published account of the 'couple who vanished' and formed the lion's share of what everybody else reported later that day and in Saturday's print editions.

We broke it – with a pen, a notepad, a bit of good fortune, and the help of an elderly lady who only wanted to talk to us.

Although in the end she had spoken to everybody, whether she'd wanted to or not. That was the game . . .

Three days after the first press conference I was sat at my desk when the phone rang. It was Estelle.

"Just making sure you got the email," she said, a little too eager to be natural.

"I've got hundreds of emails. When did you send it?"

"Just now."

I'd checked the basket – it was there, about seven from the top, under the daily Liberal Democrat digest, click-bait from public relations firms and a message from an Indian restaurant wanting a free plug in the paper.

I read it quickly while Estelle was still on the line. There would be a second press conference, tomorrow morning at the same hotel as before.

The first press conference had been Monday. Now it was Thursday.

"Will there be an update, or is it just another appeal for information?" I asked, wondering if I really needed to be there.

"Don't know," she replied. "Rob Griffin's called it. Just asked me to do a ring-around – make sure everyone knows and everyone can make it."

"The nationals?"

"Everyone, particularly the nationals."

"What's going on, Estelle?"

"There'll be a briefing, off the record, at 9.30am," she said. "After that there'll be a second press conference, we'll have something else for you. But you need to be at the briefing. The briefing is why Griffin has called it."

"I'll be there," I replied, seconds before she'd hung up.

The same hotel, the same room, the same corridor, only three days later. Press conference number two. Not expected. Not wanted. There's an atmosphere though; a weight in the air. I send Ash a quick text – something's kicking off. Will let you know.

Then we're all packed inside the smaller briefing room. It's the same room they used on Monday, only a partition has been pulled out, splitting the space in two.

Next door is for the press conference proper, we are told.

In here no cameras are allowed, no mikes, no filming. Doesn't bother me. I've got a notepad and a pocket full of biros. They can't stop me taking notes.

They settle us down and hit us with the bombshell.

There is a line running in a certain national newspaper that is putting the police investigation in jeopardy.

The line they are running is that the couple's daughter Susan . . . .

They do have a daughter.

. . . is the prime suspect in the investigation. Susan has fled abroad and police are involved in an international search, an attempt to return her to the UK.

"Is that the case?" a voice pipes up.

"Susan Edwards is a person of interest," says Griffin. "Yes. She is someone we'd like to speak to in connection with the deaths of William and Patricia Wycherley. Susan Edwards and her husband Christopher Edwards."

Two of them. Man and woman. Husband and wife. The young couple? The young couple doing the garden?

My head is buzzing.

"Where abroad?"

"Just somewhere we think we can get them back from," says Griffin. "At least we stand a chance if every newspaper and every television station, every radio station, isn't saying that they're being hunted."

In a nutshell they want a media blackout – for the press to not report what we know; which is one hell of an ask with a story like this.

There is practically a riot.

Will they confirm that they are looking for her in mainland Europe? Will they confirm . . .

Will they . . .

"No, we're not confirming anything," pipes in the Assistant Chief, missing the mood – raising his voice like he's lecturing a room full of his own.

"The purpose of this briefing is to obtain your co-operation, to gain reassurances from you all that you won't run this line."

A chill fills the room. As a journalist you tend to get to give coppers shit, not the other way round. Coppers hate journalists; always have, probably because they realise the damage we can do, and because they're a little bit afraid of us, and they don't like that.

And this lot really aren't used to being told what to do by a copper, no matter how many stripes he's got on his arm.

"We'll work with you," Griffin says, trying to calm things.

"When the time's right we'll give you the works. We'll work with you to make sure you get what you need. But not now."

"And what if we refuse?"

A voice from the back; a voice I don't recognise.

The Assistant Chief seems to stiffen.

"We're going to send round a form for you to sign before we convene the press conference," he says. "The form will ask you to agree not to run any story which states or implies that Susan Edwards is our prime suspect, or that we are looking for her abroad."

Nobody speaks.

"Anybody who refuses to sign the form will not be allowed to attend the press conference . . ."

There is laughter.

". . . or any subsequent press briefing or media event that we hold in connection with this case, now or in the future. This included media representatives from news agencies who might be routinely supplying copy to other outlets."

That's it then. Work with us or leave the party early.

There is a silence waiting to be broken. Eventually it is.

"Well I can't just say yes to this," pipes up one of the national boys. "I'll need to speak to the lawyers."

He gets to his feet and goes to the door, like somehow he's just played an ace.

"And me, sorry."

Another gets to his feet, then another.

"Take the time you need," says Griffin.

"We'll give you half an hour to call ... whoever you need to call ... and we'll reconvene at ... shall we say 11.30?"

The briefing breaks up and the coppers leave the room. People are on the phone, arguing with newsdesks, lawyers and heaven knows who else.

I take a stroll down the corridor and call the office. I'm annoyed but it's not life and death to me ... to us. We're the local rag. We've got our audience. And we need a relationship with them when all of this is screwed-up chip paper.

But I don't want us getting left behind either and I'm not putting my name to something if the rest of them refuse.

I call the office.

"They want us to keep quiet about an international manhunt," I say. "They don't want us to say that the daughter is the prime suspect."

"Is she? What's everybody else saying?"

"I did tell you about the couple, remember? Anyway, don't know. Not spoken to them. Don't seem very happy though."

"What's happening now?"

"They've broken off for a bit to let people call in."

I look along the corridor. It is populated entirely by outraged hacks talking animatedly into phones.

"Do you think they'll go for it?"

"Not sure. They seem pretty pissed off though. They're calling lawyers."

"That's nice for them. Remember when we had lawyers we could call?"

"Vaguely."

I laugh, prompting stern looks from the other hacks in the corridor.

"I think we need to do whatever the nationals decide to do," I say. "Can't be the only publication not running a line. It'd just make us look shit."

"You'll need to make the call. You're there. Just go with what you think."

"OK", I reply. "To be honest I think they'll go for it. If the cops won't confirm the line then we haven't really got anything, apart from 'it is understood', 'it is believed', 'according to sources', 'according to reports from a national newspaper'. All bollocks. And they're all carrying on like moths round a lightbulb."

Estelle passes me in the corridor and I beckon her over.

She comes, reluctantly; her eyes already shifty, just like mine, no doubt.

"So between us," I say, "is there any sort of timescale on this?"

She doesn't answer and goes to walk away.

"Off the record, Estelle. Come on. I'm trying to work with you here. You can't just expect us to sign a form and shut the fuck up. Are arrests imminent? If not, when? Tomorrow? Next week? Next month?"

I realise I'm raising my voice and I hold up my hands as an apology.

"Look," she snaps, "off the record or on the record for that matter, I honestly don't know. They only tell us what they need to tell us. But I do know that the situation is precarious. It could go either way."

"So you do know?"`

"No," she closes me down in a hoarse whisper, her face in mine. "It's just what I'm sensing from them, for fuck's sake. What if they get word they're being hunted and get on a plane to Qatar or Venezuela, somewhere we don't have extradition rights; somewhere that doesn't buy into the European Arrest Warrant?"

"But we're the bloody Chad," I snap. "You can't get us in Spain or . . ."

"You can get the internet anywhere. That's the problem. It's not print they're worried about."

I feel like a naughty schoolboy and an old man, all conveniently wrapped together and suddenly staring bashfully at the carpet.

"So how long?" I ask eventually, knowing I've really pissed her off, but sick of the awkward silence.

"How long for what?"

"Arrest."

"I honestly don't know," she hisses, looking round. "But I don't think it's going to be today, alright? Or tomorrow or this week, for that matter. Christ!"

She storms off, leaving me standing alone in the corridor; me wafting my pad about at my side, or on my face, like I'm using it as a fan.

Not this week, she'd said. Not before the next paper.

And if the national lot do agree to the blackout then they'll lose interest altogether – they'll be off chasing other ambulances. Whereas you, well you'll be left to work it on your own; just for a few more days . . . and you just think what you can do with a few more days.

It's coming crashing in; the end of this part of the story at least – a clinical couple of lines on a police email saying 'two persons have been arrested in connection with . . .'

The guillotine is being raised.

But it's Friday now and we come out on Tuesday and it's unlikely the daughter and her husband are going to be found, arrested, transported and charged before then. We've only splashed on the Wycherleys once so far and we need a second bite of the cherry . . . at least I do.

We can't say who the killers are, or who the police suspect them to be. We are silenced, effectively; holding out our own hands willingly for the shackles.

But it doesn't kill the story – not for me. We can still say what they did.

As I drive back to Mansfield, through the city, out through its northern suburbs, then into open countryside; to rolling fields full of static wind turbines and solar farms, two-for-one pubs and endless speed cameras, I think about the work that I need to do.

There is still a story to tell and a paper to get out. There are houses that have been flogged on the quiet, people kept alive when they're rotting in the ground, and a deceived community that hadn't even noticed.

I was drawn back into the room as Izzy stormed in, slamming her bag heavily onto her desk.

"Who's that twat from the local telly?"

"Which one? There's a few."

"Tall bloke, acts like a twat."

"Oh, him? I know. Why?"

"I asked him directions to the briefing and he sent me the wrong way. I nearly missed it."

"Twat."

While Izzy typed and I tried not to stand over her shoulder, I had a thought. I had a few credits left on an electoral roll search facility that I used – basically a way of finding out where people live. A decade earlier the company would have had it as standard. Now it comes out of my pocket.

I logged in.

I typed the address – 2 Blenheim Close, Forest Town, Mansfield, and it grumbled into life.

Then suddenly, there they were.

William G Wycherley.

Patricia D Wycherley.

I checked the dates.

The first record of them at the address was 1986.

Must be them. Must be.

And they were there long after 1998, which couldn't be right – because according to the cops, and if you accepted it was the Wycherleys in the ground, they were both dead in 1998 and somebody had been filling out their voter registration forms seven years later.

So who had been keeping them alive?

My mind returned to the young couple doing the garden, every now and then, regular as clockwork. Them in the garden, weeding the borders, cutting the grass, tidying the hedges, and all the time paying particular attention to the area by the patio doors; preserving the crime scene, protecting the graves, hiding the truth and letting the days roll by like nothing had happened – just an empty house, lost in time and apathy; nobody knowing what had happened behind the high wooden fences. Nobody but the gardeners.

Tuesday of week three – eleven days since the bodies had been found, four days since Griffin had closed us down; eight hours before the paper goes to bed. I've been busy. We've only had one bite of the cherry and I really want another – even if we are conspiring to hide half the story.

In the end they'd all agreed. They'd been livid, all of them ... really furious.

The press office team had circulated around the room with forms, asking us to sign them if we agreed to the blackout.

One bloke refused and had been asked to leave. He'd stood up, flustered; then he'd signed the form and sat back down again. They'd all signed, reluctantly, but they'd all done it.

I signed; told them it was fine; told them I expected them to remember the co-operation the next time we came to them with something.

They'd said they would and I'd given a supportive nod, knowing it was bollocks; knowing the promise would be forgotten the second they moved to the next signature. We really didn't have any choice, that was the truth of the matter.

We couldn't afford for relations to break down, we're not the nationals.

We can and do regularly piss them off, the police. We're not in their pockets. We'll criticise them, we'll expose their blunders and hold them to account. But we need them as well and there was a line in the sand here. We'd be living with the fallout of this long after the rest of the pack had scraped the shit from their boots and moved onto other things.

The police needed us too, day to day. They needed us to run their appeals if someone's house got burgled, or someone got robbed or raped; they needed us if some teenager didn't arrive home and their resources were being drained while they looked for them. They still needed us, the local rag, because mainly they were trying to speak to local people. They pretended they didn't, but they did. It was and is a very different relationship. It's a relationship of mutual benefit; a business relationship between sworn enemies.

To make matters worse, the press conference that followed had been crap – nothing new, just a rehash of what they'd told us a few days earlier; just a renewed appeal for information.

But that was then and this is now.

I'd driven back to Mansfield in a rage – furious at being closed down; determined they weren't going to silence us.

I'm digging. I've been digging since I got into the office on Thursday lunchtime. I've had no weekend; I've been up since the crack of dawn, in the office before it's light even.

I've got a plan, of sorts – built more on sand than stone.

I'd already done a basic digital search of the electoral roll, but I wanted to see the full paper records, held at the council officers in the town centre.

I turn up and ask to see them, expecting to be told that I'd need to make an appointment, but the girl on the desk is more than happy to help me out.

She takes me through to a side room, sits me down, and spends the next ten minutes bringing volumes of dusty records in solemn leather bindings, looking like they weight a ton.

I ask if I can help her, but she smiles and says I'm not allowed into the archive.

I make a start.

All the addresses are listed alphabetically by street name within a certain grouping of postcodes.

I start at 1985 – find Blenheim Close, but the names don't match.

So I repeat the process for 1986, and there they are.

William and Patricia Wycherley – 2 Blenheim Close, Forest Town, Mansfield. Their first appearance.

They are listed every year until 2003, when suddenly nobody is listed at the address. I make a note, I snap all the pages on my phone, thank the girl on reception and leave.

As long as nobody gets arrested we have another line, I think as I drive back to the office - another line strong enough for the front, just as long as they aren't behind bars by 6.30pm, when the paper goes to the printers; a second bite of the apple, before the curtain comes crashing down.

I call Estelle for an update – any arrests, any arrests, are we safe, are they still at large?

Eventually she loses her rag and says she will call me with any news.

"Paper goes at 6.30pm," I tell her. "After that it's out there and there's nothing either of us can do about it, so don't come whining at me if we accidentally prejudice your investigation."

I'm going by the numbers, making notes of exact times of each call, just in case I have to explain myself to a judge.

Then I turn my attention to the Land Registry – the Government organisation which records the sale of all property, both commercial and domestic in this country. They tell me that I can access the information online . . . for a small charge.

I go onto their website and start a search for Blemheim Close, Forest Town. It costs me three quid for a basic search, which I pay for myself.

If I wait to get clearance from the company to agree the transaction, there's a good chance I'll have died of old age.

It reveals a pdf of a handwritten form, showing the sale of 2 Blemheim Close, Forest Town, Mansfield, in 2005.

At the bottom of the form are two names – printed in black ink with signatures below – written seven years after they were put in the ground.

William Geoffrey Wycherley.

Patricia Dorothy Wycherley.

Somebody has sold the house pretending to be them. They've posed as William and Patricia Wycherley and they've sold the house with the bodies still under the back lawn.

A chill passes through me.

I become very aware that I'm not looking at the handwriting of William or Patricia Wycherley, the mysterious couple who vanished.

I'm looking at the handwriting of the people who killed them.

Susan Edwards? Christopher Edwards? Susan and Christopher Edwards? The gardeners.

Good at forging signatures too. Good at sending cards at Christmas.

Chapter 6

In 2012 you fled to France when the Department for Work and Pensions contacted Mr Wycherley, seeking a meeting before his 100th birthday. You returned to the jurisdiction voluntarily, in 2013, with no money – Sentencing remarks, Mrs Justice Thirlwall, R v Edwards and Edwards, June 2014.

The rumble and grumble and the rock and the rattle of the track as the train speeds up until it catches the rate of Susan's heartbeat, flying through the darkness of Northern France; her eyes closed – like she's inside the final moments of a plane before it crashes into the earth. Field after field speeds by; a flashing farmstead; the lights of a car halted by a crossing. Then, finally, the glare of the border-compound at Calais greets them; a moment of darkness followed by the sickening yellow light of the tunnel wall rushing past endlessly, like a tepid liver cancer; and they have left France.

She sits and stares at the empty seats opposite her. Chris sits by her side and occasionally squeezes her arm, or her wrist, or lays a hand on her knee.

She doesn't respond or react, she does not reciprocate. She just sits like an ice statue, staring ahead at the seats, or out of the window, at the nauseous flashing amber, like the street lighting she's always hated from their life back in Dagenham.

The carriage is empty, almost.

Three places down, a couple sit in the central isle over four seats, taking advantage of the quiet night and making the most of the extra space, their feet occasionally brushing as they lounge.

Behind them, two rows back still, Frank has got a card school going with Gary, Rock and Montgomery – shrouded in cigar smoke, their laughter filling the carriage.

Nobody else notices them. The young couple in front seem more interested in her.

Each time she looks at them, one or the other is staring at her, or at Chris.

And they don't seem to have much to say to each other either. Not holding hands. Not smiling.

Susan and Chris are both facing backwards – they have their faces to France, their backs to England. She has told him that she doesn't want to see the lights, she doesn't want to see it all getting closer, coming towards her; the inevitability and fate that is waiting at the end of the line.

It is less than a year since they made this journey in reverse, only then it was supposed to be a departure, an escape. A beginning.

They were saying a final goodbye to British shores. They were starting again, starting afresh, starting all over – running away to a new city, and closing the door firmly behind them.

Only their land of milk and honey has proved to be barren pastures, a desert of isolation, contemplation, anger and blame.

Chris clutches the suitcase on his knees – all they have left, just pictures of Gary and Frank and the others, frozen in a silver silence and suspended in a time of hair cream and sharp suits and cigarettes that didn't kill you and burned on forever.

They looked so dignified, so clean, so noble in those photos.

They are nothing like the rabble currently doing tequila shots further down the carriage, past the young couple that keep staring at her – those boys, clinking glasses, dealing another hand and taking theatrical pulls on their Cuban cigars.

She thinks of them in their studio photos again – the photos she's purchased of them; of Gary and Frank and Sammy and the rest, just to own a version of them, just to have them in her life.

Susan sees their grinning, silver faces on faded paper squares, marked by the scrawls of their lazy signatures, stroked out like a million others – to Helen, to Judith, to Sandra, to Susan. To nobody I know.

How she wants a cigarette now.

How she wishes she had smoked her lungs out all these years.

How she wishes she had been dad, smoking his way through sixty-a-day, all paid for by the state from the healthy bundle of benefits he collected.

Another peal of laughter from the back, and Monty is pushing in his chips, then throwing in his cards, sinking back in his seat, sulkily.

How Susan wishes she was spread out now like Monty, spread out and stoned on ganja and gin, slumped in the back seat of a red '57 Chevy, cruising down Sunset Strip – no Frankie at the wheel, no Dean or Sammy or Gary, not tonight.

Tonight it's Monty's turn – pretty little Montgomery Clift at the wheel. Monty who was dead on drink and drugs at 46, whisking little Susie to some show or other; where all the boys would flirt with her and want her, and she would get the pick of the litter.

And tonight it's Monty's turn, the poor, vulnerable, little doe-eyed boy.

She's getting tired of Sammy and his tapping feet, Gary and his moody stare, Frank and his twinkling eyes. But she's most bored of Sammy. More bored of Sammy than dad now. So Sammy can go and join Elvis and dad in the closet.

Never did a day's work in his life, dad, and still had the money for sixty fags a day, every day.

Her going without, always.

Not mum. Never mum.

Mum always had her gin and a drag on dad's fags whenever she asked for one – although he preferred to give her the end bit.

But it was Susan that had nothing, Susan who starved, who never went out, who never had friends, never had anything – because she had scruffy clothes and needed a wash and a hairdresser; because dad used to make mum cut her hair to save a few coppers – while he smoked his fags and she slugged her gin in the kitchen, looking through to make sure Susan didn't see, didn't know, even though she knew all along.

And as she grew into a woman, or as near to one as she ever came – without breasts, without hips, without looks – Susan withdrew into her own room and her own mind.

There she threw herself into books and pictures – too frequently contemplating her stern, pointed, witch-like face; her hair that would never grow properly; the clothes that looked like her mother's; the life that was far from glamourous; and the life that she knew she should have had.

Not the Susan of gin joints and parties, not the Susan lounging on the back seat of a Hollywood cruiser, letting Gary and Monty take their turns.

Not that Susan.

The real Susan.

Her.

How did it come to this?

Susan looks over at Chris. He is still staring straight ahead, clutching the suitcase full of Gary and Frank and the others, occasionally closing his eyes – but opening them rapidly each time, because it makes him want to cry, it seems. His lip quivers, his face strains, and then his eyes snap open and he stairs out, once again, at the facing seats or the sickly view through the window.

His face is decorated with beads of sweat. He can't speak. He can't move. Susan doesn't want him to.

Chris looks nothing like Monty, nothing like Deano, nothing like Gary, or dad. He looks like a killer about to be arrested by the police. That's what he looks like. He looks like a killer, like a cornered ferret. Gary smiles at her again, tips her another wink, downs another shot, then gets back to his cards. He doesn't see Susan smile back . . .

Sat on the swings in the back garden of a house in West London a lifetime ago. It is sunny and bright. It is the height of the summer. Susan watches dad flirting and joking with his nieces, Vivien and her friends – her laughing like a giggling schoolgirl, even though she's already a woman.

Dad looking like Cary Grant – sharp suited with a cigarette pressed between his lips, his hair slicked back smart and a forgotten drink in his hand which he sloshes around as he holds court.

Mum sits away on a step on the patio, silent and stern, taking guilty sips at her gin and lime, pretending not to see, not daring to notice.

They had walked there, Susan remembers now all these years later, walked miles because dad didn't want to take a bus or the tube. Couldn't afford his fags and the bus ride, so the fags had won. The fags always won.

Walking down sweltering streets next to mum, not holding her hand because mum never held hands, so Susan never asked, not anymore.

Both walking behind dad, always ten paces behind, never daring to get closer, while also fearing his rebukes if they fell too far behind.

Dad's back, walking alone, fag in hand, nodding at passers-by, never stopping to talk. Dad didn't have friends, dad had too many secrets for friends, too many lies washed around and passed out as truths.

Susan hopes someone will give her a push, but she sits on her swing unnoticed, invisible.

She looks up at dad but he is gone from the garden, the pert little arse of one of aunty Viv's friends disappearing through the back door in a sparkly red dress – her, casting her eyes towards mum to make sure she hasn't been spotted.

But mum had just stared at her shoes as the girl disappeared inside, leaving Vivien to rule the roost. They are gone for a while, dad and the girl, and Susan wonders if they are queueing for the toilet. Then dad comes back, brushing down his hair, refreshing his glass and sparking up another fag.

Soon the friend is back as well, nursing the creases out of her skirt, smoothing it down towards her knees, her eyes always on dad. They both seem to glow, flashing occasional glances back and forth.

They'd pay later, Susan and mum. He was always worse when he'd been drinking, always worse when they got back to the house and the reality of his life sunk in again – back inside his familiar four walls, his ugly daughter and ungainly, hunched wife, living on the social, hiding from the rent man.

He was always worse when he couldn't strut like a film star, playing the role of exotic uncle Bill, who worked undercover in the War and didn't come back to Blighty until the early 1950s – even though he'd actually fled to Canada to avoid the draft.

He was a coward, Bill Wycherley, her dad. And deep down everybody knew it. He even had the gun which he'd brought back after the War, which he claimed had been his Special Forces service revolver, although he actually bought from an American GI in a bar.

That was dad's secret. That's why he never made friends, never let anyone get close. In those days, when families were still grieving loved ones lost just a decade-or-so before, nobody had any time for a coward – only his family.

Bill's family would have forgiven him anything, and regularly did. He was a black sheep, was uncle Bill, and that's why they'd loved him so much.

Another couple move down the train, taking seats a couple of rows behind. Susan can't see them. She can only hear the sound of their hushed voices, the shuffle of their feet on the rough carpets, the sound of their breathing, the rustle of fabric and the creak of plastic as they sit down.

Susan wonders where they have come from and why they have moved – this train has only two stations, the one they've just left and the one Susan hopes never arrives.

The card school has died down now and the boys are all sleeping off the whiskey, apart from Gary, who looks dreamily out of the window, pulling on what's left of his cigar.

She can sense the couple behind her, staring at her, their whispers undetectable to her ears; murmurings which may be English, may be French.

Susan glances round, quickly, and meets their stares. She doesn't smile. Neither do they, but they stop talking until her eyes are no longer on them.

They had left their French flat in a manner similar to their home in Dagenham, only without the thrill of new adventures and expectations for the life ahead. Now there is just the inevitability of their situation.

Chris had shut the door solemnly, and left the key in the lock for the landlord to find. They waited until they heard his door slam below them, after they'd peered through the foggy attic windows, watching him cross the street and head towards the Metro down the street.

This is the time, their eyes had said to each other, and they hurriedly put on coats and shoes, and grabbed the suitcase which had long been packed and ready by the front door. They were taking Gary and the others with them. They had to come. They were all they had left.

They couldn't afford the Metro. Chris scanned the handful of coppers he had pulled from his trousers, fumbling together enough to buy a baguette, which he roughly tore in half.

They gnawed on it, famished, as they wandered through the streets towards the main station – no longer noticing the architecture which had wowed them such a short time before.

They drank water from a public fountain to wash down the bread.

Not much of a last meal, all things considered.

Dad always kept their wedding photo in pride of place on the mantelpiece. Him looking handsome and dapper, mum ungainly and slumped, embarrassed by the occasion – doing her best to hide the swell in her belly with a tatty bouquet.

They were standing outside the Baptist chapel in Fulham where they still went on a Sunday – where dad would get all fire and brimstone and pious, then leave her and mum on the steps of a pub round the corner while he went in for a stiffener afterwards.

They made for a strange pair, even then, and you had to think, with his film star looks and her heavy and ungainly frame that he knew what he'd been doing all along.

He wasn't getting himself a wife, more a packhorse for now and a nurse for later on. He didn't want a pretty little floozy – he could have one of those whenever he ventured out alone, and Susan knew he regularly did, right up to when she was a young woman, and even with her limited knowledge of such things, she could detect that glint in his eye and the stink of other women on him.

And that's why he hated mum so much as he got older – when his looks more collapsed than faded in his early fifties and the floozies stopped lining up. Then all he had was mum, his ugly and mannish wife, who he forced to walk behind him – less out of religious conviction now, although he'd never have admitted it, and more out of embarrassment and contempt.

And as dad crept towards his mid-sixties, his plan for a nurse also failed him, as mum's back played her up more and more, and dad found himself to be her reluctant and vengeful carer.

But in the photo his eyes still sparkled, like all his Christmases had come at once. Susan often wondered, then, when she was a girl and through into adult life, what the young William Wycherley would have thought if he'd known what he would grow to become – a coward, a hypocrite, a womaniser, a penniless shirker.

What hopes must that young man have had when he first fled his home in the mining communities around Mansfield, when he packed up his bags and ran away to London one day when he was still a boy, hoping for a whole new life away from the clapped out temperance halls and the prospect of a life set in darkness, deep below the ground, where he'd have broken his back each day for pennies.

No. That was no life for the cultured young man who loved God and loved playing music, who would perform with his brothers and sisters at chapel events each Sunday, soaking in the praise and the applause of the rough-handed miners who used their one day away from the coalface to come and worship the Almighty.

No, that was no life for William, and he first fled to Canada – he would tell others it had been as part of a child migrant programme, which was a lie, because really he was just running away.

But Canada hadn't worked for dad that first time and he was back in Britain within six months, this time settling in London with his brother who had also fled the Shirebrook coal seams.

That lasted until the war, when dad had once again upped and offed back to Canada, abandoning his brother and the window-cleaning round they had set up together, quick as a flash before his call-up papers could drop through the letterbox.

Dad only ever had one answer to the problems he faced. His only solution had been to run away; an instinct he carried throughout his life.

* * *

Chris had spoken to a guard, shown his passport, shown Susan's passport which he also kept in his top pocket. There was a hushed conversation, before they were let through. Then they were on the train and sitting down. Gary and Frank and Monty and the rest were already seated. Just those four, with Sammy loitering by the window, looking out.

They chose the quietest carriage so they could talk – but once they were settled there was nothing left to say, and as the young couple joined them, seating themselves a few feet away, the chance had gone, perhaps forever.

But that was for the best now, thought Susan. Silence was the best option. They had talked for days, for days and days – about the past, about their lives together, about mum and dad and that horrible night, about what happened that horrible night.

"We are victims," Chris had said. "We are the victims," over and over, until Susan had almost believed him.

They flew to Graceland, Susan and mum and they had the best of times – mum who always loved Elvis and was grief-stricken when he died on the toilet at 42. Susan, who liked Elvis because mum liked Elvis.

But Susan was just giddy with the money in her pocket after granddad passed away and she decided there and then that she was taking mum to Graceland with some of it.

They were like fish out of water in America's deep south, her and mum, standing at Elvis's grave, buying mementoes to take home to dad, even though dad hated Elvis, along with everything else.

They would walk through the streets of Memphis, her and mum, amazed at the yellow school buses, stopping to watch the coloured musicians strumming the blues in the streets or on porches outside bars, looking at the police on their motorbikes, wearing mirrored sunglasses and carrying guns in their holsters.

They didn't want to go home, ever.

Susan booked the tickets not long after granddad died, after she found out that he had left her ten thousand pounds, and not a penny to dad.

Dad was furious and made it clear he was furious.

It was his money, he had said. It had been his father. It was his father and his fucking money. His fucking money and she was a fucking Judas bitch and she'd get what was coming to her.

Only Susan kept the money and for a while she thought she might use it to escape from him for good, to take it with her to America where Frank of Dean or Gary would meet her in a bar on Sunset Boulevard, and fall madly in love with her, and say that she could keep the money, because it was hers and they had plenty.

But instead she had taken mum to Graceland, where they had stared at Elvis's grave, and bought dad a litter bin with a photo of The King on the side, which she had found by the dustbins the day after they got home.

In the end it was just her, mum and dad, after she'd flown to America and felt young and special and rich. But dad kept his tantrum going for weeks, and months.

So, after the trip she counted up what was left and there was a little over seven thousand, which was a lot of money in the 1970s. Enough to buy a house, or at least to go a long way towards it.

So to calm dad down and to make mum happy, Susan had found a house for them to live in, in Edgware – only it was ten thousand pounds and she felt guilty now about taking mum to Graceland. It felt fickle and excessive, and it felt foolish.

So she told mum and dad that she wanted to buy a house for them to live in, to get them off the estate and to put a roof over their heads that belonged to them and not the council.

Only she needed them to find four thousand pounds as she didn't have enough for the one she'd seen.

Dad hit the roof at first, and said it was her fault and if she'd not been such a selfish fucking cunt and buggered off to America then she might have been able to buy it for them outright.

And for almost the first time she had stood up to him, she had put him in his place and he hadn't liked it one bit; but he'd had to swallow it, because deep down he wanted them to buy the house and he couldn't afford it without Susan's money in the pot.

She'd said, alright, well, if you feel that way, I'll just take the money I've got left from granddad and buy myself a nice little flat. You can come and see me, come for Sunday dinner, as long as you call first and let me know to cook.

And suddenly mum had a thousand in her savings, and dad cashed in an insurance claim from when he fell off a ladder, the last time he'd been working, and they had a house to call their own – mum and dad and Susan, a happy little family.

Flying back into Heathrow, she had drunk Champagne with mum, clinking glasses over the Atlantic and laughing, giddy, like best friends.

And that was the last time Susan could remember her and mum being happy together.

Dad always was miserable and cantankerous; relentless almost. He never used his fists on them, not after Susan was eleven and as big as him. Mum was always bigger than him, and as he got older he was frail and doddery. But he damaged them all the same; especially Susan, who he inflicted harm on in ways that she found difficult to define or comprehend.

In her 20s, Susan would look at him, sat on the sofa in the house she'd bought him, spouting bile and hatred at anybody who would listen, smoking fag after fag, and stubbing out the ends in a silver ashtray on a stand, so he could flick his ash without raising more than a spindly arm.

One day those fags will come back to haunt you, and the cancer will get you. And let's see who cares. Not mum, not when you're in the ground and gone – the soil muffling your moaning and bitterness.

And not me. I'll dance on your grave for everything you've ever done and said, you evil, vindictive old man.

Then one day she'd brought Chris home, and on that day her world had ended, at least as she knew it.

Out of the window, the amber cancer of the tunnel suddenly slips away and is replaced with the domineering darkness of the Kent evening, purple skies turning inevitably to black.

Susan looks at Chris, but he doesn't look back.

Dad had hated Chris from the start, but he'd have hated it if she'd brought home Clarke Gable; more even. Susan never knew whether he hated Chris more because he was so ordinary, or whether it would have been worse if he'd presented more of a threat – if he'd possessed the film star looks that gravity and nicotine had stolen from her father too early in life – leaving him frail, puny and white-haired.

Chris wasn't much, but he was more of a man than dad ever was.

They never talked about how they met, her and Chris, and as the years went by it faded away into an awkward unmentionable.

You only met someone through a lonely hearts column if nobody else wanted you. That's how Susan felt anyway. Even when she was a woman, even when she part-owned her own home and had a job, the men in the office never looked at her in the same way they looked at the other girls, never flirted with her, or teased her; certainly never asked her out or tried it on with her. But why would they? She was just plain Jane Susan Wycherley, the lonely spinster in waiting.

Even mum had found somebody, even if that somebody had been dad, and look how that had turned out.

Susan wanted control and as she moved into her 20s, she felt the need for more independence from her parents.

She wanted a partner and she wasn't going to end up saddled with someone like her father, with his roving eyes and hands, replaced by his bitter and lashing tongue as age and gravity got the better of him.

No, Susan was in control. She would decide who she was going to be with, from whoever responded from the agency she had paid fifteen pounds to join.

And in the end, that person had been Chris – little Chris with his soft voice, his awkward manner and his social unease. Chris, who liked military history and shooting guns and had a steady job in accounts.

There was part of Susan that thought, hopefully, mistakenly, that Chris and dad would hit it off – dad could tell Chris about his experiences in the War, working on merchant ships out of Canada, away from all the fighting.

He could show Chris the gun he kept in the top drawer next to his side of the bed, and Chris could impress dad with his knowledge of the War, and De Gaulle and Churchill and all the others.

But it wasn't to be, and deep down Susan always knew.

Dad hated him from the outset, set about bullying him as soon as he set eyes on him – even tried to throw him out, told him to fuck off and leave his daughter alone. He didn't want the likes of him meddling with her.

"This is my fucking house, you pathetic little cunt, so fuck off out of it," he'd said the first or second time Chris came round, or something like that.

But Susan had put her foot down and said that actually it was more her house than dad's, and she would invite whoever she pleased.

After that she invited Chris round just to annoy her father, to show him who was wearing the trousers round the house these days.

"I'm not your nurse. I will never be your nurse," she had said to herself, over and over again.

And when Susan was being really honest with herself, as very occasionally she was, she'd admit that she probably only married Chris to get back at dad once and for all, after he started taking himself upstairs, or into the garden shed in the Summer whenever Christopher called.

She feared that without her father's hatred, their dreary little romance would have quickly faded to nothing.

They married in 1983 – Susan was 26, Chris was 27. Dad didn't attend. Mum did, but said she'd pay for it when she got home.

The train has slowed now, creaking on British rails back towards the London they had fled for good, less than a year ago, the London they had said goodbye to, hoping to never see again.

"Won't be long now," Chris says, like he's talking to a bored child on a day trip back from the seaside.

It's the first time he's spoken since the train set off from Lille.

Susan doesn't reply. The anger has built up in her again. Anger at dad. Anger at mum, and anger at Chris – because he's the only one left, and because *he*'s got them into this. Only he hasn't, not really.

For a while, a year maybe, Susan had felt empowered, in control. She had fled the nest and lived with Chris in their little flat in Dagenham, and she had dad on a leash because she part-owned the house he was living in. It was one quick call to the estate agent to turn his miserable old bones out into the street.

She'd go to visit, sometimes even taking Chris to prove a point, and because she knew dad would go out she could sit and talk to mum. Although mostly Chris stayed away because he didn't want the hassle of it and all the rows and abuse; first with dad and then from Susan on the way home, taking out her own frustrations on him. Dagenham was about as far from Edgware as you could get while still being in London, and that suited Susan perfectly.

It took over an hour on public transport and mum and dad never came calling.

To this day Susan didn't know why she agreed to sign over the house to them, why she gave them every penny she'd ever had. Perhaps it was the first euphoria of new marriage, that sense of growing up, of being independent, of not wanting to be controlled by her parents, and of not wanting to control them. But part of her also knew it was a severing of ties – all they really had that joined them now was their three signatures on the deeds to a house in Edgware, and if she removed her name then she was setting herself free in a very real way.

And besides, what was seven grand when you were content? Chris had a steady job and earned a decent wage, so to hell with the house, and to hell with mum and dad; well, dad, anyway.

Only Susan hadn't realised until their second year of marriage that Chris was useless with money, really bloody useless. He didn't drink much and neither of them smoked, but he kept buying things, things he wanted but didn't need – first for himself, his Churchill first editions and his De Gaulle letters, and then for her. He'd turn up with a new picture of Gary or Frank or Rock or Monty, and he'd hand it to her like a sheepish schoolboy who had just brought a painting home for mother.

Susan would gush and he'd peck her on the cheek.

"How much was this, Chris?" she'd ask.

Only he'd never say; he'd just tell her not to worry, that she was worth every penny.

But then they couldn't afford to pay the rent, so they'd have to take out a loan and get more into debt; but still he'd buy things – more books, more pictures, more letters, even a gun like the one dad still had to use at the gun club.

Then the letter arrived, fluttering onto the mat.

Dear Susan,

It has been some time since we have seen you, so I felt it appropriate to write, what with neither of us being on the telephone.

After giving it very careful consideration, and as I now feel I am entering the final chapter of my life, mum and I have decided to move out of London.

I have long missed the town I grew up in and am now eager to spend my final days back in the community that made me.

We have therefore accepted an offer of £36,000 on our house in Acton and have purchased a property in Mansfield for significantly less. This should afford us both the opportunity to live out our lives in relative comfort. Mum agrees.

Your father.

That spidery hand, that insect-like scrawl of his, which Susan could imitate perfectly, from all the time he'd made her answer his correspondences, to the doctor, to the council, to the bastards at the dole. And whenever she wrote in his style, she felt all of his venom, all of his hatred and poison pouring through her.

She felt it now as she read the letter again in her mind, every word perfectly preserved in her thoughts; her father's final insult, his final betrayal. He was having the last laugh, he was taking control. He was doing what he always did when his back was against the wall. He was running away.

And as the years went by and Christopher's debts grew and grew, and the bailiffs came round, or the electricity was cut off, or the council threatened them with eviction; and they had to take out more loans or sell off more of the collection, or all of the collection, to get by, to make ends meet; it was then that Susan's hatred had started to grow.

Her father had betrayed her, and her mother had let him – she had taken dad's side, like she always did in the end.

And even after mum and dad had moved to Mansfield, and they had got themselves a telephone, and so had Susan, they would make her life miserable from afar, calling to pull her into their squabbles and fallouts; dad on the phone in the small hours after a night on the whiskey, telling her what he thought of that cunt of a son-in-law; mum calling at the end of her tether because dad was being so vile.

Then Susan did hate, in a way that she had never been capable before, despite everything he had done to her. She hated dad for the way he was, she hated mum for betraying her, for stealing from her, and for other things beyond mention. And she hated Chris for being weak, for being impulsive; and she hated Mansfield for giving her father his last laugh.

Up ahead, Susan could see the bright lights of London drawing ever closer. She closed her eyes, determined not to cry.

A bright Tuesday morning in Mansfield, and Susan walks through the centre of town, heading to the bank, clutching a letter with instructions in mum's boxed hand.

It instructs the manager to open up a new account in mum's name and that of her daughter, Susan Edwards. It also authorizes the transferral of £40,000 into this new account from another joint account she holds with her husband, William G Wycherley.

Due to my husband's failing health and declining years, we have decided that it is time for all financial burdens to be spared him, in order that he can make the most of his final months and years.

The bank carries out Patricia's instructions without question, and Susan strolls out through the Market Place and relishes the breeze and the radiant sunshine on her face. She looks at the shoppers, scuttling around this sad little town, and she wonders whatever possessed dad to move them out of London to this place. He didn't know anybody here. He didn't like anyone here.

It was the first time Susan has walked these streets in six years, since she and Chris had paid a visit in 1992 and there had been another blazing row. Dad had been pissed by the time they arrived and proceeded to get more pissed and more abusive as the long hours crept by.

Eventually Chris had bitten, told dad to show people a bit of respect, but that had just been like a red rag to a grumbling old bull.

Stumbling to his doddering feet, bearing his once-broad shoulders on his week and trembling legs, he prodded a boney finger hard into Chris's chest.

Mum was crying, Susan didn't know where to look, and she just wished Chris would stand up for himself.

'Well this is my house now, old son," dad's rasping, fag-damaged voice had croaked. "So get out. Get out now."

Chris had almost risen to it, almost, but in the end he'd stepped away, grabbed for his coat.

"That's it, piss off, you sniveling little shit," William had roared as he tried and failed to follow him around the tiny, sun-starved sitting room.

"This is my house. This is my fucking house."

But not anymore, thought Susan, pressing the button and waiting for the green man to flash before she crosses the road.

Long walk back to Forest Town.

Hot day.

And so for once she'd splashed out and took the bus.

The train comes to a shuddering halt back at St Pancras. It looks calm and quiet in the dead of night, as Susan glares through the filthy window – just a few late-night travelers sipping cocktails at the Champagne Bar, a couple holding and kissing on the platform, a young man in an overcoat, carrying a briefcase, standing alone.

As the engines quieten and the doors open with a hiss, nobody moves, not Susan, not Chris, not the young couples to their front, or the young couple to their rear.

The boys have all gone now, back to Hollywood.

Nobody is in any hurry to step from the train, least of all Susan. It is a waiting game.

Part of her hopes that if she waits long enough, the train will turn around and take her back to France.

Finally Chris touches her knee.

"We need to get up," he whispers, placing the suitcase on the table before them as a statement of intent.

"We've done nothing wrong. Remember that, Susan. Remember what we've talked about."

Susan, finally on her feet, using the headrests of each seat to help her stay upright. She senses eyes from one young couple on her as she nears them, and they rise suddenly, blocking her path as they make their way slowly to the door; Susan now feeling the presence of the other pair behind them, driving her down the aisle like an old horse headed for the knacker's yard.

Onwards she moves, towards the door, and she's finally spurned on by the chill air that sweeps in from the platform. One foot down, then another, and she turns to wait for Chris.

But straight away there's movement from the couple in front – taking her hands, twisting her arms behind her back and snapping metal bracelets around her skeletal wrists.

She sees more police running down the platform now, armed police carrying guns.

"Susan Edwards?"

She doesn't answer; but instead watching as Chris is bundled from the train by the other couple, the young man and woman who had been sat behind them, who lead him from the carriage and restrain him until the uniforms take over.

"Are you Susan Edwards?"

"Leave him alone," she screams. "Leave us alone."

"Are you Susan Edwards?

"ARE YOU SUSAN EDWARDS?"

"Yes. Yes, I'm Susan Edwards."

"Susan Edwards, I am arresting you on suspicion of the murders of William Geoffrey Wycherley and Patricia Dorothy Wycherley. You have the right to remain silent . . ."

Through her screams she can hear the same caution being shouted at Chris, like a sickening echo over the noise of the train's dying engines and the chatter in the station.

Susan is frogmarched unceremoniously down the platform, bent forwards, head down, the pain in her wrists unimaginable, crowds gathering to watch the show, her blushing at the shame of it.

Then she is bundled into the back of a waiting van and the doors are slammed behind her, silencing her screams to the world outside.

Chapter 7

*It was that detail which painted a very different picture,
one that involved premeditated murder, likely driven by a
long-harboured financial grudge and the opportunity to
get themselves out of debt – Detective Chief Inspector Rob
Griffin, post trial press statement, June 2014.*

Another late night – although for once not the fault of
Susan and Christopher Edwards. Out for a few beers with
the lads – the ones that aren't coppers, the ones he still
knew from school.

A long-arranged night out, which Rawlins had almost
bailed on, because of Susan and Christopher Edwards. But
in the end he'd gone, straight from the station and down to
the boozer, just to be back in the real world for a bit,
surrounded by people who knew little of the darkness of
his working world.

The thought of a few pints in the pub, then back home
to cozy up to the girlfriend; falling asleep on the sofa to a
recording of Saturday night's Match of the Day.

Just a few hours away, in a world where you laugh and
joke about days gone by – about the long-haired English
teacher who walked like he needed a hip replacement;

about the dumper truck some of you nicked off the building site and drove through the estate after school, back in the days when you were still young enough to get away with a ticking off from the local beat bobbie; about the girls you'd chatted up, and felt up if you were lucky, on the long and lazy, late-summer walks home from the classroom.

You make smalltalk about how the wife is, how the kids are, how the new house is doing; you hear all about the last holiday, all about the next holiday; how the job is going . . . without ever giving anything away. All good. Up for a promotion. Got some leave coming up . . . and nothing more.

And him the copper, him the billy-big-bollocks with an armful of stripes that nobody ever sees, all human and real for once – down the pub with the boys, blanking out what's really making his head spin.

Then back home to the Victorian terrace in a plush part of town, bouncing off a wall as he rounds a corner, lurching with every step, relishing the chill air in his listless lungs.

He fumbles a key into a door, he creeps in, not knowing what time it is, and kisses the girlfriend who hadn't expected to see him anyway.

He takes a shower and has a shave; sees the bed and thinks about crawling into it, just for a second, while the booze is still spinning his head enough for him to close his eyes and step away for a few hours.

But all the time he can sense the Holmes Room at St Ann's nick, just a short walk away, pulling him back, refusing him his life back for good until this is over ... at least for now. He puts on a clean shirt, a different tie, and neatens his hair. Then he climbs back into the same suit he'd kicked into the corner of the bedroom a few minutes earlier.

He kisses the girlfriend again, on the forehead this time because she's now spark out in front of the telly. Then he walks to the main road and hails a cab a little after midnight, flashing his warrant card at the driver when he says he wants to go to St Ann's at this time of night.

He settles into the back seat, closes his eyes and wonders what the fuck he's doing.

He hates himself for his absence; hates the force for the hold it has on him; hates the Edwards more for their demands on his time.

But for now he's punished himself enough through the freezing cold shower and the harsh slaps to the face he'd administered to bring himself back. There would be plenty of time for reflection, plenty of time for making up. Now there was work to do.

He can't let things rest, he has to be there – sat through the night at St Ann's Police Station, just yards from where Danielle Beccan was gunned down in a turf war a couple of decades before, waiting for the phone, or the flat beep on his laptop when a new message pings its arrival.

Rawlins is there just in case – just in case he's missed something; just in case ...

There are questions; so many questions that need answers, and Rawlins is sitting on a mound of intelligence from a room full of coppers, and somebody has to steer the ship. Somebody has to find the answers. And he won't find them with his feet up, sipping on a Merlot and watching last Saturday's football with his slippers on, or down the boozer with the boys. That will come later.

He checks the date and realises it's Wednesday, just, and he can't remember whether there'd been a weekend or not.

He's on his own, obviously, and the phones are silent, the chatter is gone – there is just the occasional hum from the coffee machine, or gurgle from the water cooler.

The case has gone quiet and the press have moved on; the warning off of the week before has diverted their interest. Now it was just the local rag still snooping around, still poking its nose in; writing about house sales and electoral rolls, still throwing in the line about the mysterious young couple, those doing the garden all those years ago; doing the garden every now and then, telling the neighbours that the Wycherleys were off in Morecambe . . . or somewhere.

It is still unclear whether police have identified the mysterious young couple who neighbours said had turned up to do the garden after the Wycherleys disappeared.

Pushing their luck. Always pushing their fucking luck.

But then, it was just the local rag. And they were playing the game . . . just.

Eventually Rawlins looks again at the grainy CCTV footage – a busy St Pancras Station, people rushing and loitering, browsing at shopfronts, tinkering on pianos, buying tickets, looking lost.

The Champagne Bar, people quaffing down bubbly at twenty quid a glass, going down a treat as they prepare for their holiday jaunts to Paris, or Brussels, or Lyon.

Young couples, looking loved up; happy mid-lifers, kids off their hands for a few days and hoping to rekindle something; nervous businessmen in suits, looking shifty and sitting with girls half their age; wannabe backpackers, splashing out their parents' cash to avoid an overnighter on the ferry out of Dover. Then . . .

A solitary woman, sitting on a bench, wringing her hands and looking around like an abandoned child; her hair cropped short, like she's done it herself, her clothes worn and threadbare, like she's bought them from a charity shop.

There is a suitcase rested at her knees that she keeps a hand on, cautiously eyeing anyone who walks by – nervous, timid, terrified.

Rawlins looks, and looks, and looks. Her flickering greyness on the screen, her hand forever going out to feel for the edge of her case, the nervous yet endless craning of her sparrow neck as she looks around.

He has watched it a dozen times, but he'll watch it again, over and over.

She is joined by a man, little and slumped, his hair white, wistful and balding. He offers a hand and helps her to her feet, then he picks up the suitcase and leads her away from her bench, away from the station, onto the platform, onto a train.

Susan Edwards.

Christopher Edwards.

Rawlins has photographs of them now, supplied by relatives, pictures from long ago, when they were young, when they were recently married, when their hair was still dark, and when they still smiled.

They're older now but it's still them; it's Susan and Christopher, and they're leaving England for Europe.

It's the day after his firm lent him ten thousand quid; the fortnight before they reported him missing a little under a year before.

Their faces.

They're going away and they're not coming back.

Their faces are the same as someone jumping on a plane and leaving for a new life in Australia; the same mixture of glee and sorrow in the grainy images of Susan and Christopher.

Only there's more.

As they both step onto the train and cast back one final glance at the station, the last glimmer of England they hope to ever see, Rawlins sees something else. He sees relief. Then he sees them smile. They are their suspects, Susan and Christopher, and they are holed up somewhere in mainland Europe.

In her statement, Elizabeth Edwards says that Christopher had told her they were in Lille.

But then, would he really tell her where they were, unless he needed her to wire him money because he no longer had a bank account?

Otherwise that was stupid, really amateurish?

Rawlins takes a slug on his stone-cold coffee and rubs his eyes.

'But they were amateurs,' he thinks. 'At least they were amateurs at running away.'

Or were they?

I'm in Lille, Elizabeth. But please don't tell anyone, especially not the police.

They could be bloody anywhere, Rawlins thinks, slamming down his pen.

Once they were on the other side of the Channel, they would have been able to access a real spider's web of rail networks to anywhere on the planet. They could have got as far as Istanbul, further probably, without ever showing a passport again.

And that's if they'd stayed in Europe; if they'd not caught a flight to Thailand, to Bolivia, to Ecuador, or Brazil – to places where wafting a British passport at customs got you through the front door and ten grand in your back pocket went a bloody long way.

And even if they were in Lille, if that was as far as their limited scope could carry them, they could still flee; they could still find money, and they could still be gone. Even now they could be on a plane to 'God knows where'.

Her parents are dead. Her parents were never reported dead. There was never a funeral. The extended family believed they were still alive. They have two skeletons, retrieved from the back garden of their own home.

And that's still not enough for the Crown Prosecution Service, still not enough for a European Arrest Warrant.

They'd made a lot of money out of not reporting her parents dead – Susan and Christopher. They'd swindled cash from a flotilla of institutions, organisations and businesses over a long period of time ... and they weren't coming back easily.

The web they had built was substantial.

Rawlins stands up and rubs his aching back as he walks

to the window and looks at the early morning skyline, turning from light-polluted black to dingy grey.

He smiles, conscious that his paranoia has kicked in.

They've still got resources, they've still got the full support of the command team.

But for how long? How long before a girl gets pulled out of the Trent with stab wounds and leaves clogging her throat? How long before another small-time pusher gets a bullet through the back as he cycles through the Meadows, or Radford, or any of half a dozen city centre inner suburbs? How long before there's a spate of rapes on one of the estates and division are screaming for resources? How long before someone tells him his resources are being cut back? How long before a fifteen-year-old double murder can no longer be a priority?

In his guts, Rawlins knows they may have just days, hours possibly, before the investigation is scaled back, reduced, parked – before the curtain comes crashing down.

They'd spoken to Christopher briefly – got his number from Elizabeth Edwards and taken a punt; got him on the phone for a brief chat, although he'd hung up as quickly as he answered.

"Sorry, I can't talk, it's not convenient," he had bumbled, before hanging up.

'Still chasing phone records,' thinks Rawlins. 'Still chasing rainbows.'

He flicks through a pile of interview transcripts from relatives. They're shocked. They're mortified. There is a strange type of guilt in them – the sort perhaps only truly known by estranged families.

"When was the last time you saw William and Pat?"

Twenty years; twenty five years; when I was young. But they always kept in touch?"

Regular as clockwork. Occasionally. Usually just a card at Christmas.

'It all depended on which account you read,' Rawlins thinks. 'Did they target certain relatives? Or were the responses just reflections of family hierarchy?'

"And what did these letters say? Were they always written by William?"

Yes, until he got older and a bit confused, then Susan would write on his behalf; no, mainly from Susan; always from William.

"When did you last see Susan?"

Some had never met her, it emerged, they just knew she was Bill and Pat's daughter; never really even read the letters to be honest.

I remember her at a family party, donkey's years back, sat on a swing, looking lost, sipping squash like it was nectar. Funny child.

"And what did they say in these letters? In these cards?"

Rawlins pulls open a file, flicking at heavy, plastic-coated pages, until he finds the letters, the cards. Not the real ones. They're already bagged and sealed and locked in the evidence vault. These are just copies, blurred, but good enough to read.

He reads the first one he sees.

"I realise my father travelled the world in his younger years, well it is like he is having his second youth

– because when he does speak now, he speaks of travel, and travelling.

I really cannot keep up with where he's planning to settle.

He and mum like to travel in the Irish Republic particularly. I tend to think it is all a yearning for past years, to do all those things one never got around to before.

But I've never seen him with such zest . . ." – A letter written to Vivien Steenson by Susan Edwards in 2011, two years before they fled to France.

And another, from December 2007.

"I enclose a Christmas card for you – on behalf of myself and my parents.

As for your letter saying your card was returned from Blenheim Close, I am sorry about that, but not to worry.

I should explain that – with my father getting elderly and my mother not always in the best of health – they have been travelling around Ireland, because of the good air, off and on for some years. Eventually they decided to sell the home, and they are thinking of settling in Ireland permanently."

Rawlins grabs at a different file, flips it open at a random page, then searches back and forth.

An earlier note, written in a more boxed, awkward hand, dating from November 20, 1998, three months after the Wycherleys were murdered; signed by William.

"At present I am sent order books for payment of my benefits in cash at the Post Office.

However, it has become troublesome for me to get to the Post Office to cash the orders.

I understand from reading some benefits agency leaflet that it may be possible to have my benefits paid directly into a bank or building society account. If this is the case, I would be obliged if you would send me the appropriate application form in order to arrange this."

There's more.

Routine letters to doctors, dated October 2005, written as Bill, declining an invitation to a chest clinic.

"I'm feeling better, and I will be visiting with relatives over the next months: for that reason it is not convenient to make an appointment."

Another from December 2006, again posing as Bill, declining a pneumonia vaccine.

"As I will be staying with relatives, I would prefer not to be sent letters offering me vaccines I will not want."

Endless.

Letters to banks, letters to opticians, letters to the DWP, letters to the council – but all reactive. Every official letter, apart from the early ones where William is settling his affairs, are responses to requests.

Do you want a flu jab?

No, fine thanks.

We note it's been some time since you've had your eyes tested.

Eyes are fine, old boy. I'll call you.

Would you like to come to a chest clinic?

Would you like to bugger off and leave me alone?

Even the final letters, that short interchange between William and the Department for Work and Pensions, are all reactive.

We need to meet you to examine your benefits.

Oh, no need, all going swimmingly thanks, just keep sending the cheques.

No, we really need to talk to you.

A final letter from Susan, then only radio silence, for the past ten months, nothing but silence – until now at least.

Rawlins wades through more files; dull stuff, financial evidence, but crucial all the same. These files contain the spider's web, all slowly being drawn together into a single, sticky thread. That's when they'll have them.

Bored and frustrated, he flips ahead to the end of the section, to the footnotes made by the investigating DS from financial crime.

"It would appear that on the Tuesday after the bank holiday in May 1998, Susan Edwards attended the Mansfield branch of the Halifax Building Society and set up a new account in the names of her mother and herself.

It seems that slightly more than £40,000 was redirected from accounts held in the joint names of her parents – William and Patricia Wycherley.

There is evidence that the Edwards received William and Patricia Wycherley's pensions from the time of their deaths in 1998 to the point that they departed for France in 2013. This figure amounts to around £150,000 over the period.

An attempt was made to cancel the pensions in 1998, but this was not followed through after a letter was sent to William Wycherley, informing him that his pension could be paid directly into a bank account. It would seem that the bank account given was the joint account held in the names of Susan Edwards and Patricia Wycherley.

They also claimed industrial injuries benefits, winter fuel payments and Christmas bonus payments, with a total expense to the public purse of around £175,000.

In 2005, the Wycherley's home in Blenheim Close, Forest Town, Mansfield, was sold for £67,000. The signatures on the relevant documentation are those of William and Patricia Wycherley.

We have been unable to source an original signature for Patricia Wycherley, but the signature of William Wycherley is a forgery, albeit a relatively competent one.

Later in the financial history, beginning shortly after the sale of Blenheim Close, we see a new trend developing.

Patricia Wycherley begins to take out loans in her own name. She also acts as a guarantor to a number of loans taken out by Susan and Christopher Edwards.

There were also credit cards, in both the names of Patricia Wycherley and Susan Edwards – typically those held in Susan's name had her mother listed as guarantor.

It would seem from initial investigations that significant effort has gone into keeping Patricia's financial background squeaky clean.

We cannot establish this beyond doubt at this point, but there is evidence that money was ferried into accounts associated with Patricia, often at the expense of other debts that were owed independently of her by Susan and Christopher Edwards.

For my summary on outgoings, please see appendix five."

Rawlins flips back, thumbing heavily at the laminated pages, looking for appendix five.

He happens across a silver photograph of a matinee idol, the authentication certificate tells him it is Gary Cooper. It also states that it was purchased for $2,500 in April 2010 by Christopher Edwards.

Another of Frank Sinatra; and a letter, dating from May 1960, heavy and fudged typewriter setting, faded yet expensive paper.

"Dear Miss MacPhaie,

Now that I am home again, and have a chance to go through my mail, I want to say how wonderful and kind it was for you to write me and send all these good wishes which I know helped me to recover. We never know how many good friends we have in the world 'till some adversity gives us a slap in the face and we realise that friends are one of God's greatest gifts.

Thank you so much,

Sincerely,

Gary Cooper."

His signature is scrawled beneath. One of hundreds, produced on a production line no doubt, the actor just scrawling his heavy name as an afterthought to Miss MacPhaie.

A month before, Cooper had undergone surgery for prostate and colon cancer, a margin note states in the file. He died almost a year to the day after the letter was dated.

On the opposite page is a receipt, stating that the letter had been purchased by Christopher Edwards in 2009, for a little under £2,500.

Electronic copies, retained by the vendors for proof of sale.

God knows what's happened to the originals.

"We are still building a full profile of expenditure over the full period of investigation, which is obviously a significant piece of work.

However, from later transactions, from 2010 onwards, it would appear that a significant amount of money, estimated at around £15,000 was spent by Christopher Edwards on film-related memorabilia. This behaviour carried on until late 2012.

By examining his work emails, it would appear that all of these purchases were made from his place of employment. All correspondents list his home address as the point of delivery.

We have found some initial evidence of sales from the same email address, although from an earlier period. These periods would appear to be highly active, over as little as a week in some instances. It would seem that Christopher Edwards was selling a number of items, often items of significant value, frequently for much less than their market value, and for much less than he had purchased them. There is evidence of the sale of a book written by Winston Churchill, and a letter written by Charles De Gaulle, although these investigations are still ongoing."

These are repeat cycles, Rawlins thinks. A slower period of accumulation, of purchase; then a rapid and panicked period of sale – the Edwards regularly clearing out a dozen-or-so items over a couple of days. Buy and sell, buy and sell. That is the pattern.

A spider's web.

"They were terrible with Money, Susan and Christopher," he thinks. That's what Elizabeth Edwards had said. "Always in a pickle, he was – always coming with his begging bowl out. That was our Christopher."

'If they weren't so terrible with money,' thinks Rawlins, 'they'd probably have gotten away with it.

'Although, in fairness, if they weren't so terrible with money, they'd probably never have killed the old dears in the first place.'

Slowly Rawlins gets up and rubs at his spine again until the ache goes away, then he walks to the window and looks out at the early morning for a second time, the streetlights have gone and the morning is there – pre-sunshine in all its dismal greyness.

In the distance, beyond the concrete monstrosity of a 1970s shopping centre, some redbrick mansions long ago turned into flats, offices and shops, he can just make out the Victorian dome of the council building; standing on the skyline like a poor-man's St Paul's.

It's not as picturesque as Venice or Berlin, but it's a handsome enough skyline. Only that's not Nottingham. To know Nottingham you have to be down on the streets, scraping it off the soles of your boots. And Rawlins has trod every filthy corner of it; driven the roads of its dysfunctional estates and kept the peace in its conservative outer-suburbs.

But he's out in the sticks now. He's well and truly out in the sticks. He's away from the sickly street lights and highrise flats, he's away from the organised crime, the drugs, the rapes and the muggings. He's fifteen miles south of a ravaged, former mining town where the remains of two elderly people have just been dug up in their own back garden.

Here, in this city, people die out of poverty, out of want, out of circumstance or association.

But not at Blenheim Close. There they died out of greed, out of hatred, and out of indifference.

'And that's the reality,' thinks Rawlins. 'They were killed for money. They were killed *because* of hatred. But they were killed *for* money.'

What frustrated Rawlins most, after spending every waking hour getting to know Susan and Christopher Edwards, without existing for a single second in their company, was a simple question.

'Who was the driving force?' Who, at some point, between 1983 and 1998, sat the other one down and said: "You know what? Why don't we just kill the miserable old bastards? Why don't we blow them away? Why don't we bury them in the back garden of their own home and spend all of their money? The money that was ours all along. The money that they stole from us. It had to be one of two people,' thinks Rawlins. 'It had to be Christopher Edwards. Or it had to be Susan Edwards.'

Christopher, the unlikely gun-toting marksman, the boring and unnoticed distant relative, who married his ugly duckling and lived a quiet suburban life, collecting his first editions and his letters, reading his history, and occasionally taking a selection of firearms to a gun club in Earls Court, where he would spend many a happy hour blasting the daylights out of human targets. He knew how to shoot, did Christopher Edwards.

Or Susan? The hateful and hated daughter? Conned, bullied, ripped off by her own father over the house she bought for him; abandoned by him with a bumbling idiot of a husband who could hardly keep a roof over his own head, let alone hers?

And was he really that bad, William Wycherley? Was he bad enough to kill, and throw into an unmarked grave, dumped into an unmarked grave?

In someone's eyes he was – in Susan's eyes, or in Christopher's? In somebody's eyes, he deserved a bullet. It had to be both of them. It took them both to do the deed. It took them both to build the web. Patricia was collateral damage, because they came as a pair, did Bill and Pat. Hate and money; money and hate. The act of murder binds the Edwards. But did they share a motive?'

Rawlins scratches heavily at his scalp, massages his eyes and works his jaw. Then he slumps back in his chair and closes his eyes, sleep almost taking him before he forces himself awake. He looks at the ballistics file again.

Point 2.2 round, probably shot from a Second World War Revolver, most likely a Colt Commando – standard police issue firearm, adapted for military use when the Yanks came into the War in 1941. Christopher Edwards is registered as owning a Colt Commando, along with two other weapons. Following the Dunblane massacre in 1996, when the Government completely banned hand guns in the UK, Christopher Edwards turned in two firearms. But not the Colt Commando.

A gun club nut had turned his revolvers on a school full of kids just two years before the Wycherley's were shot, and Christopher Edwards had kept a gun; he'd kept the same make and model of gun that William Wycherley was rumoured to have kept in his own bedside cabinet.

A spider's web.

Rawlins computer pings periodically as emails arrive – picking up in momentum as the world comes back to life for a new day.

He's managed to ignore them until now, but the latest ping grabs his attention and he clicks at the screen.

His eyes are drooping now, he is thinking about getting a cab, or getting some probationer to drive him home, to his girlfriend and his warm bed, just for an hour or two; just as the early risers start to filter into the office, all grey-suited and clutching coffee in cardboard cups.

Then his phone pings. A text from Griffin.

"Check the email I've just sent you. I'm calling a briefing for 9am."

And suddenly Rawlins is wide awake.

He checks his messages, finding Griffin's at the top. There is no separate message. Just an email from a third party, forwarded on to Rawlins.

From: Christopher Edwards, the email reads.

To: Chief Inspector Robert Griffin.

Subject: Surrender to UK Border force at Lille Europe Station.

Priority: High.

The chatter in the background from the early arrivers fades; Rawlins can hear nothing but the slowed-down thump of his own heart hammering in his chest; the laborious rising of his ribcage as his lungs fill with air.

"Dear DCI Griffin,

Later on today we are going to surrender ourselves to the UK Border Force authorities at the Eurostar terminal at Lille Europe station.

We would prefer to do this since my wife is already sufficiently frightened. Please could you notify the UK Border Force at Lille Europe so that they may expect us.

I would also ask that you call or SMS me to confirm that you will do this. If you cannot get through to me (my last top-up having expired a few days ago) please e-mail me, so that we may be certain that we are expected."

A spider's web.

Rawlins sits silently for a moment; tapping a pen on the edge of his desk; staring at the faded monitor when the sun finally blurs his vision as it breaks over the skyline.

A spider's web, drawn into a single thread.

He reads the message again. Then he picks up the phone.

Chapter 8

A reclusive Forest Town couple were shot dead by their daughter and son-in-law, who buried their bodies in the back garden, stole from their bank accounts and conned relatives and neighbours into thinking they were still alive . . . Andy Done-Johnson, Mansfield Chad, Thursday, June 5, 2014.

It had come over me like a creeping mist; like a mustard gas, hardly noticed until I was on my knees in no man's land, clutching at my throat and gasping for air. By then it was too late.

I hadn't seen it coming, maybe just its presence, beyond my lines of sight, somewhere over my shoulder; a lingering and stalking darkness.

Eventually an explosion had come; an intolerable buildup following by an eruption, a blanket of fury like a grenade being tossed into the air.

I was done.

It had started with a row, a tantrum probably; an irrational mind misfiring and throwing bile and fire round a half-empty newsroom.

Before I knew what had happened I'd hit the bottom step, barged through the glass door and I was out into the car park, vaguely aware that I'd left an unfinished row halfway down the stairs.

I'd climbed into the car, gunned the engine and screeched away; rage blinding me as I steered the vehicle at the tepid street lighting on the main road; on autopilot almost, my body going through the motions while my mind tore itself apart within the contours of my skull.

I'd driven home, aware only of the darkness, the thump of the engine and the stream of car lights coming towards me.

I fumed, I cursed and I swore; I blamed everybody, apart from myself.

It was a row over nothing; a row over nothing that had been brewing for months.

Finally, eventually, it had been a row about a story that should have gone on the front page; a story that was buried at the back to pull me down a peg.

But I was done.

I was finished.

I was out of the game and I was glad.

Fuck it.

Only I was also in the dark of no man's land, gasping for air . . .

The last I could remember of it was a committal hearing.

I was on a tram, chugging into Nottingham, looking at my watch, nervous and late . . . again. Nottingham's trams move at about ten miles per hour. They are packed. They are packed and they are slow. I was late, and it was making me later.

191

I was heading to town to cover a story – the Edwards, now finally arrested, were making their first appearance at Crown Court – but really I was just going to look at them, just to see them in the flesh.

The final tram stop was five minutes' walk from the court, although it took forty minutes to get there from the end of the line, and I wandered down the road, past the side entrance where the prison vans pulled in, past the scrum of snappers, waiting for the transports to arrive, flashing their cameras at blackened windows as they passed.

Then round the corner to the main entrance, past the camera crews and the reporters talking into phones or smoking fags and chatting.

I stood around for a minute and savoured the buzz – taking me back to my first steps down Blenheim Close now more than three weeks before.

Then I walked through the heavy glass doors and joined the back of the security line, looking at my watch and cursing the queue.

That was the last time it had been clear – standing in a queue with a purpose.

Three months later and I was sat in the darkness of a December day, waiting for the light to go and the street lights to flicker into life; the rush-hour traffic to pick up past my front window and the school kids to shuffle past on their way home, their hands thrust purposefully into heavy winter coats.

Dark days and lonely wanders in the park, avoiding other walkers whenever I saw them, if ever they strayed too near. Emails from the office enquiring about my health, largely unanswered. Regular trips to the doctors to check on my progress, sending off the sicknotes to keep the pay coming in; checking on the medication, meeting with the councillors and having nothing to say to them.

Phone messages from friends, concerned, appealing – all left in limbo by a man who had done with the world; just the small matter of a still-beating heart to overcome to finally find peace.

Under the ground, forgotten and alone as the world travelled onwards; as forgotten as the Wycherleys, just a diary entry in history.

Cloaked in darkness; a solitary figure wandering through the shadows of the world, living in my own head – a terrifyingly lonely place, full of hatred and regret and contempt and fear and fury. Always alone, even with my family around me, their efforts unacknowledged, unheard; their voices just echoes somewhere in my broken mind.

I'd sit in the gloom of my front room, huddled in a blanket; no lights, no noise, staring at the dying embers of a fire; occasionally noting the movements of the neighbours, or strangers wandering past the house.

Nights staring at the ceiling, my wife's gentle breathing and my son's occasional unconscious cries my only company through the darkness – before falling asleep only when the light came, surfacing in the afternoon and slumping on the sofa; then forcing myself out on another walk, another lap around the same damp earth, the drizzle on my face or the frost in my breath, waiting for the night to come and swallow me once again.

I was broken. I was done. I was over.

I'd think about the man who had loitered at the door of court number two waiting for his moment, wondering where he had gone, because that had been me just weeks before; someone lost in time to me now; someone I used to know.

That person, standing at the door of court number two, waiting for the usher to open the door to the throng.

Susan Edwards.

Christopher Edwards.

Committal hearing.

I'd barged my way in – as the usher came out and declared the court open, ahead of the media clamour, ahead of the stampede as seventy arses did battle for the same ten seats.

You needed to be to the right of the double door at court number two, just loitering, looking like you were just leaning against the wall because there was nowhere to sit.

You blanked the hacks that you didn't know, smiled a nod at the ones you did. But you didn't move, not for anything.

You didn't move because as the doors opened and the usher stepped out, he'd briefly block the path to everyone but you, the only one standing behind him now, the only one with a free run at the press bench down the aisle to the left, as you ducked behind him; coat flung heavily over one arm, briefcase in the other, filling the aisle, making sure nobody else got past.

You aimed for the best seat while the rest were still forming a disorderly scrum behind you.

This is my seat. This is the best seat ... and it's mine.
This is my patch, my turf; it doesn't belong to some visiting
chancer up from the smoke.

I was right on the corner by the aisle, with the best view,
with the best chance of catching what the judge had to say,
the best view of the Edwards' flickering eyes and their
clasping hands, if ever they appeared.

The place had packed out behind me until every seat
was gone.

It was a free day out at the theatre, and I'd been given
the Royal Box.

A minor, childish and futile victory; nothing more than
a tomcat spraying piss up a wall.

I was another victim of the Edwards, in truth.

They had done for me like they had done for Bill and Pat
Wycherley. They had sucked me in like all those distant
relatives over all those years. Only I was a voluntary victim;
I had done it to myself. I had put myself in the shadows,
the no man's land of their murky world.

They had gone away and left me to the mundanity and
mediocrity of my working days before their arrival; left
me, the lonely madman wandering in a storm like a
Shakespearean lunatic.

For a while I'd kept myself busy enough, launching an
investigation into the operations at Sports Direct, the cut-
price sports retailer which runs its main warehouse and
head office from a drab and prison-like facility just over
the Derbyshire border from us in Shirebrook – a modern-
day gulag in a forgotten corner of England.

A migrant worker had given birth in the female toilets

on New Year's Day – too terrified of losing her job to ask to go home, too terrified to stay at home in the first place. She may have left the baby under the sink and tried to return to her duties, or to go and seek help. Nobody knows but her. But the police were called and reports filtered out that the baby had been abandoned in the toilets.

It caused a storm and it sucked me in and, for a while, I'd almost forgotten about poor old Bill and Pat; the two of them lingering somewhere in the recesses of my mind.

But it was a brief interlude and it's wasn't enough; it was nowhere near enough.

Soon I'd been frustrated and bored by the routine of the day job – back to the weekly rock-up at Mansfield Mags' to report on the shoplifters, the drug addicts and wife-beaters; I'm covering the mundane again – the charity fundraisers, the bike-rides to Skegness, political spats in the council chamber.

I'm a madman, stumbling blindly towards a raging storm on a mountainside; Tom O'Bedlam, shivering at his keyboard, roaring and rallying at the approaching squall, my voice all but drowned out.

Then I'd picked up a story about a couple of ageing rockers – both well into their fifties – who had been pepper-sprayed at a charity pub gig by an over-eager copper. A fight had broken out and they were just trying to get a panicking daughter to safety; only he'd emptied a full canister in their faces, and confiscated the phone of a bystander who'd filmed it. The rockers were in court charged with resisting arrest and affray, but really it was the copper on trial.

I thought I'd struck gold again – police corruption, a cover-up, abuse of public office; arrogance. Bizarrely the police had insisted on carrying on with a prosecution and it was open season – their dirty laundry aired in a public court.

I'd thrown myself at it, insisted on three days out of the office to cover the trial; losing friends at a rate of knots. I was narky, irritable and miserable. I snap, I over-react, I lose my rag and I criticise the hierarchy too loudly, too publicly, too often.

So my story was dumped in the middle of the book and I walked away into a dark corner.

I was gone five months, locked away in my dark place, cursing the job, hating the company, loathing the bosses, despising myself.

I drove to the house sometimes, to Blenheim Close, just to see, just to remember – just to park up and look at it; somehow still seeing the police tent, the tape, the scene of crime vans and the satellite trucks.

Only there was nothing left now but a flimsy 1960s box, a neglected hedge, a greying sky, a row of sightless curtains, and fresher fish and chip wrappers thrown onto the ground around it.

But I was surrounded by calm and peace and a feeling of the world moving on here; while really I was still stranded two miles away and four months ago when I'd been raging on the stairs, storming into the night with a final 'fuck you' as I'd slammed the door behind me; falling into the driver's seat, gunning the engine, fumbling for a belt and driving blindly at the darkness ahead.

Raging!

I'm out in the wilds now; in the wilderness.

I'm Tom O'Bedlam, screaming at the elements and trembling in the shadows, cursing at the darkness; shivering in the corner.

The foul fiend, he follows me.

He bites my back.

Poor Tom.

Poor Tom's a-cold!

A dark place.

A lonely place.

But slowly it had faded and the sun had broken through. I started to venture out willingly. I walked the dog for miles, seeing the world around me for the first time; the glare of the early-Summer sun now forcing me to screw up my eyes as I filled my lungs with the fresh, sweet air. I breathed in the smell of blossom, of herbs and honey, with the first buzzing of the bees vibrating in my ears.

I started to mend. I'd got through the worst of the winter.

I travelled to Oxford to catch up with an old university mate, just for some different surroundings. And as I sat, half-pissed in a sun-drenched beer garden somewhere in the city, I realised I needed to go back.

We'd been catching up, nattering about the old days, mutual friends and debauched behaviour. We talked about books and plays and music, and somehow I told him about the Wycherleys and the Edwards, the bodies and the back garden; and the old couple who vanished.

The Wycherleys, the Edwards, and the bodies and the back garden. And it occurred to me that the trial must be coming up.

It was mine.

It always had been mine.

It was still mine.

And I was going back.

I remembered their faces from all those months before when I'd first seen them at the committal hearing.

They'd looked dazed and confused, deprived of sleep and daylight, like they'd just been worked over by the KGB. They had been brought up with the jangling of keys and the yielding of a heavy lock. They followed a female guard, who showed them to the seats at the front, removed their handcuffs and retreated into a corner.

The public benches had been packed, but the court itself was skeleton staffed; just a circuit judge and junior counsel doing the formalities, trainee solicitors scribbling onto forms, a clerk, an usher, and Susan and Christopher Edwards locked away behind a perspex screen.

The charges had been put to them. They had said nothing.

No plea was being entered at this stage, junior counsel informed the judge.

No application for bail was being made.

They would be remanded into custody until their trial date.

The curtain had come down.

They were both formally accused of double murder.

They would be going to trial, and all I could report was their names, what they'd been charged with, whether they'd entered a plea, and what they were wearing. Apart from that I was gagged, and from there the darkness had descended.

I'd watched as Susan and Christopher Edwards were led away, back down to the holding cells, away from the world for almost a year – their departure marked with the slamming of an iron door.

I saw her face as she was led away, sallow and twisted and bitter and shocked. I saw her face and it stayed with me; haunting me in my darker moments, but ultimately drawing me back; Susan's face.

It's the face that I'm looking at now, almost a year down the road. Same face, same clothes, same room and heavy glass screen. Christopher by her side, as before, small and slight, like a dormouse, only clutching a plastic bag nestled in his slight hands.

A year has slipped away in the time it takes to blink, it seems.

It's press night at the theatre, the cast are starting to assemble, and it's a full house.

Beginners please.

It is a strange setting for a piece of drama – the cast facing away from the audience, instead focusing on a raised and solitary figure, holding court in a scarlet red robe and a frayed shoulder-length wig, as the support players shuffle around the stalls in tattered black capes, bespectacled and grey, clutching at their lapels and striding like buzzards and bloated cockerels in the dirt.

We have come to hear a tragedy – the story of an old man, bloodily dispatched before his time by his cold and heartless daughter.

So say the prosecution.

For this is high drama, after all.

This is tragedy.

I am here, somehow – off the drink, on the wagon, on the pills.

Not back, but on the way; perched on the press bench in a formica courtroom, all light wood and the sort of heavy carpets you get in business hotels; staring at the jury shuffling their feet in the rows opposite.

I've been treated to a distinguished cast:

Mrs Justice Kathryn Thirlwall – a High Court Judge up all the way from London for the occasion.

Peter Joyce QC for the prosecution – a wise old buzzard with a sniff of Rumpole about him.

David Howker QC for Susan Edwards – subdued and brilliant, a twinkle in his eye – who would die months later during a family holiday in France.

Dafydd Enoch QC for Christopher Edwards – stern and quiet, meticulous and reserved.

His junior, Andy Easteal, who represented Susan and Christopher at their committal hearing all those months ago; before they went away, before I went away.

Behind them sits an army of bit players, solicitors and secretaries and legal executives, all shuffling at papers and talking in hushed voices.

And behind them, on the other side of the perspex screen, sitting separately and staring ahead, or at their shoes, are the main attractions; our villains – Susan and Christopher Edwards.

There they are – small and frail; wearing the same rags they'd been dressed in a year before.

201

Susan looking down now, wringing her hands together, her shoulders crumpled and bent.

Christopher alert, looking ahead; making notes in a pad they've allowed him to bring in.

They are a picture of misery.

He wears a green pullover and awful burgundy trousers.

She wears a plain navy skirt, a grey cardigan, and a white blouse with a simple collar.

I look at them in their stillness. I think about two bodies, shot and dumped in their own back garden, buried with less dignity than the family cat.

Are they killers?

I just don't know.

Probably.

Maybe.

Maybe not.

Griffin is sat behind me in the gods, surrounded by an entourage of plain-clothed coppers, occupying seats the public have been booted out of.

A fat security guard sits idly in the dock.

The houselights fade. Papers stop rustling.

It starts with a battle, if only a battle of wills; a legal scrap playing for advantages, while the jury is ushered out before the first soliloquy can even be uttered.

Sighs from the press bench with the theatrical throwing down of pens.

Howker on his feet once the jury are out.

Susan Edwards will plead guilty to the manslaughter of Patricia Wycherley due to diminished responsibility. She asserts that she played no part in the death of her father.

Then Enoch.

Christopher Edwards will plead guilty to disposing of the bodies, and financial matters following the deaths, if that is acceptable to the prosecution.

Joyce shakes his head and rises to his feet.

It is not acceptable.

It is the prosecution's case that Susan and Christopher Edwards jointly planned and executed the murders of William and Patricia Wycherley, disposed of the bodies in an unmarked grave and conspired to profit from the deaths.

This is the case they will take to trial.

And so it begins; the jury are returned, we pick up our pens, and Joyce – who has been slumped in his chair like he's taking a nap – returns to his feet and takes the floor.

He raises his slender frame, erect yet slumped, he pours over his podium, flicking through a speech he has long since memorised; Lear, proclaiming to his court.

When he speaks it is with a voice graveled by a lifetime of fags.

"On Tuesday May 5th, 1998, the first day that the banks were open after the May Day Bank Holiday, a joint Halifax bank account was opened at the Mansfield branch in the joint names of Susan Edwards and her mother Patricia, giving her mother's address for correspondence – Number 2, Blenheim Close, Forest Town, Mansfield."

Joyce leans back, relaxes, glances down once again at his meticulous notes, glances at the jury, then settles into his narration.

"At the same time two joint accounts in the names of Susan Edwards' parents were closed and cleaned out. More than £40,000 was taken and has never been traced."

Joyce raises an eyebrow, and turns once again to the jury, holding a regal pause while they hang on his every word.

Meanwhile we shall express our darker purpose.

Joyce speaks only of fact, only of detail, only of Bill and Pat and Sue and Chris – but between the lines he tells the story of a twisted old man; fallen, forgotten, abandoned and murdered by a vengeful daughter.

How sharper than a serpent's tooth it is to have a thankless child.

"The prosecution case," says Joyce, "is that all the money taken from the accounts went into the pockets of the defendants. You will hear later in this opening of many further transactions amounting to very substantial amounts of money stolen by the defendants."

My hands already ache as I scratch down every word into my notepad with my decrepit shorthand, cursing the months I've taken away.

"The reason Tuesday 5th May is significant is that Susan Edwards' parents, William and Patricia Wycherley, were shot and killed by the defendants over that May bank holiday weekend.

"They carried out those killings using a .38 revolver owned by Christopher Edwards, and it was then covered up by burying their bodies in their own garden.

"Over the next 15 years, in order to continue stealing money payable to the dead parents, had they been alive, and to cover up what they had done, they lied to family members, they lied to neighbours, they lied to doctors and financial institutions, creating and using many false documents.

"They lied to everyone to deceive and trick them into thinking Susan Edwards' parents were still alive. They could then cover up the killings and continue to fund their own lifestyle and help solve their own financial difficulties."

Joyce takes a breath, takes off his glasses and gives them a polish, adjusts his wig and strokes his eyebrow like he's toying with a fine moustache. All eyes are on him.

"Neighbours described the deceased as reserved and had little contact with the outside world," he says. "Neither of the deceased were seen alive after May Day 1998. The reason for this is plain – on that weekend they were shot dead by the defendants, and buried the same weekend in their own garden."

Joyce takes off his spectacles yet again, gives them a wipe and leans more heavily on his podium.

"And what is the background to this?

"Susan Edwards and Christopher Edwards were the daughter and son-in-law of William Geoffrey Wycherley, born on November 6th 1912, and Patricia Wycherley, born on May 22nd, 1934.

"William and Patricia lived at 2 Blenheim Close, Forest Town, Mansfield, from 1987 to their murder over the May Bank Holiday weekend in 1998.

"On October 10th, 2013, the bodies of William and Patricia were found by the police wrapped in bedding and buried in the rear garden of their address, in a grave measuring between 90cm and 110cm in depth.

"A post-mortem examination revealed that each had been shot twice in the upper body and had been facing their assailant at the time."

I look at the Edwards, motionless through their Perspex window – like they're staring out of a kitchen window.

Christopher's eye occasionally flickers to Susan, who doesn't look back. She never reciprocates. He occasionally shuffles in the carrier bag he keeps at his feet, pulling out a pad, scratching a pen back to life on its cover.

"When matters came to light," says Joyce, "each of the defendants gave an account that had been carefully hatched and rehearsed, in the hope of escaping justice and avoiding liability for the murders.

"Matters came to light after the defendants received a letter from the authorities stating that they wished to see William Wycherley because he was approaching 100 years of age. In a panic they fled to France. When they ran out of money, Christopher Edwards contacted his step-mother and asked her for money, but went on to give an account of what happened all those years ago.

"The defendants married in 1983, and for much of their relationship they were in severe financial difficulties, and suffice it to say that by the time of their arrest, they owed in excess of £160,000 to their creditors."

Joyce doesn't look at the Edwards, he doesn't acknowledge them.

"From the very beginning they had the means to channel all monies payable to the deceased into their own hands, whether by way of state benefits and pension payments, or by obtaining credit in the names of the deceased, or by selling their house.

"Between 5th May 1998 and the defendants' arrest, £173,767.40 was diverted from benefits and pension payments, and a further sum in excess of £66,000 was obtained by the illicit selling of the Wycherleys' home."

Joyce outlines some of the loans: money borrowed from the Halifax in Patricia's name in 2000 for £5,000; two credit cards in 2004, again both Patricia's; money moved from account to account, Susan using various branches around London.

Then Joyce looks at Susan and Christopher Edwards. He looks at them for a very long time.

"After the May Bank Holiday in 1998, the only people seen at the premises were the defendants, who were there on a regular basis maintaining the garden, but not the house," he says.

"Lies were told to the neighbours to cover the absence of the deceased, and to allow them to continue withdrawing money from the account.

"Christopher Edwards pretended to be the nephew of the deceased and told neighbours that they had retired and gone to live in Morecambe.

"They told others that the deceased had gone travelling, or that they had gone to Blackpool due to ill health.

"In 2005, when a vehicle crashed through the fence of the property and damaged the rear lawn, the defendants attended immediately and paid for and repaired the damage themselves, rather than making an insurance claim and having others attend the property to carry out the work.

"Christopher Edwards subsequently told the neighbours that as a result, he had been contacted by the owners in Blackpool who told him to sell the address as quickly as possible."

Joyce halts, pours over his notes, looks at the jury, then pushes his glasses over the bridge of his nose.

"The police became involved after the step-mother contacted them," he says, "telling the police that she had been told by her son, Christopher Edwards, that he had been responsible for assisting Susan in the burial of her parents.

"They got away with it for 15 years, until they ran away and ran out of money. But it was a joint plan – a plan that Susan and Christopher Edwards concocted together, and committed together."

Joyce sits to a silence that holds in the air like a mist, before the general hubbub of the court slowly creeps back in.

We look around, us in the cheap seats. We stretch, lifting our arms and cracking out our shoulders.

I've been sat down for too long, writing for too long. My knuckles sting and my brain is fog, my backside aches from the wooden bench.

You do me wrong to take me out o' the grave.

I look at Susan Edwards, her face fixed forwards, staring blankly through the glass.

She turns her head and she looks back at me just for a moment, her poker expression utterly unchanged, and then she looks away.

Chapter 9

Neighbours described the deceased as reserved and had little contact with them. Neither of the deceased were seen alive after Mayday 1998 – Peter Joyce QC, R v Edwards and Edwards, Nottingham Crown Court, June 2014.

Susan sat bolt upright to the sound of the muffled crack shaking the walls of her flimsy room, vibrating in her chest and splitting the darkness – forcing her feet to swing instinctively from the bed, out of the covers, finding the warmth of the carpet with her curled toes.

She stared, blinking into the gloom of the early morning, forcing her eyes to see.

A second bang, tearing through the night, unexpected, making Susan jump again.

"Mum," she called out, jolting to her feet, fumbling against the walls, feeling for the switch or the door-handle, whichever she could get her hands on first.

Finally she clutched at the handle, her fingers locking round it, before swinging it blindly open onto the pitch black of the poky hallway, illuminated only by the yellow sickness of the street lighting which perforated through the flimsy and dust-covered laced curtains; a dagger-like shaft of light jutting out from under the door to her parents' room.

They didn't sleep together these days, not willingly, not for decades, but Susan's presence has forced them into the same bed.

"Mum?"

Susan heard shuffling from the other side of the slender door.

She knocked.

"Dad?"

Nothing – just a frozen silence, a scene in freezeframe on the other side of the woodwork and at the forefront of Susan's mind.

"Are you alright?"

Stifled breathing.

"Mum?"

"Go back to bed, Susan."

Mum's voice, breaking, scared, terrifyingly calm.

Susan pushed open the door, forcing it over the resistance of the bulge in the poorly-fitted carpet.

Inside, mum was standing upright, rocking, trying to stay on her feet, one hand over her mouth, a smoking revolver hanging limp in the other.

Dad was on the floor, two gaping holes smoking in his chest, blood fountaining out to match the rhythm of his dying heart, splashing and forming in pools around him on the floor. Susan had gone to him, but only a faint step.

He was rasping for breath, his eyes were fluttering, rolling; his mouth trying to form a word, but he only managed a solitary red bubble, a final rattle, and then silence.

Mum dropped the gun heavily on the bed, collapsing to her knees.

"I couldn't stand it anymore," she said. "I just had to be free. I just needed to be rid of him."

She feels like a medical experiment strapped to a slab, a terrified mouse confined to a glass bowl, the needle about to penetrate her chest. It's like a Victorian dissection; the experts, the interested and the voyeurs crowding around as the surgeon prepares to take his first cut; or schoolchildren watching open-mouthed as a biology teacher takes apart an unfortunate frog.

She had lived in a bubble for almost a year now. Each room she occupied could be seen into, but not seen out of. Here she could see out, but only to the wider four walls of this court chamber, a glimmer of brightness forcing through a skylight.

The judge, all in red, facing her, looking down on her; the backs of the heads of four rows of lawyers, the one to the front right on his feet – a slumped crow of a man, bent on his scrawny legs, motioning back at her without ever turning his head.

To her left is the jury, stern and serious, not meeting her eyes – only looking when they think her eyes are elsewhere.

The journalists, she thinks, laughing and joking when the judge steps out; her whole life nothing more than a day out of the office for them.

I am a mouse in a cage, she thinks; a fish in a bowl.

The little hunchbacked man is talking again, pouring over his plinth like a spider nestling over its eggs.

He talks and he gestures, jokes and lectures, and all the time he is telling a lie; turning her into a killer, or a monster, or both. She is a fantasist. She is a freak. She is a liar. Then he pauses to clean his spectacles on his cloak yet again, like some bit-part Hammer Horror actor from when she was a girl.

"She stated that her husband was not involved and did not know about the deaths until a week later," says the little bottled spider.

"She then made no comment to questions asked, until she was asked about the part of her prepared statement relating to her husband. She then repeated that he had no involvement in the deaths, was in London at the time, and wanted to tell the police when he found out a week later. He was appalled."

In the corner of her eye, Susan senses Chris looking over at her.

Gary made a great lawyer. Sat in the interview room with her, making notes, occasionally scratching at the stubble on his chiseled jaw, stubbing out a cigarette before lighting another.

Sometimes he rubbed at his eyes, when he was tired, and Susan could see the creases on his face; after the police had done sweating her, working her; trying to force it out of her . . . like in a film.

It had all been in a silver sepia too; Susan the dumb broad accused of cashing in on her father's murder; Gary the world-weary criminal defender, there to save the dame.

"It wasn't my fault," she told him. "I had a bullying father and a spineless husband. I was just a girl in the wrong place at the wrong time."

Sat in the holding tank, Gary with her, pulling on endless cigarettes, offering Susan one, which she waved away.

Only she couldn't remember this film, and she thought she'd seen all of Gary's movies a dozen times or more.

He'd leaned in, real close, placing a consoling hand on her quivering knee,

"Here's the thing, Suzie," he said, flicking his ash on the floor. "The cops, they just ain't buying this 'Chris wasn't at the party' line."

Susan flashed her eyes, all doe, then looked at the floor like she was going to cry.

"But they've got to believe me," she pouted, "because everything I've said is the truth."

She'd given a statement, she'd told them exactly what happened. So why didn't they believe her? Why weren't they letting her go?

Gary had sat silent, lost for words for a moment, the smell of tobacco and booze on his breath.

"You've got to give them something else," he'd said, eventually. "You've gone 'no comment' in there for the past half-hour. You need to spill some more Susan, just enough for me to help you."

She'd pulled away then, wanting to run, but locked in this tiny interview cell.

Only she'd relented. Gary was always right.

So they called them back in and she told them about the gun, keeping her voice steady, her manner calm.

It was a black revolver that she had never seen before, not until that night, when mum had thrown it, still smoking, onto the bed.

She didn't know where it came from, the gun, but she suspected it was her father's.

There were always rumours in the family that he had a gun – something he'd brought back from Canada, after the Brits said they wouldn't prosecute him for cowardice; a prop for him to reclaim his deserted manhood.

"But Chris had guns, didn't he?"

Montgomery Clift was playing the cop, all wild-eyed and broody; sweat on his brow, anger in his glare.

"No comment."

But Monty had continued, undeterred.

"Chris has a gun very like this one. Colt Commando? You ever seen it, Susan? You ever seen a gun like that?"

She'd shaken her head, placing her fingers on the edge of the interview desk.

"I don't know anything about guns," she gasped. "I couldn't tell one from another. I hate guns. They terrify me."

Monty slammed a fist into the desk, then shouted, like he was losing his cool.

"Well, that was the murder weapon, Susan, and Chris had one just like it. We got documents."

Then Gary had blazed in, on his feet with his stern jaw right in Monty's face.

"Come on. The lady just told you she knows nothin' about guns."

"I never went with Chris," Susan blurted suddenly, her voice cracking with the strain.

"Not to the club. I hate guns. I've always hated guns. Chris always wanted me to shoot with him, but I never wanted to go because I hated the bangs, they frighten me. I'd never seen that gun before and I don't know what sort of gun it is."

Two bodies on the floor – mum and dad, Bill and Pat.

Susan stood over them, the smoking gun dangling from her limp arm now.

Mum bleeding out, pints of it coming out of her, already dead eyes staring back accusingly before she'd ever hit the carpet; her legs going from under her with the second shot.

BANG!

It had just gone off in Susan's hand the first time, hadn't it?

There had been shouting and screaming, screeching and raging at each other, both of them hysterical, her and mum.

How long had it gone on for? Could have been minutes; could have been seconds – mum pulling her straggly hair back over her scalp, like she always did when she was stressed; when she was at her wits' end; when dad had been going at her for days.

Susan had put her fingers up after a while, stretched them outwards, appealing for calm with the flat of her palms.

"I need to call Chris," she had said. "Chris will know what to do."

But mum had just raged more, like a banshee on the fells, and Susan realised for the first time in all those years just how much mum hated Chris as well.

It wasn't just dad.

And as she raged she seemed to angle towards the bed, or the gun on the bed; her hands together, like she was in prayer, and they were pointing at the bed; they were pointing at the gun on the bed.

She's going for the gun. She's going for the gun.

But suddenly mum had backed away and Susan had felt the weight of it in her own hand; the coldness of the metal against her nighty, the course grip of the handle on her sweaty palm.

And the filth coming out of her mother's mouth, and the things she'd said about dad, and about Chris. And about how she . . .

The gun was in Susan's hand, pointed vaguely at mum; strange, because the last she could remember it was still on the bed. She lowered it a fraction, but she couldn't quite bring herself to put it down, to drop it.

"I need to call Chris," Susan had repeated, trying to stay calm.

"Chris? What could Chris do, Susan? Always was bloody useless? Good for nothing. Good for bloody nothing."

"Don't say that," Susan was suddenly, screaming, the gun raised again.

"He just wound your dad up, he did. Couldn't stand him. Drove a wedge in this family, he did."

"Don't talk about Chris like that," Susan, or thought; she couldn't remember, but the hammer had been cocked back.

"He's a good man, Chris. He's a better man than you think he is. He's a better man than dad ever was."

"He was no better and no worse, in bed or out. I only found that out the last time you came to stay."

Had she said that? Had she just said that? Susan had wondered every day for the next 15 years.

Did she just tell me she'd slept with Chris?

BANG!

And then the room was spinning and Susan blinked away the blackness in her vision, rubbed at the burns on her cheek and on her hand as the gun had whipped back and almost smashed her in the face.

Her ears rang and her knuckles stung from the sparks that spat out of the side of the revolver.

Mum clutched at her chest, staggering heavily over one knee, trying to talk, reaching out, her eyes already glazing.

Stop looking at me.

BANG!

STOP LOOKING AT ME.

And mum had, hitting the floor with a thud.

Eventually Susan had dropped the gun on the carpet and sunk to her knees.

Still in the fish bowl, Susan sits, trying to keep composed, paying no mind to the lies he's spouting, the slanders he's hissing; that beastly, horrible, little man – cleaning his spectacles, motioning theatrically back at her without ever looking her in the eye.

Her, the specimen in the jar, soon to be put out of its misery with the stab of a needle, the squeeze of a syringe.

"A second prepared statement was read out," he says. "She stated that the weapon used in the shooting was a black revolver with a brown handle that she had never seen before, but she suspected that it belonged to her father. She disposed of the gun and the bullet casings on the day after the shootings."

The journalists have their heads down suddenly, scribbling frantically in their silly little notebooks.

"After the killings, pension money paid to her parents built up and questions were being asked. Susan Edwards wrote to the Department for Work and Pensions pretending to be her parents, and opened an account in her name and her mother's name to pay the money into."

She wants to scream.

I didn't want the money. We didn't want the bloody money. But we had to take it because if we didn't take it then people would start asking questions . . . and we'd have been found out. And we couldn't be found out, either of us, even when I dragged Chris into this, because I couldn't face jail; we couldn't face jail . . .

"I was sitting on the stairs, hours later. I was sitting on the third step and my feet were planted on the floor. I was rocking back and forth, I remember that, my head clasped in my hands and I was tearing at my own hair, retching at it, trying to pull it out in clumps – only it wouldn't come.

"I could hear screams, distant screams that seemed to be coming from another world – only they were coming from me. There was a little window in the front door – a little distressed glass rectangle, that let light in but you couldn't see out of because it was so deliberately warped. I sat for hours just staring at that rectangle of glass, looking for the flicker of blue lights; listening for the distant screech of sirens.

"I sat there all night, just rocking, crying . . . thinking.

"It was like I'd fallen into a coma – not awake, not asleep, but somehow still conscious, like I was squatting in somebody else's head.

"But I was there all the time, thinking about mum and dad lying dead on the floor upstairs, about what mum had said, right at the end – about dad, about Chris.

"Then the gun had gone off, gone off twice, and mum, falling down dead at the second shot, her eyes going grey before she'd even hit the floor.

"I sat through the darkest hours, until the early morning forced its way through into the hall, through the little warped window on the flimsy front door, filling it with a desperate half-light. But there were no sirens. There were no blue lights.

"There was nothing but me, shivering on the stairs, and mum and dad lying dead in the room above me. I opened the door and looked out; it must have been four, four-thirty perhaps. And I just stood there breathing in the cold morning air and looking out on their bleak little world, in its early dawn greyness, and I couldn't quite work out how any of us had come to this.

"How had I ended up so bullied and miserable? How had dad got away with taking it out on me and mum for so many years? How had mum known so much for so long, and never said a word? Living with all that knowledge festering inside her – just letting it rot away at her mind and her innards; but never challenging, never standing up to him. Not for either of us.

"And mum knew everything that had happened and she said she'd slept with Chris, just before we all had that big row back in 1992 when we went back to London, and had to fork out on the train.

"And they think I killed them both? That's what you're saying? They think I killed them both?

"You know what? Sometimes I wish I had. I wish I had killed him as well as her. I wish I'd meant to kill her. I wish I'd bloody well meant to kill them both. I wish I'd planned it and got Chris to fire bullets into them. Only I didn't."

There was a knock on the door then and Gary put his finger to his lips, beckoning Susan to silence.

"We good?" said Montgomery, swinging his head round the cell door.

"Five minutes," Gary replied, waving him away with a dismissive hand.

Susan's new world has no blue skies and no pretty views; just prison corridors that stink of sweat and disinfectant, a boxed cell she gets to herself – she is on remand so her living conditions are better than the convicted prisoners – but it's still a life of bars and locks.

Her crown court appointment is the first time she's been out in the world for months. She's been looking forward to it, in a perverse way – just to be away from the claustrophobia of the prison corridors, to see greens and blues.

Only she doesn't.

In the end it had been prison, then into a van where she was handcuffed to a railing in a tiny cubicle, not even able to stand up to see out.

After the long and painful ride, which concluded with flash guns popping at her window as the van slowed to allow the court's rear security gates to swing open, she steps down and a blanket is immediately thrown over her head.

Then she is frogmarched indoors once more; herded along corridors like livestock being taken to the slaughter rooms and into a holding cell, where the door is slammed heavily behind her.

And even now, in this box, where Susan had pictured green fields and golden skies, she is still encased in bricks and mortar.

There is no light. There is no sky. She could be beneath the ground for all she knows, just like poor old mum and dad.

Finally she is led upstairs, chained to a podgy guard, and through to a goldfish bowl where she stands next to Chris, the circus freaks brought out to be examined, the little ringmaster at the front working the crowd against her.

"There had been no contact with the deceased after a visit went sour in 1992," he says.

And she remembers that row. She has thought about it every day since 1992; her and Chris heading up all the way from London, feeling duty-bound to go, to see Bill and Pat.

Chris had been as reluctant as ever, knowing what to expect, but going along all the same, just to keep the peace.

221

Dad had been vile, exceptionally vile, and Chris eventually grabbed his coat and walked to the door, opened it silently and stepped out into their lifeless little cul-de-sac.

She'd gone after him, catching him on the corner of Blenheim, only Chris wouldn't stop walking; his face crimson, his voice strangled by fury.

"I can't do it, Susan," he'd said. "I can't do it anymore, putting up with him and his vicious tongue, his bullying, his . . ."

"But it's only one more night, Chris," she'd replied. "We're half way through. Be a year before we have to do it again."

Chris had faced dad's lashing tongue dozens of times over the past decade, and he'd always weathered it before, laughed it off almost – quite enjoying the fact that his presence made the old man so irate.But not that day. Not anymore.

"You can stay," he said. "But I'm going back to London. I can't do it, Susan. I just can't do it anymore."

So Chris had sat on the broken-down seat on the shabby little park just down the road while Susan had gone back to the house. She'd packed their tiny suitcase and walked heavily down the stairs, hoping someone might meet her at the bottom and plead with her to stay.

But there was nobody, so she walked into the front room in as stately a manner as she could manage. Dad was leaning back in his armchair, smoking a fag triumphantly. Mum was crying, looking away.

"We're going now," Susan had said. "We're going now, and you probably won't see us again."

Anger had seized her then, welled up in her throat and burst from her in the form of stinging tears, which she hated herself for; hated them for.

"I don't understand why . . ."

But she hadn't been able to finish the sentence. Somehow there seemed little point. So she'd walked along the hall silently, closed the door behind her silently, like she was closing a book at the end of a particularly heavy chapter; or shutting the door on a relative's home for the last time, after they'd died, or after they'd been taken into a home.

"In 1998, Susan had been contacted by her mother who was now acting as carer for her father, and persuaded her to visit. She visited over the Mayday weekend, she had said in her statement. She had called while there to say the visit was awful."

That call from mum after six years, six years after they'd all but been thrown out of the house.

They'd changed their number after that, Susan and Chris, but somehow mum had got hold of the new one.

Crying, pleading, begging almost.

"I need to see you, I'm sorry, we're both so very sorry. Please come, Susan. Please, can't we leave things in the past, let bygones be bygones?"

So she'd agreed, grieved, furious and relieved in equal measures that mum and dad were back in touch after so long. And more than that; they were sorry, they wanted another chance.

Chris hadn't said anything, not after she agreed to go on her own.

And with hindsight, she wishes she'd stayed away; that she'd put down the phone the second she recognised mum's voice.

They should have stayed away, not let mum and dad draw them back in.

Her fingers had trembled so much she had to fight the coins into the slot when she'd escaped to call Chris from the phone box down the road.

"I just needed to get out," she told Chris. "It's vile. I can't cope. I want to come home."

And Chris had said that she should, that she didn't need to ask his permission.

"Just come home, Susan. Just walk away like last time."

She'd been silent for a long time then, the only sounds her stinted sobs and the clunk as she fed more coins into the slot of the payphone.

"They control my every thought, Chris, my every feeling. Everything I do is to please them, or to spite them."

"Then come away. Don't be a martyr and come home."

But something had stopped her; taken hold of her and led her back inside the house.

"I want to Chris," she'd said, "I really do. But I can't. Mum's so miserable and . . . oh, Chris, she's just drunk all the time now, always got a gin in her hand; and she's in pain and dad's just so bloody awful . . ."

"It's not your problem, Susan. They've dug their own grave."

Susan hung up the phone and put on a forced smile for mum.

They'd drunk gin and even laughed a bit, after dad had gone to bed.

They talked about Elvis and Graceland, and the musicians playing on the porches and outside bars. They'd even sang a bit of Elvis, and one that might have been Johnny Cash.

Then they'd drunk more gin and mum had got all weepy and sad, saying she couldn't stand dad anymore, couldn't stand his bullying, and his whining and his hatred.

She'd spoken about how he'd driven Susan away from them by everything he did; and the bullying and the nastiness, and how he was to poor Christopher.

How he'd been vile to her, never loved her, only wanted her for a nurse to wipe his arse when he couldn't manage it anymore.

Only he'd made a bad choice, because now she was ill and in pain with her back, and she needed him to care for her, and how he was livid about it.

"Tripped me, one night," she said, "just as I was getting up to go to bed, and he stuck out a foot and tried to trip me into the fire. He denied it, said he didn't; said it was my big, clumsy feet. But I knew. I know he'd done it on purpose."

Then mum had gone to bed, downing the dregs of her gin and stumbling to the door. And Susan had sat in silence for a while, drinking more gin until it had almost all gone; shocked and dazed when she looked at the clock to see it was already gone midnight.

"Eventually, after hours sat on the stairs, the early morning cold was making me shiver and I'd gone up to see mum and dad. It was light now and they were lying where they fell, the blood on the floor darker than before, turning to black – dad on his back, mum on her front, where they'd fallen, never to move again, not on their own. Somehow I was still surprised. I half expected them to be asleep in bed; the night before just a bad dream.

The bubbles of blood that dad had been blowing had dried into a maroon crust on his lips and down his cheek, his eyes were open and grey, like mirrors. Mum was face down, her hair matted with blood soaked under her like she'd wet herself.

I couldn't understand why the police hadn't come after I'd waited all night for them. I'd have told them everything if they'd come that night, how mum had shot dad, and then somehow I had shot mum.

But they hadn't come, so in the harsh morning light I somehow realised I had to do something. I couldn't leave them like that; it just wasn't respectful.

"I just didn't know what to do and the sun was coming through, making the day unseasonably warm; smothering me, suffocating me.

I could only think of Chris; about how he'd know what to do, how he'd bring order to the lunacy. Only I couldn't tell him over the phone, I needed him to see for himself, so I'd hatched a plan, of sorts, to make him my partner in crime.

I needed to take control and I needed to do it there and then, so I climbed to my feet from the corner I'd suddenly found myself slumped in. I pulled the sheets and blankets off the bed and tore the cover off the duvet.

I wrapped dad up first, then mum, the blood coming out of them as I moved them around and soaking through the bedding; farting out of them almost in congealed, black-ened pools.

I'd thrown the blanket down first and rolled dad onto it, face down now. Then I'd thrown the corners over him, hiding him from the world; a temporary resting place.

After that I moved onto mum, which was more difficult because she was heavier and bigger boned. I threw a duvet cover over her back and pressed it firmly into her shoulders, then I turned her over, her innards gurgling and squelching and finally covering her too; hiding her sightless and accusing eyes."

Monty launched to his feet and thumped his slender fist on the desk, leaning into her.

"That's a heap o' s . . ."

Gary had risen to meet him, staring him in the eyes.

"Well, that's what she's saying, buster. That's her statement."

Gary took a final pull on his cigarette, then stubbed it heavily into the ashtray, breathing out the smoke as he leaned back, folding his heavy arms.

"I'm not buying this crock, sister," Monty had fumed, running a hand through his dreamlike locks.

Susan said nothing, instead staring at the mass of paper scattered over the desk detailing her account; her version of events.

"You've asked me to tell you what happened detective, so I'm telling you," she said, no life in her voice.

"I suggest you let the lady continue."

Monty had thrown up his hands, slumped back down in his chair and motioned Susan to continue.

"I'd walked the final few steps with a sense of dread . . . of inevitability. I just knew that absolutely nothing would have changed. And I was not mistaken. I'd walked through the front door after giving it a slight tap, out of politeness. I'd shouted hello, wiped my feet and walked down the hall, sensing the smell of his burning cigarette somewhere deeper in the house.

When I found him he was sitting on the sofa in the front room, ignoring the telly; stubbing out one fag and digging for another.

His eyes were cold and distant; and I knew immediately that mum has only asked me there for herself. He was still as bitter as he'd ever been.

He touched a flame to the end of another unfiltered Park Drive, took a drag, spluttered and wheezed, then took another pull to help his lungs settle. He looked like a corpse.

I hadn't missed him, not for one day, not for one minute.

I hadn't missed mum either, if the truth be told – I'd even started to tell people on the estate in Dagenham, if I ever spoke to anybody there, that they were both dead – dead and buried long ago.

He still managed to make me cry that day, even though he never knew it, as I saved it for the dingy, poky little spare room upstairs, which I was sharing with all of his clutter and detritus.

Then I cried – after he'd called me a slut and a whore again, after he'd insulted Chris just for good measure and shouted at mum, who stormed from the room; who I'd found sobbing in the garden, smoking a fag she must have stolen from him.

If any of you actually knew just what a vile man he was . . . if you only knew."

"Okay doll, we get it," Monty said, throwing a pack of cigarettes onto the table. "He was a nasty piece of work. You hated him. Seems to me that's all the more reason for you to kill him."

"I'd have killed him gladly," Susan replied calmly, pushing the cigarettes away from her. "If he'd run at me with a knife and I was able to defend myself. But I didn't kill him. Mum did."

"So, take us back to the bedroom."

Susan did.

"They were lying at odds to each other, like in a makeshift morgue. I panicked and wondered what would happen if someone came into the room, if burglars came and stumbled over the bodies. I wracked my brains, wondering where I could put them, to hide them, just in case. I'd already used all my strength to wrap them in the bedding and turn them over, so the thought of moving them far or even getting them into the loft or something was beyond me. It was only when I sat down on the bed in despair that it came to me. There was nothing I could do there and then apart from hide them away, then hide them for good when I had help, and for that I needed Chris. It had to be Chris because he was the only one who would help me, the only one I could trust. Otherwise I was going to prison and I was going to prison for a very long time.

Sooner or later they'd start to smell and one of the neighbours was bound to report it to the council. And I was beyond calling the police now because they wouldn't

229

believe me; and why would they? I was in the house with my two dead parents, a gun on the floor, and shells scattered over the floor. Plus my fingerprints were all over the gun. I thought about just walking away and going back to London, just pretending I'd never even been there.

But you'd know, wouldn't you officer? You'd have a way of finding out. Someone would have seen me at the house, someone would remember seeing me, off to the shop or at the phone box.

And you can find out things, the police. You could have found out from the bus tickets that I'd bought or from the cameras at the stations. I had to hide them, and the only place I could think of was under the bed, just in case of the burglars. So I clambered to my feet, took a deep breath and grabbed dad at the shoulders, holding the blanket tight in my fists, and I dragged him a foot at a time across the carpet and towards the bed; black blood seeping deeper into the cloth with every strain of my body, leaving a gory trail across the floor.

I pulled the mattress aside and leaned it against the wall, then I pushed the wooden bed frame onto its side, so it was standing up against the open window, its legs facing into the room. I fought dad into the place nearest to the window, straining and groaning, his head banging on the floor every time I shifted him another few inches. Then I collapsed into the wall, my breath gone and my heart thumping erratically in my chest.

Mum had taken longer, even though I didn't have to move her as far, but eventually they were side by side, and I'd dropped the bed frame back over them, like I was sealing them into a tomb; pulling the mattress back and fighting it straight. It looked like an empty room."

"And the gun, Suzie? What did you do with the gun?"

Monty pulled out another smoke and put a flame to it, snapping his zippo shut and blowing out fumes.

"I almost forgot about it, until I saw it on the floor; so I rushed to it in a panic, like somebody else was going to see, and I picked it up with its heavy wooden handle, scooping up the shell cases as well that were scattered around it.

I went down the stairs, into the kitchen, and dug through the cupboard under the sink where they kept the carrier bags.

I selected one, a big, thick department store bag – solid green plastic that you couldn't see into; and I threw in the gun, tipped in the shells, and sealed it with some tape I found.

I walked the streets, wildly clutching at the bag and its sharp innards into me, looking for somewhere to put it, somewhere to hide it.

Finally I passed a bin and thought that was as good a place as any, so I threw it in."

"You did well, Suzie," said Monty, stubbing out his cigarette. "Into a council bin and straight to landfill; buried somewhere in an underground city of garbage. Almost like you'd thought it through."

"Well I didn't," Susan snapped. "I just wanted to get rid of it and I didn't know what else to do. I was worried that if I hid it in a hedge or threw it in a stream it would be found. Children might find it and I didn't want that."

Monty stared at her long and hard, tapping a pencil annoyingly on the edge of the desk, like he still didn't believe her. Susan tried to maintain his stare, but she couldn't and looked away.

"Then you went home to Chris?"

"Yes I did. That's just what happened."

Monty paused and stared at her again, seeing into her like an oracle and forcing her mouth to go to work once again.

"I went home. I locked up the house and I made sure all the windows were shut, and the blinds were down. I popped the front door key into my handbag and I walked all the way into Mansfield town centre. And I caught the bus back to London – the 10.35am National Express, calling at Nottingham, Leicester, Milton Keynes, Golder's Green and London Victoria, followed by another hour-and-the rest back out to Dagenham."

"And what day was this?"

"The Sunday, I think, or the Monday."

"And it was definitely the 10.35?"

"Yes, definitely. Why?"

Monty leaned forward and clasped his hands together, massaging his fingers over his knuckles.

"It's just, the thing is, Susan, that we have evidence that you were in the Mansfield branch of the Halifax Building Society at 11.17am on the Tuesday. You were setting up an account in the joint names of yourself and your mother?"

"Was I? Then I must be mistaken. It must have been on the Tuesday."

"Later than 10.35am?"

"Yes, sorry, I'm getting confused. That must have been one of the other times I went up there."

Nobody spoke for a very long time, it had seemed. Monty had spent a lot of time writing notes, not looking at her, pausing occasionally to think, his mouth working as he did.

Gary was motionless in a room filled with a threatening silence . . . which Monty broke.

"Tell us about the bank, Susan. Why did you set up the account?"

"No," she replies. "I don't want to talk about the bank."

"On the Tuesday you went into the Halifax Building Society and you opened an account in your name and in the name of your mother, Patricia Wycherley. You transferred funds in the region of £40,000 into this account from other accounts previously held by your mother and your father, William George Wycherley."

Silence.

"Why did you do that Susan?"

"No comment."

"Why did you write to the pensions office, pretending to be your father and mother?"

"No comment."

It was the Halifax and it was sunny and I walked all the way in from mum and dad's, and I felt free and brave – like I had a plan that would let me carry on with life. I had a hand-written letter from mum clasped in my sweating palm saying we were going into business together. I had to keep them alive, all the time, forever; because while they were alive and sending letters and cards, nobody would be looking for them. While they were alive nobody would be wondering who killed them.

"And what about the pensions office, Susan? Why did you pretend to be your father and mother in letters you sent to the Department for Work and Pensions, transferring funds into the newly-created account in yours and you mother's names?"

"No comment."

The door swung open, some bit-part actor coming in and whispering into Monty's ear.

Only it wasn't Monty anymore; it was a young-looking detective, older than his years, speaking to her – smart, youthful, strong-jawed, but not Montgomery Clift.

"Susan Edwards," he said. "I have to advise you that an application has been made to Nottingham Magistrates' Court, for your further detention. Susan, they've granted us the right to detain you for a further 60 hours, due to the grave nature of the charges you face and the evidence you have detailed so far."

She looked at Gary for help; only Gary had gone – replaced by a pasty, narrow-shouldered little man who looked like he'd spent too many years of his life locked away in police interview cells.

A scream then, silent at first, but becoming deeper, more vocal, more shrill; her head in her hands now, her body slowly rocking, like all those years ago on the bottom steps at home.

"Can we have a moment, do you think? My client is clearly distressed and not capable of answering your questions at the present time."

A sigh.

"Okay, interview suspended. It is now 10.30pm on Friday, October 31, 2013. Present are Susan Edwards, her legal representative, myself: Detective Inspector Tony Rawlins, and Detective Sergeant . . ."

Chapter 10

*I think cold is a better word to describe them than evil –
cold and calculating. I don't think either of them showed a
single thread of remorse – Detective Chief Inspector Rob
Griffin, post trial press statement, June 2014.*

The same CID office, the same faces, only more buzz now,
like they were nearing the end of a long journey; same suits
and haircuts – just a few weeks older now, faces more tired
now, a bit less tolerant and moods more snappy.

There was also a strange heaviness to the air; a sense of
treading water, or wading through treacle. But there was a
focus; an awareness that their targets were banged up in
separate cells in the Bridewell down the road, and the
curtain would soon be coming down.

People were heading home, in a flurry of rustling coats
being pulled on, and bags being thrown over shoulders.

"Fancy a pint Tony?"

They only called him sir if a more senior officer was in
the room.

But Rawlins waved the voice away with an apologetic
"maybe next time". And probably he would; when the
days were a bit more routine, when they'd got the Edwards

banged to rights. There was nothing quite like a night out with the boys; apart from a night in with the girlfriend.

Only not tonight.

Tonight was less than a fortnight after they'd dug up the pensioners; and not two days since the Edwards had surrendered themselves to British custody and been carted up to Nottingham in the back of a van to answer a good few questions.

"I'd love a pint," he shouted just before the door had closed. "Only I've got work to do!"

They laughed sycophantically and waved goodnight, as Rawlins settled at his desk and waited for their chatter to subside.

Not tonight.

"Yes, I'd been extremely concerned about Susan. She hadn't seen her parents in six years, she hadn't spoken to them as far as I knew. Then out of the blue she got a telephone call and she said she had to go up for the weekend. I remember to this day the look in her eyes as she left the flat, pecked me on the cheek and squeezed my hand. She looked haunted, like she was going out to face the hangman's noose.

"It's a terrible thing, duty – especially when it's duty towards people who don't deserve your loyalty. He was truly vile, William Wycherley. He was a bully. He was a coward, a spineless coward who did awful things and treated people in awful ways. I hated William Wycherley and I hoped I'd never have to see him again; and as it turned out I didn't – at least while he was still breathing.

I'd wished him dead many times but I didn't kill him. He wasn't the way he was with me because he wanted to control me, or dominate me or put me in my place.

He just didn't want me in his life. He didn't want me in Susan's life. He just wanted them both to himself. There was nothing I could do to fight that. There was no way of finding middle ground. It was an absolute position. Just fuck off, was all he ever had to say to me.

William Wycherley was a fraud and he lived a lie. They all made out they loved him, when they responded to the cards and the letters, but who missed him really? Who came to see him? Nobody. Nobody came to see him, not in 15 years. Nobody missed him in 15 years.

One of Susan's relatives got a letter returned once, probably around the time we were thinking about selling the house. They wrote to Susan, and that was that. I think that was when we came up with the idea that they were traveling around Ireland. It seemed to keep them permanently out of people's thoughts. But it was a simple decision in the end. We had to keep him alive . . . them alive. They had to exist on paper, both of them; two spirits fluttering through the files of Government central, and the filing cabinets of doctors' waiting rooms.

"I wanted to call you people as soon as she told me, as soon as she showed me. But Susan had been frantic, falling to her knees, screaming, pleading, begging with me. She'd screeched, 'If you call the police they'll think I did it. And now you're here they'll think you did it as well. The only way we're safe is if people think they're still alive'.

And nobody cared anyway – certainly not the neighbours, they didn't speak to the neighbours if they could help it. The relatives were scattered all over the place, pretending they were doing their duty with a Christmas card and the odd letter. And Bill and Pat would reciprocate, with details of their own adventures. I'm quite an expert in the family correspondence of the Wycherleys. Nobody ever suggested a meet up, or invited them to anything. Nobody ever hinted that it would be nice to see him. Not one invite, ever. And nobody ever questioned how a man supposedly approaching his hundredth birthday was still gallivanting around Ireland. Nobody but the Department for Work and Pensions, anyway.

He was out of sight to all of them, out of sight and almost forgotten; bitter, cowardly old Uncle Bill with his bashful, bullied wife. They probably held a party when he announced he was heading out of London; they'd have thrown a collective sigh of relief. I breathed one, I can tell you, despite how upset Susan was.

"They sold that house from under her nose. It was Susan's house really; mostly Susan's house anyway. William bullied her out of it, and then they sold it from under her nose. She was furious, but as far as I was concerned it was money well spent. Susan was devastated but I'd have paid double to get rid of him, if I had it, to get the old man a few hundred miles from us.

I'm not sorry he's dead, you know. In fact, I'm glad. But I didn't kill him. Patricia killed him, and Susan killed Patricia by mistake, because Patricia forced her hand. She'd lost her mind, I think; been locked up with William for too many years. I'm actually quite surprised she didn't do it sooner. It's just a shame she waited until Susan was there before she picked her moment. She could quite easily have just smothered him quietly one afternoon, then pleaded provocation. That would have made life much more simple for everyone. But she didn't. So in the end we had to keep them alive, Susan and I, and the only way we could do that was by writing letters, cancelling appointments, and taking the money. We wanted to cancel the pensions, but it was impossible. So in the end we decided we needed to cash them in, and everything else they had left as well. And we took the money, and we kept taking the money, because we didn't have any other way out."

Rawlins sat in the dark of an empty office, exhausted, wired on coffee, listening to endless recordings of interviews as they landed in his in-tray, in the form of little black memory sticks. They looked like a shoal of dead fish, each marked with a number, flickering their black bellies against the harsh overhead strip of lighting.

This was the night shift that followed the day shift – all worked by the same team; all as bleary-eyed and coffee-drenched as Rawlins.

One lot were working Susan, the others going at Christopher; all reporting back to Rawlins, who was reporting back to Griffin – an all-controlling, silent ringmaster.

The night shift; working through the dark and frozen hours, taking on the Edwards robotically; turning over every rock.

Rawlins had put in an appearance with Susan – just to look her in the eyes. But he'd had no time for Christopher; instead listening to hour after hour of endless recordings – Christopher Edwards giving his version of events.

His voice was gentle and clipped, with a neutral accent. He didn't lose his composure once. He sounded like he was doing no more than talking his way out of a difficult situation; a parking fine or a littering offence.

"I returned from work and Susan was just sitting there, staring out of the window with a tumbler of gin in her hand. I knew something was wrong, but I assumed she'd just had a hard time of it. I knew from experience just how demanding and difficult Bill and Pat could be; especially Bill. So we passed a few pleasantries and I went to make a cup of tea, just to give her a bit of space because I could tell she felt a bit awkward and I didn't want to put any more pressure on her.

She's very fragile, Susan. She's had a huge amount to contend with, and she actually copes with it all very well, all things considered. But you can't pressure her. She'll tell you in her own good time. If you pressure her she'll just clam up. We'd spoken a few times while she was away, calling from a phone box somewhere on the estate. She said that if Bill knew she'd been speaking to me it would just agitate him, make him worse. She'd say she was just popping to the shop, or just going out for a walk around six, because she knew that I'd be home by then. And usually Bill was starting on his Scotch by then and was a little bit gentler; it usually took a couple of hours for it to make him turn nasty.

But every time she spoke to me – if I remember correctly, she managed to call me every day or almost every day at least – she'd end up in tears on the other end of the line.

It wasn't because he'd been a bastard, at least most of the time. I think it was just that Susan felt helpless; lost. It was her mother, I think. She hated her father but she'd become almost apathetic towards her mother, especially after that big argument some years before, and I think seeing her mum again after all that time, and what she'd become, just brought it all back. She felt torn.

Her mother always sided with Bill, after we got married, even when he was being particularly awful. It had been very different back in the day, before we got married; when Susan and Patricia worked together they could just about maintain the upper hand. They could gang up on him, I suppose, tell him he was being an arse and almost make light of it – or back each other up at least.

But that was all gone now. Once Patricia backed William over the sale of the house, that was it, and the bond between Susan and her mother faltered. Susan felt betrayed. She felt like she'd always been there for Pat when it really mattered. She was always around. She was dutiful, and they really weren't easy people to be dutiful towards. She spent a considerable sum of her money taking Pat to Memphis, and the rest of it on giving her a home to call her own. But Bill was always resentful about the money that Susan had been left, and he'd never have been happy until he'd taken it from her; which he did, without any objection from Pat. I don't know why – either out of exhaustion or fear, I suppose.

Only Susan always saw it as a betrayal. It just said to her that, in the end, her mother also resented the money she'd inherited, and I honestly don't know whether Pat did, or whether she was just too scared of Bill to stand up to him. I'll tell you something though. Those six years, between the fallout in 1992 and the weekend Bill and Pat died, were the happiest of Susan's life. Those years when Bill and Pat were shut away in a little box at the back of her mind, when they were a hundred or so miles away; then she was calm, she was content. Only then they drew her back in and destroyed everything for her, again. But there's a duty with parents. It doesn't matter how horrible they are, it doesn't matter how frustrating they are, or how hateful they are, they still pull at your heartstrings. Susan felt guilty, I think, more than anything else. She didn't want her mother to be lonely, or desperate, or miserable. She needed to try and do something. That's not love though. It's duty, or genetics, or something. No matter who she was, no matter what she'd done, you can never quite leave your own mother to rot, can you? It's probably to do with chemistry or something."

It had almost been a relief to get up, stretch his legs and shoulders out and go for a slash, getting away from Christopher Edwards' narrative for a few moments.

On his way back, Rawlins grabbed another coffee from the vending machine, which would join the army of other forgotten or largely untouched plastic cups littering his desk.

But even away from his screen, Christopher's voice had still gone round in Rawlins' head – his calm and reasonable voice, a bit like a diplomat.

Rawlins studied a photo of him, his arrest photograph; a bland face with heavy spectacles which magnified his eyes, delicate features and a thinning hairline. He looked more like an accountant than a killer; which didn't mean anything, only it still did. He looked at the image again; Christopher wearing the clothes he'd been arrested in; the pale blue shirt with a peak of white vest showing through at the neck, his face cultivated with grey stubble.

Anyone can kill. That is the reality. Absolutely anyone.

Back at his desk, Rawlins ran his hands through his cropped hair; rubbed at his eyes, wondering yet again what the fuck he was still doing there, as he looked out at the blackened sky and the deserted incident room – a sea of abandoned paperwork and forgotten plastic cups.

Then he pressed the play icon on his screen once more, allowing Christopher Edwards' calm and, somehow soothing voice back into his ears and head; wishing he could just go home – knowing he could, and also knowing he couldn't.

"I don't recall when Susan mentioned about us going to Mansfield, but it wasn't that first day, I do know that. It was most likely the day after, or the day after that. I know it wasn't the first day because she'd been terrible when she got back, and when she told me she'd been brighter; and she was brighter after that first night back. I remember she told me that Pat had called and said they wanted us to look after the house for them while they went away for the weekend. It was like the past six years had never happened. But what could I do without looking like I was being difficult? I was reluctant, of course I was. I really wasn't interested in having William Wycherley back in my life, or doing him any favours. I certainly didn't want to come face to face with him, if I'm totally honest. But I just assumed they'd built some bridges while she was up there, Susan and her mother, so I went along with it for a quiet life.

It was sickeningly hot and stuffy on the coach up there – we never took the train because it was too expensive, and we both felt heavy and sweaty by the time we got up to Golders Green, not even out of London yet. But it was a lovely day and I just looked forward to getting out in the fresh air when we finally got to Mansfield.

We slogged up the motorway at a snail's pace, not breaking into the sandwiches we'd made ourselves before we passed Milton Keynes. I had cheese and lettuce. Susan had salmon. After about four hours of plodding up the motorway we made it to Mansfield. It was a mile or so out to Blenheim Close from where we were dropped off, and we sauntered out towards Forest Town. It was still sweltering but we were just happy to be off the coach, feeling the wind on our faces, and blowing cold on the sweat patches under our arms and over our clothes.

We stopped on the way and bought fish and chips, which we had wrapped to eat when we got to the house. It hadn't changed; the same dull cul-de-sac with brown, patchy lawns, faded fences and dog excrement all over the place. Susan pulled the front door key out of her purse, which I thought was strange because I couldn't think how she'd got it. Usually they'd just leave it in a plant pot around the side.

But in we went and we sat at the little table by the window and ate our fish and chips straight out of the paper. Then when we'd finished, Susan scrunched up the papers and took them to the bin and came back with a cloth to wipe the surface.

After that she sat down opposite me and I remember her massaging at her knuckles, and it was then that I knew something was amiss, because she only ever did that when she was nervous and had to tell me something bad. I remember it perfectly. After a moment or so, she just looked me in the eyes and said 'Chris, mum and dad are upstairs'.

I was flummoxed. I didn't want to see them, either of them, but I didn't want to make a scene.

'Well, what are they doing upstairs, Susan?" I replied. 'Why don't they come down and say hello'.

I got to my feet then like I was going to greet them, or confront them, but Susan reached out and took my hand, like she was begging me back into my seat. 'They can't come down,' she said. 'They can't come down because they're dead. They're dead upstairs.' And then she started to cry."

There was a madness to Christopher's account, Rawlins thought as he pauses the tape and looked at the grey morning coming through the skylight – but also a calmness, a clarity; he sounded like a witness who'd already been mentored through his day in court.

Rawlins had seen it before; only they tended to be the career criminals, the ones you couldn't intimidate or scare, the ones who wouldn't sweat it at a ten stretch behind prison bars.

Only Christopher Edwards had no previous – apart from a troubling financial history he was squeaky clean; not even a caution or a speeding fine. But this wasn't the silver screen and the killer didn't need a dark cape and a top hat, or lurk in darkened alleys.

"There had been no smell in the room at all, nothing beyond the lingering stench of William's stale fags.

At first I couldn't see them, even after Susan turned on the light; not until she motioned under the bed. She lifted back the mattress, which was folded over the side nearest to me, like children had become over-excited playing trampolines on the bed. I was in shock, you have to understand that, so everything I'm telling you is tainted because I don't know if I'm telling you what I remember, or what I think I can remember. I'd never seen a dead person before, and certainly not in those circumstances.

Susan moved away, back to the door – like she thought I was going to hit her, which I've never done and never would. I peered down, like I'd just run over a cat and I was looking under the car to see what sort of mess it had made. All I could see was blankets at first – they could quite easily have been a couple of sleeping bags stuffed under the bed, only I could see the staining, the black coming through the cloth, tar-like and flakey.

I don't remember much after that for a while, only the next thing I recall I was sitting in a heap on the floor with Susan hugging me, rocking me like a colic-stricken newborn

– crying hysterically. I couldn't believe the mess we were in. I was blurting, I do remember that; not really what I said – something about calling the police and getting it out in the open – but more the panic and the rage and the fear in me – rolling me around like an old ship in a storm. Susan had been screaming and pleading and begging; holding my face and talking to me like I was a child having a tantrum.

She had cradled my head; forcing me to look deep into her eyes. 'You can't tell them Chris,' she had said. 'You can't tell anybody. If you tell the police they'll think it was me . . . worse, they'll think it was us. They'll find out about the house and the arguments, and dad being so vile to you. They'll never believe that I only killed mum because she drove me to it. They won't believe that we didn't plan this; to kill them both. If we tell the police now then it's the end of our lives; they'll lock us up and throw away the keys. We can be free of them. We don't have to go to prison. We don't have to be apart'.

So together we lifted the mattress off the bed and lugged it into a far corner, then Susan asked me to help her with the frame, and we just lifted it onto its side, away from the bodies.

I had to see them. I had to see their faces, I don't know why – I still couldn't believe it, I suppose. I couldn't believe that it was them. I just needed to know. Then Susan sat me down and told me everything that had happened – all of it, even about what Patricia had said about us having sex, which was a lie.I held Susan tight and promised her that it was not true, and we cuddled and cried and hugged on the floor while Bill and Pat lay motionless in the far corner of the room. I asked Susan where the gun was, and she told me that she didn't know – only that she'd wandered the streets and dumped it in a bin along with the shell cases.

It was hot, it was still light, even after we'd been sat hugging and weeping on the carpet. Then I remember saying, 'If we're not going to tell the police then we need to hide the bodies', and Susan had replied that she'd thought about the attic, only they were too heavy and they'd start to smell and the neighbours would call the council, and then we'd be done for.

We thought about setting fire to the house at first, but we didn't know if the police could tell if they'd been killed before the fire started. It was in the days before everybody had the internet so we couldn't check things easily either. Then Susan said we should dig a big hole and bury them in the back garden; and that we had to keep them alive, at least on paper. And I think it was then that I understood that Susan had thought this through already, and I felt betrayed, like she was using me as a pawn in some awful game of chess.In all of this I was just protecting Susan, from the police, from her father, from the world; so we closed the door on Bill ant Pat, then we went downstairs to watch the Eurovision Song Contest, just to pass the time until it got dark. Dana International won that year. Funny what you remember."

Rawlins stopped the tape and checked the date Christopher had given – Eurovision Song Contest winner 1998, he tapped into his grimy keyboard.

It was the 43rd, it tells him – held in Birmingham after Katrina and the Waves won for Great Britain the year before. It took place on Saturday, May 9, 1998.

And Israeli transexual Dana had indeed won the competition that year.

Rawlins flicked through files, his composure abandoning him – sheets coming away, falling to the floor in a skimmed heap.

Both accounts stated that Susan Edwards visited her parents in Mansfield over the May Day Bank Holiday of 1998. That was Saturday May 2 to Monday May 4.

Then they returned together on Saturday May 9 – Susan told Christopher everything and they settled down to watch Dana International win on the telly.

So all of Christopher's dates match up and his account is credible.

But that meant that Susan must have opened up the new bank accounts four days before she told her husband that her parents were dead, and in Rawlins' mind that didn't fit.

Then his phone rang. The entomology report was in.

"Susan woke me a little after midnight and reality rushed in – where I was, what had happened, and what I had to do.

I must have dropped off watching the news, although I don't know how. We'd decided that we needed to bury them as close to the back patio door as we could. We didn't want to be seen, and we also knew they'd be heavy. Susan shook me awake, holding out a cup of tea on a saucer. I drank it down and went out to the shed and found a spade from Bill's small collection of tools, propped up at the back behind his hand-push lawnmower.

There were just the bare essentials in there, just in case he fancied a potter in the fresh air. So I took the spade, which looked barely used; first to prize up the double depth of slabs just outside the back door, and smash away at the flimsy layer of sand-heavy concrete, until I could see the soil below.

Only the earth was hard, like rock. It had been a magically warm Spring and they were already talking of hose-pipe bans and water shortages. The ground was hard work, harder to break through than the concrete – I was chipping away at it, an inch at a time at the start with the edge of the spade, the soil coming away in flakes. Then further down, after maybe a foot or so, it slowly dampened and softened, although the heavy clay made it painful going.

I was dripping with sweat, wheezing and clenching at the pain in my shoulders and wrists and I was maybe only a foot-and-a-half down by the time the sun was coming up. I'm not a big man. I'm not a strong man. I was not made for manual labour. I should have stopped then, as soon as I spotted the sun breaking over the houses. I should have retreated then. I should have found a shady place away from the daylight, but on I went, until the sun was up above the buildings, curtains were starting to twitch and dogs were barking to be let out. I heard the clink of milk bottles from far away, a car being shuddered into life by a grating ignition. I heard a back door opening too close by; the shuffling of feet on the lawn of the houses behind. Then Susan was at the patio door, beckoning me in, pulling me out of the light.

I could see William Wycherley's eyes in my mind, staring out lifelessly like Jacob Marley in his box, still full of poison and hate; no warmth in those eyes of his. And it was that look, those eyes, that face that made me keep thrusting the spade down and down into the earth, time after time, until I just wanted to weep with the agony. William's cold and lifeless eyes, his grey skin, sweating death into his rank coverings, carrying his contempt through all time. Nothing but hatred; nothing but hatred and self-pity.

I told Susan we'd have to wait it out and she nodded, led me through to the sofa and sat me down. I was spent. The television was off and it was quiet. I thought back to the evening before, sitting in the stuffy, fag-smelling front room, after we'd closed the door on Bill and Pat and made our way gingerly back downstairs – sinking into the furniture and not speaking for a long time."

The entomology report landed on Rawlins' desk. He wanted to read it but his brain was still swirling around with Christopher Edwards.

'He's offering me a non-confession, Rawlins thought. 'He's saying he's innocent of the murders; his own defense, the less-serious crimes he's putting his hands up to. Fraud. Disposing illegally of human remains. Five years, maximum. Out in two-and-a-half, less, maybe; a month of lock up in a Category A, then out for two years of gardening in some cushy open prison in the country with day passes out.

'He says he didn't kill them, that Susan was accidentally involved, that she only killed her mother under extreme provocation. He's admitting burying them. He's admitting spending the money and conning the taxman. He's here because of duty to his wife. He wants us to believe he's a victim. And perhaps he is.'

Rawlins played the tape back a notch, and listened again to Christopher's description of entering the Wycherley's bedroom, flipping off the mattress, pushing up the frame; Susan telling him that she'd thrown the gun and the discarded shells into a bin, early in the morning the day after.

He made a note.

'Gun? Does the murder weapon discard spent shells?'

He looked, once more at the entomology report, encased in a Manila file, being teased onto the floor by his elbow. But his mind wasn't there yet – not bugs, not just yet. He'd got a better offer; and he hit the play button again.

"I woke calmer, the room darkening with the fading sun. I could hear Susan moving about and it could have been any Sunday morning. Only I was on the sofa and my neck ached; the stale tobacco stench still in the room, like Bill was sat in the corner glaring at me. I drank my tea and ate some toast that Susan made from the stale bread in the kitchen, and I watched the sun go down over the houses at the end of the garden. It was a long wait, hours almost, or so it seemed. We were way beyond the long, dark nights of winter, and I could hear the chatter of the neighbours sitting out in their gardens until the late-Spring chill drove them indoors, retreating with the clatter of wine glasses.

There was the singing of the birds, the occasional moped buzzing around the estate, the shudder of windows opening, or closing. Then it was dark again and time for me to resume with the digging. My arms and shoulders already ached, my biceps and triceps stung, for what they were; twitching and failing. But I carried on through darkness and into early morning, until at last the hole was as deep as my waist, as deep as it could be, and as deep as I had the strength for. It didn't look like a grave. It looked like a pit; an opening to Hell in the deep blue of the failing night.

I went inside and washed the dirt from me, splashing tepid water onto my grubby face. Susan was motionless, clutching her knuckles together, pushing her fingers like needles into the backs of her hands.

I don't remember the next bit, but I do remember being back in the bedroom – Bill and Pat as before; the room reeking of old people and Park Drive. So we helped William Wycherley into the earth. He was slight, weightless almost between the two of us at first, and as stiff as a board. I took his shoulders and Patricia had his feet, and we lugged him through the door like we were moving an old coffee table. I walked backwards along the landing and down the stairs, fighting his rigid body around every corner. We set him down at the bottom of the stairs and rested, breathing heavy, not speaking. His weight got heavier the longer we had to hold him.

Then we'd started again, working him round the corner and into the living room by pulling at his shoulders and pushing at his feet until he was stretched out flat under the radiator beneath the front window. We got our breath for a while and then we went back upstairs for Patricia. She was heavy from the outset, more limp; blood gushing and blurting out of her, air creaking around her insides and bubbling out of the holes in her chest, us retching with every escaping creep of stagnant air.

We couldn't get a proper hold on her because she was so limp and sagging in the middle, and we ended up bumping her down most of the stairs, forcing her round corners and dragging her by her feet until she lay, face down, next to William. Then we sat on the sofa, looking between Bill and Pat and their awaiting grave, Bill as stiff as a board, Pat all slumped and folded – an arm sticking out of her shroud, all white and cold."

'Rigor mortis,' Rawlins wrote on his pad, followed by three heavy question marks. He knew the answers already, he knew them off by heart, but it wasn't his job to say it. Coppers took statements. Coppers built cases. They needed experts to say things, experts who were neutral, who were believable and didn't have a vested interest.

Christopher Edwards had described William Wycherley as in a state of rigor mortis, Patricia most probably in a state of primary flaccidity.

Harder to prove that, but he described blood gushing around in her – suggesting that full lividity has not yet occurred.

Rigor mortis typically sets in from between two to six hours after death, but it starts in the smaller organs and the body's extremities; the eyelids, the nose, the lips. Slowly the body's muscles are starved of lactic acid, turning it to stone, for a while. Rigor mortis can last for up to five days, but is typically complete in three. The smaller you are, the quicker it sets in.

A mouse could be as stiff as a board in minutes; a human, less so. A small man quicker than a large man, or large woman. Rawlins remembered the summary from the manual they'd handed out on the first day of detective school.

Lividity, or liver mortis, is what happens to the blood post death. For its entire existence blood in a human body has travelled, round and round, like a never-ending roller-coaster. But suddenly that all stops, and the only place for the blood to go is down. After death, blood obeys gravity. It sinks to the lowest points of the human form, coagulating and congealing, creating deep bruising where it comes to rest . . .

"We dragged them towards the door, labouring them across the carpet, over the little step and out onto the soil. William stayed in his shroud, but Patricia was flopping loose and in the end I just grabbed her by her clammy wrist and pulled her across the carpet; Susan standing open-mouthed just staring at me. The hole wasn't wide enough to bury them in side by side, but it was just about deep enough for them to lie one on top of the other.

The pit was narrower the deeper it went; its sides forming a gentle slope, I realised then. William was first, me with his shoulders again, Susan at his feet, and we struggled with him to the edge of the grave and dropped him in. Only he didn't quite fit, so I had to climb down into the hole with him and work him into its widest points; corner to corner where he could just about lay flat. I sat down on the grave's edge and breathed air back into my lungs, looking out at the darkened skyline for signs of life, but there was nothing.

Then we turned our attention to Patricia and, I'm sorry to say, just rolled her down on top of him. She tumbled over with a rasp of escaping air and came to rest face-down over her husband, more blood seeping into her shroud.

Then Susan made us a cup of tea and we sat, drinking in silence, apart from the occasional clink of china. My hands were caked in blood and soil, while Susan's remained largely clean, and I noticed I'd left grime around the sides of my cup. Then I placed it down on the coffee table and walked back to the garden, conscious the night would soon be abandoning us again, as I saw the first light of day streaking over the rooftops.

I got back to work and shovelled dirt over them with manic sweeps of my spade, stamping heavily into the soil, compressing it down as best I could; the weight from my sole packing the soil tight around the bodies. Then I piled in more soil and repeated the stamping until the grave was full. Finally, I slapped the ground flat with the bottom of my spade and dragged the slabs back into place over them. As the light came flooding in and the world started to return to life, as I retreated back into the house once more, it looked no more suspicious to me than an emergency repair to a burst water pipe."

The blowfly is the most effective means of establishing how long a body has been left out in the open before it is buried. The blowfly community can only exist because there are dead things around; dead things left out in the open – a badger hit by a car, an old fox that lays down and dies under a shed, a blackbird that smashes into a patio door; a drunk hit by a car on his dark walk home and flung into a ditch. They take their final, gasping breaths, they die, they cool, and the blowflies move in.

Blowflies can sense a dead body from miles away. They can also sense that something is dead a long time before other breeds of flies, insects and beetles – which are more common in bodies that have been left out in the open for a much longer period.

So, the dog or the fox or the badger or the blackbird or the human dies, and the blowflies party. They first feed off some of the seeping fluids that come out of the body, but they can't consume it all because they don't live long enough.

A human body, if undisturbed, could maintain generation after generation of blowfly; laying eggs that become maggots, which gorge on the flesh and the innards, and then, only when they are fat, do they morph into the next generation of blowfly – on and on, undisturbed until nothing remains.

Finally, after weeks or months or years, long after they have been joined by a legion of other flies, beetles, bugs, worms and foxes, will they head off to colonise new worlds.

But they leave a trace, and they date a body. A body left out for a week, you'd expect the presence of flies, the early signs of inhabitation; even in a closed room, if somewhat less so. A body left out for a week, or a month, or a year even; well you'd expect much more. Rawlins had read all of this years before in a forensics manual, when he'd first moved from uniform to CID. But he remembered it all again now as he thumbed through the report he had finally forced himself to read – the introduction to the document at least, written in the more technical hand of Dr Martin Hall, forensic entomologist at the Natural History Museum, London.

"We slept late into the morning, both of us, until the sun was high in the sky; long after the morning commuter traffic had rumbled past, long after the chatter of children heading back to school, a bell ringing distantly somewhere. I bathed and cleaned off all the grime in the same bath that William had once sat in, then I placed all my filthy clothes in a bin liner and found replacements from my travel case.

After that we strolled into town, to the B&Q store, where we bought shrubs and plants to place over the burial site. It wasn't a sentimental act, it wasn't us dressing the graves of two loved ones. It was simply a practical decision; it was cover, nothing more than a new feature to an already well-tended little garden.

I planted the shrubs and the plants, being careful where I dug; not wanting to disturb the soil or expose the remains, as any odour would have betrayed us. After an hour or so of gentle pottering the work was done and I slapped my hands together to shake away the soil.

"Inside, Susan was going through drawers, pulling out pictures and paperwork, bills and letters, demands and invoices. The paperwork went into one pile, the photographs into another, and she packed all the letters away into a Manila file and said we'd take care of it all when we got back to London.

Then she looked at me, her eyes suddenly distant. 'But we'll need to come back here,' she had said. 'We'll need to make the house look tended and lived in. And if people get suspicious and ask where they have gone, we will have to tell them that they've moved away – to Bognor or Blackpool, or Ireland or Australia. We shouldn't tell people who we really are – we should just tell them that we're their niece and nephew, if they ask, and we're just looking after the place for them while they're away. And these carpets will need to come up because they're caked in blood. And when we come in future, we'll need to bring an empty suitcase; to cut up pieces of carpet and carry it back to London until it's all gone. We can dispose of it down there by tipping it into the bins, a little at a time'," she had said.

"It had been like an out-pouring, like she'd been thinking about it all week. And suddenly I felt like she knew what she was doing, and that we could get through this. She had thought very hard during that week, I realised, as I watched her take all the photographs and drop them into a metal bin, throwing in some scrunched-up newspaper for good measure. She carried it outside into the garden, set it down and touched a match to it. Once the fire was blazing high and there was nothing left of William and Patricia but bills and correspondence, Susan went to the fireplace and gathered up their framed wedding photo. Then she tossed it into the burning bin as well, and we watched as the flames shriveled their union into history and ash, and bubbled Elvis's face into blackness on the outside of the can."

Rawlins rubbed heavily at his eyes, pulling the skin taught over his cheeks; working his jaw to force life back into it. Outside it was light now, and the early birds from Major Crime were just beginning to filter into the Holmes Room – filling kettles and turning on creaky old desktops; hanging up coats and laughing about adventures from the night on the piss before.

On the notepad under his palm there was the word 'bullets', followed by heavy question marks. Beneath that he had written 'decomposition rates' and 'blowfly activity', again flagged by question marks.

He picked up his phone and dialled, letting it ring for a long time before he was finally greeted with a reluctant, 'Hello!'

"It's Rawlins," he said. "Can I speak to Adamson please?"

"This is Adamson," replied the voice. "What is it?"

Rawlins struggled with his words at first, exhaustion kicking in, he supposed, with too much to say in a single sentence.

"I think we're onto something," he managed. "There are some contradictions between the suspects' version of events and the physical evidence. Can I come and see you?"

There was a silence on the line then; nothing but breathing until Adamson replied, "I'll come to you," and hung up the phone.

Then Rawlins had slumped back into his seat, rubbing at his stubble and massaging his eyes once again. He sank into darkness; floating into an endless pit; losing his breath in the blackened, heavy water which took him down.

Suddenly, like he had been asleep for hours, a voice drew him back; a delicate hand pushing his shoulder. "Sir, wake up."

Rawlins' eyes rolled and he forced himself to sit upright.

"Sir, the CPS have just called. They've given us authority to charge."

"I'll let the chief inspector know," was all he could think to say.

Then he closed his eyes again, betraying a faint smile as he finally dozed off.

Chapter 11

Due to the historical nature of the murders, the lack of CCTV footage, the lack of a murder weapon and the generally poor state of the bodies, the work of forensic scientists and other experts played a massive part in the police investigation . . . Andy Done-Johnson, Mansfield Chad, Saturday, June 21, 2014.

His hand didn't shake, not at all; that was the first thing I noticed. His back straightened and his shoulders broadened. He grew in stature. He looked into the middle distance, his hand pointed straight at the jury as he made a makeshift revolver from two fingers. He mimed firing it, mimed the recoil – but his eyes never faltered and his hand remained steady throughout. His improvised firearm returned to its starting position again, and again and again, as he fired one shot, then a second, then a third and a fourth; finally lowering it to his side and letting his fingers stretch out.

There was a murmur around the court then, a couple of jurors gave each other uneasy looks. Joyce remained unmoved, but if you peeled away the mask you'd have seen a grinning joker. Christopher Edwards had just shown the court that he was a highly skilled marksman. Christopher Edwards had just shown the court that he was capable of gunning down two people with extreme precision. Christopher Edwards had just shot himself in the foot.

It was nearing the end of a long day of cross examination for Christopher Edwards, when out of the blue Joyce hammered the first nail into his coffin lid. Christopher had been on the stand for hours – first taking the gentle yet firm questions from his own counsel, Dafydd Enoch QC, then those of his wife's barrister, David Howker QC, playing a game of halfway house – siding away from the prosecution but looking for any crack in the wall that might be to Susan's advantage.

Then Joyce clambered to his feet, pulled his gown down firmly by its collar, checked his notes briefly but deliberately and straightening his wig; then calmly, clinically and masterfully, he laid into Christopher Edwards.

At first it was the money – how it was hidden, how he didn't know, how he was just helping, just protecting his wife.

He told the court he was unaware that Susan had opened a Halifax Building Society joint account in her and her mother's name on May 5th 1998 – the day after the May Bank Holiday weekend when they died; the weekend Christopher Edwards insisted he was in London.

But he couldn't remember at what point he *did* know about the bank account, if not from the start. He told the court his wife had returned to London later the same day, on the Tuesday; that she didn't tell him that her parents were lying dead upstairs until the following weekend, when they had returned to Mansfield to look after the house.

We walked into the house. We ate our fish and chips. Then Susan had said that mum and dad were upstairs, and that they were dead.

So far the prosecution had tried and failed to convincingly pin much of anything onto Christopher Edwards; certainly not to the point where 'beyond reasonable doubt' was established, and there was a nagging and growing view on the press bench that Christopher was going to walk free.

We'd heard how the Wycherleys were shot, but nobody had definitively proved that Christopher pulled the trigger; only that somebody did. We'd heard about the type of gun that killed them, and that Christopher owned a weapon of that type . . . only, potentially, so had William Wycherley.

All the time *reasonable doubt* was fighting its corner, coming out slugging; preventing the firm judicial finger from clearly pointing out Christopher Edwards.

That was until Joyce asked Christopher about his love for guns, about where he went to shoot, and what first got him started with it. And Christopher talked about his hobby, about his passion for it, about how Susan didn't like it, didn't like guns; how she squealed and put her fingers in her ears on the one occasion he'd taken her to the Earl's Court shooting club he used.

He described how he'd owned three handguns, and how his obsession had come to an enforced end in 1996 when the ownership of handguns for sport was banned after the Dunblane school massacre in Scotland, where Thomas

Hamilton, a licensed handgun owner, murdered 16 children and a teacher before turning his revolver on himself.

"Could you show us how to fire a gun, Christopher? Could you show us how you would stand, what you would do; if you were practicing at that gun club of yours?"

And Christopher had, happily, while his own barrister sat quietly with his head in his hands.

The entire room seemed to be thinking the same thing. Christopher Edwards had just fired four perfect rounds from his imaginary weapon.

For a moment in my mind, Christopher Edwards was no longer in the dock, he was in a bedroom fifteen years ago and twenty miles away; his revolver kicked back, sparks spitting out of the side with a crack, smoke spluttering from the barrel; the first two shells hitting Patricia Wycherley square in the chest; the second two, shortly afterwards, William.

In my pad, next to my shorthand, I scribbled: "How could Susan have shot her mother if she was so scared of guns?"

Beneath that, I added a word.

"GOTCHA!!!"

The jury is out now, after three-and-a-half weeks. They have been locked away in a little room to discuss and debate, to decide the whole future of two people's lives; to settle on their guilt or their innocence. The judge has instructed them on their duty and the rules they must apply to reach their decision.

Christopher and Susan Edwards are innocent until proven guilty. It is the role of the prosecution to prove their guilt beyond reasonable doubt. It is not their job, or that of their counsel to prove their innocence. They are innocent, unless the prosecution has proved their guilt ... beyond reasonable doubt.

If the members of the jury are not satisfied that the prosecution has proved their guilt then they should return a verdict of not guilty – they should acquit and let them walk free.

I have heard this speech a thousand times, spoken by a hundred judges. It is the basis of our law, our liberty and our freedom.

But each time I heard that instruction, I always knew we were all over bar the shouting, the talking was over and the long wait was about to begin. We pace the corridors of the court complex, drink coffee until we feel sick, watch for the comings and goings of Joyce et al – rising en masse from our perches in the central waiting area each time one counsel or another heads into Court 2.

We joke and we natter, we exchange stories; desperate for the lunchtime recess, where we know we can get out into the fresh air for an hour without the fear of missing anything; and we plot each other's downfall, all fighting for the killer interview at the end of it all.

Suddenly the Edwards' defence started to feel like an English batting collapse at Trent Bridge, just a mile or so over the river from where we were sat. It was a story so meticulous, so rehearsed, so perfect that it seemed almost credible. Almost.

But then the lawyers and the scientists had started poking at it with a stick, shining a torch deep into its

267

innards, looking hard into its frozen eyes, and from there it unravelled.

For the first time I could see the beautiful accuracy and polish of it; the work that had gone into it. But that was when I saw it for what it was as well. It was a bare-faced lie; it was a story; it was a fantasy; it was a dream. It was smoke and mirrors. It was armour full of chinks.

Other than Christopher's theatricals, the science didn't fight their corner.

Firearms expert Khaldoun Kabbani hammered in another nail.

A total of four bullets were found with the remains of William and Patricia Wycherley, he told the court. They were both shot twice and the bullets that killed them were found within their skeletal remains. Both the Wycherleys had skeletal damage caused by .38mm bullets, one of which had been found lodged in Patricia's spine.

They had most likely been shot by a Second World War Colt Commando revolver, which fires low velocity bullets. Based on the ballistic fingerprints found on the retrieved bullets, it was almost certainly this make and model of gun that killed them.

Certain guns fired certain types of ammunition, so if you had the shells it was already a much narrower search. These were .38 rounds; fired commonly by maybe a hundred different revolvers. So, by comparing the markings on these bullets it was possible to conclude that they came from a Colt Commando, Kabbani said.

"If we'd had the firearm involved then we could have established its credentials," he added. "We could have stated beyond reasonable doubt whether it was the murder weapon or not, only sadly we don't."

'Thrown into a bin 15 years earlier,' I think.

"And could you describe how you would load and clear this type of weapon?" said Joyce, a circling buzzard.

"They were shot with a revolver," Kabbani replied. "The only way to either load or remove bullets from a revolver is to break the weapon, or remove the cylinder."

"Break? Sorry, could you . . ."

"A revolver has a cylinder at its centre," he said. "As the name suggests, it revolves. A cylinder typically has between five and nine chambers into which you place bullets. The cylinder revolves one notch each time the trigger is pulled. Bullets are inserted individually into these weapons, although a professional user may opt for a moon clip – a ring-shaped devise that holds multiple rounds at the appropriate placing and spacing, allowing the user to reload the weapon much more quickly. Some revolvers break in the middle, on a hinge, like a shotgun. Others allow you to remove the entire cylinder by pulling on a leaver, an ejector, which flips it out of the side of the weapon. If you've got a couple of fully-loaded cylinders in your pocket, this again allows for a quick turnaround."

Joyce let Kabbani talk himself out of steam. The man knew his revolvers.

"And, to your knowledge," he asked, "do revolvers ever expel shell cases onto the floor?"

Kabbani looked almost perplexed at Joyce's question; dumbfounded.

"I'm sorry?"

"Are there any sorts of revolver that spit spent cartridge shells out of the side when the weapon is fired?"

Kabbani took a breath then, like he was thinking hard; like he was about to explain something complex to a child.

"Revolvers don't manually discard spent shells," he said finally. "Revolvers don't do that. An automatic pistol spits the spent shells out of the side, but not a revolver. You have to manually take them out."

A pause.

Joyce.

"But we have heard that Susan picked up the spent shell cases off the floor."

"No. What she's describing is the action of an automatic pistol," said Kabbani. "The weapon discards the spent shells each time it is discharged. You load a clip into the butt of the gun and it fires the lead out of the barrel, simultaneously flipping the spent cases out the side and onto the floor."

"But the Wycherleys weren't killed with an automatic pistol, were they?"

"No. The Wycherleys were killed with a .38 Colt Commando revolver."

"And that weapon doesn't discharge spent shell cases out of the side, onto the floor?"

"No, it doesn't."

"And there is no possibility that the Wycherleys were killed by any other sort of handgun?"

"No! None. "

"And so why, would you say, would Susan Edwards describe picking up spent shell cases off the bedroom carpet in the hours following the death of her parents?"

The longer the jury are out for, the more likely it is that they will come back with a not guilty verdict – at least that's what we always say. There's a logic to it – someone's guilt should take as long to discuss as their innocence. But often guilty verdicts come back in minutes, before you've even made it to the front of the queue for coffee. Not Guilty always took longer. Deciding someone's innocence takes more consideration, it would seem.

Once they'd been out deliberating for a day, the judge would usually bring them back in for an update; ask if they'd reached a decision on which all 12 of them could agree?

If the answer was no, the judge would ask if, given more time, they could reach a decision on which they all agreed?

The ideal is a unanimous decision – 12-0 either way. Everybody agrees. Guilty or Not Guilty. That's how it works.

However, if the jury had been out for a really long time, a day and a half perhaps or two days, then the judge would bring them back once again and ask them whether they are likely to reach a decision? If the jury foreman indicates a firm difference of opinion, the judge would then give them the option of returning a majority verdict – 10-2 either way, 11-1 even better.

With a case like this, a double and premeditated murder, a majority verdict wouldn't be put on the table for a very long time.

It could be days, and we hadn't even reached lunchtime on the first morning of deliberations.

Like any proper bug expert, Dr Martin Hall from the Natural History Museum looked like he'd been locked in a darkened room for much of his adult life, stitched into a shabby lab coat and looking at dead insects through a microscope.

He wore a tidy beard and talked with the passion of the academic, blinking at the daylight almost – a giant beetle wearing tweed. And he knew his blowflies. He really knew his blowflies.

He described their distinct ability to detect death, long before any other form of insect, and the breeding and feeding cycles post-mortem. From a forensic point of view they left a trace. They allow scientists to accurately date human remains not buried after death, from hours to days to months.

"And was there any evidence of blowfly activity on the bodies of William and Patricia Wycherley," asked Joyce?

"No, there was not."

"None whatsoever?"

"None whatsoever."

"And tell us, Dr Hall, how long would a human body need to be left out in the open for blowfly evidence to be present?"

The doctor sighed, like he was explaining to a child.

"It's impossible to give an exact time," he said, after a moment's thought. "So much depends on individual circumstances – on the weather, on the time of year, on the vicinity of the body to established colonies, on whether the body was outdoors or concealed."

"Well, what's the shortest time?" Joyce almost snapped. "In your professional opinion?"

Hall rubbed at his beard.

"Typically, a body left out in perfect conditions, that is to say a body left out in the open at a time of year when flies are more productive, then it could attract interest almost immediately."

"Almost immediately," Joyce echoed.

"Yes, literally minutes," Hall continued. "It's the females that smell them out – it's almost like a sixth sense."

You could feel the pressure in the room then, all eyes trained on Dr Hall, including the Edwards; especially the Edwards.

"It's how blowflies exist; their very lives depend on it. They need to forever be looking for new sources to feed on and lay their eggs, so they can make more blowflies and carry on their species. It's an instinct.

"As humans, our most basic instinct is a need for water, followed by food, followed by safety, followed by reproduction. But water is our most basic need because without it we die, and we die relatively quickly. We, however, are much more complex creatures; much more capable of adapting. All a blowfly needs to survive is something else to die. And death is all around. I would expect in general terms for blowflies to be present at a recently deceased corpse between several minutes to several hours post-mortem, depending on the unique circumstances. I would expect to see evidence of eggs shortly afterwards and evidence of first

273

stage maggots within 23 hours. This is how we detect the time of death. Second stage maggots will be present at about 50 hours post-mortem, third stage maggots anything from 72 to 130 hours after death. After this the maggots burrow down into the surrounding soil and mutate into the next generation of blowfly. That is why the ground is checked around the corpse as part of the process."

"First stage maggots? Second stage maggots?"

"First stage maggots are tiny, like grubs in an apple," continued Hall. "Third stage are huge; big and fat."

"And if the body was inside, locked in a room, would that prevent the presence of blowflies? If that body had been left locked in an upstairs bedroom, say, with all the doors and windows shut? Would that have stopped blowflies from being present?"

Hall thought for a moment, not looking for an answer; more looking for a way of explaining it to someone without a PhD.

"It would have delayed it," he said, finally, "but not prevented it."

"How long, would you say?"

"Again," said the doctor, "there is no exact answer. It would depend on all manner of circumstances."

"Would it be possible for blowflies not to be present in a dead body shut away in a room for a week?"

"No," Hall said firmly. "No, that would be impossible, not even in cold weather. Even in cold weather I would expect blowflies to be present in those circumstances within 96 hours, less in warmer weather. And according to the records, it was very warm over that time period."

"And would it be possible, in your opinion doctor, that Christopher Edwards could have entered that bedroom and not been aware of the presence of flies?"

"I don't believe so, no," said Hall. "Even in the circumstances described, you would expect to see first-stage maggots by that point, and a lot of fly activity."

"And so, Dr Hall, say that someone dies naturally, with their doting families at their bedside, after a long and fulfilling life – how do these people prevent their loved-one from being desecrated by blowflies. How do we stop the maggots from defiling them?"

Hall thought long and hard, like he was being asked to comment outside of his remit.

"Well," he said, "in Western culture, after death, we keep the deceased at a low temperature, usually in a sealed container in a clinical environment, until they are released back to their loved-ones for the funeral."

"And what about in a culture where it's hotter, or where they don't have the facility to keep bodies cooled?"

"Then they get them into the ground or burn them as quickly as possible. It's built into the religion in many cultures, if you think about it."

The vultures are circling as the hours creep by outside Court 2. I endlessly check my phone, or wander to the window and watch the furious traffic, crawling along three lanes of clogged up road outside; the ugly 1970s bus station opposite the only view available to speak of.

When the jury's out it is static time, dead time; life in limbo until you see the barristers pouring back into court, coppers looking edgy, hacks climbing to their feet; pretending they're stretching their legs. It's deep into the afternoon of the first day now, the jury are deliberating, and there's nowhere to go and nothing to do. It is a hell of formica chairs, white walls and mindless, stripped lighting.

I try not to think about the verdict, to keep a neutral mind, but this is high stakes poker and a guilty verdict is what the readers want; little has changed since the old ladies knitted and watched as the guillotine came slicing down on French aristocrats.

My head spins with questions.

Will they walk or will they go down? Will Christopher go down but not Susan? Unlikely. Will Susan go down but not Christopher? More likely. Will they both go down? Most likely. Or will they both be acquitted? I've seen it happen more than once. And what will they get if they are both found guilty?

And there is a question to pass the time.

I tap into my phone and start to do some research, just for my own amusement really.

It has to be a minimum of 15 years. If you're convicted of murder then the very least you can get, the very least you can serve is 15 years. Only it's not cut and dry even then. If you're convicted of murder you're sentenced to life imprisonment and that is what it means, officially. You get life. Only mostly you don't, because it's too expensive on the taxpayer. The judge has to set a minimum tariff – the number of years a killer must serve behind bars before they can be considered for release. So if you're sentenced to serve a minimum of 15 years, that is what it means. You don't just chalk off the days on the cell wall then grab your bags at the end of it. You have to go before a parole board, which must assess you and deem you suitable for release back into society. It must establish that you are no longer a danger to others, that you are no longer a killer. If they deem you unsuitable then you stay behind bars until your next assessment, or the next, or forever. Mostly murderers get released after15 years, but this is just a starting point.

At the top of the scale is a 'whole life order', which does what it says on the legal tin.

You won't ever get out. You will die in prison. You will not see daylight or ramble over open fields ever again.

Peter Sutcliffe has one – although bizarrely it wasn't issued until 2010. Ian Brady had one.

Myra Hindley had one – until her death in 2002, as did Donald Nielson (the Black Panther) and Harold Shipman – who only served two years of his before stringing himself up from the ceiling of his cell.

There are dozens of them, I discover: contract killer John Childs; wedding murderer Arthur Hutchinson; Jeremy Bamber; south coast railway murderer John Duffy; 'Gay Slayer' Colin Ireland. Rosemary West.

They were all given whole-life terms by politicians – by the Home Secretary, to be precise. Then in 2002 this practice was ruled unlawful and since then only judges have had the authority to order someone to die in prison.

Not that things have slowed down much, to be fair. Since 2002, Paul Glen, Andrzej Kunowski, Phillip Heggarty, Thomas McDowell, Mark Martin, Mark Hobson, William Horncy, Kenneth Regan, Paul Culshaw, Glyn Dix, Daniel

Gonzalez, Viktor Dembovskis, John McGrady, Stephen McColl, Rahan Arshad, David Tiley, Michael Smith, Steve Wright, Levi Bellfield, Douglas Vinter, Marc Chivers, Peter Tobin, Royston Jackson, Ernest Wright, Anthony Hardy, John Maden, Desmond Lee, Winbert Dyce, Stephen Griffiths, John Sweeney, George Johnson, John Cooper, David Baxendale, Andrew Dawson, David Cook, David Oakes, Stephen Farrow, Mark Bridger, Dale Cregan, Gary Smith, Lee Newell, Jamie Reynolds, Anwar Rosser, Ian McLoughlin, Michael Adebolaja, Joanne Dennehy, Paul O'Hara, Ryan Matthews, David Mitchell and Jason Gomez have all been told by judges that they will never see the light of day, that they will take their last breaths behind bars. It shocks me just how many truly terrifying people there are out there, in our so-called civilised world. And suddenly Susan and Christopher Edwards don't seem too terrible. Not that terrible.

The Edwards aren't in this league; or anywhere near some of our most notorious killers.

Roy Whiting, who murdered Sarah Payne in West Sussex in 2000, had his whole-life term reduced – first to 50 years, then down to 40 years minimum. Police killer and former US Marine David Bieber had his hacked down to 37 years.

Dennis Nilsen, who murdered at least 15 young gay men, chopped them up, and stuffed the body parts down his drains, was given a minimum 25-year term – although more than 30 years later he is still inside.

Paul Hutchinson, who abducted, raped and strangled Nottingham schoolgirl Colette Aram in 1983 and was finally jailed in 2010 through advances in DNA was given

25 years minimum. Like Shipman, he took the easy way out and killed himself shortly after his conviction.

Michael Stone, who murdered mother and daughter Lin and Megan Russell in 1996; Soham murderer Ian Huntley, who lured 10-year-old Holly Wells and Jessica Chapman into his home before killing them and hiding their bodies, all escaped whole life orders.

Based on everything I read I guess, if found guilty, Susan and Christopher Edwards will go down for between 20 and 30 years; *if* they are found guilty. Although after a day parked on a bench and the court complex starting to empty towards the end of business, I'd have gladly seen them walk, just so I didn't have to come back and sit it out again the following day.

Home office pathologist Dr Stuart Hamilton took to the stand, tapped the microphone and nodded to the judge. He had done this before. When asked, he confirmed that he carried out the initial forensic examination of the Wycherleys' remains. He confirmed that this examination took place at the Queen's Medical Centre, Nottingham, in the hours following their exhumation from Blenheim Close.

Following his own investigations, he called on a number of other specialists to ascertain the cause of death, necessary because of the historical state of the find, he told the court.

Both bodies were found with bullets within the chest cavities – two in each. One of Mr Wycherley's ribs had a groove in it where a bullet had hit the bone, while Mrs

Wycherley's remains had a slug lodged in her spine. The location of the bullets suggested they would have passed through major organs and, in Mrs Wycherley's case, her aorta, killing her almost instantly.

"Now, Dr Hamilton, said Joyce, flicking at his notes, "can you tell me this?"

I leaned forward onto the slender press bench, my pen poised, expecting something significant. I wasn't disappointed.

"Christopher Edwards has described looking at the bodies of the deceased before he buried them. He described Mr Wycherley in particular as appearing clammy and grey, but with no further signs of composition. What is your professional opinion of this?"

Hamilton answers immediately, without any thinking time.

"It doesn't describe the state of a body left out in the open for that length of time," he said. "After one week I would expect to see marbling in the skin on the face. That would have been obvious. The body also bloats grotesquely as gases are forced out. The skin blisters and comes away from the body easily. If you took the hand of a person, for example, or the wrist of someone who had died a week ago and tried to pull them, to drag them, there's a good chance that a lot of the skin would have come away at that point. The body will also seep black bile from its orifices, if moved."

Hamilton paused briefly, waiting for another question, but when one didn't come he carried on.

"And obviously, if it's hot, this process is speeded up; and according to the records it was unseasonably warm over the stated time period. After a week in the open, the faces of the deceased would have been, frankly, unrecognisable."

"But Christopher Edwards described pulling Patricia Wycherley by the arm through the front room in his testimony," said Joyce, suddenly animated; giving the impression the question had just come to him.

"Indeed," Hamilton replied, taking a sip of water.

"When Christopher Edwards first entered the room containing the bodies of William and Patricia Wycherley, he describes no smell beyond that of stale tobacco. Is that a credible description?"

"No," Hamilton responded, again almost immediately. "No, it isn't. Two human beings left at an average of 12 degrees over that length of time would have created a smell that would have overwhelmed everything else. If you left a chicken out at that temperature for a week it would create a smell that overwhelmed everything else, and here we are talking about two adult human beings. It's pungent, it's foul and it's pervasive – on opening the door it would have been instantly apparent. It is not a subtle smell."

It's pushing four o'clock when I finally crack and go to find a coffee. I wander up a flight of stairs to the cafe, as others begin to wander as well, to the toilets, or out for a fag. There is now a collective view that deliberations will spill over into tomorrow. There just isn't enough court day left to get the jury back and the verdict heard. We're coming back tomorrow.

I walk into the canteen, to the fading odor of the now distant lunchtime and smattering of court detritus killing

281

time – a few relatives and witnesses wearing suits, barristers and solicitors huddled into the window seats that are reserved for them, and Hilary Rose and a man who I assume is her husband. I have watched her out of the corner of my eye for weeks – in the public gallery every day; silent, shocked, timid and anonymous.

'And why shouldn't she be?' I think, as I join the back of the coffee queue. 'She and her family have been indirectly accused of apathy by the 'red top' press; a snaking assertion that they somehow failed their elderly relatives by not being interested enough.'

The best part of a year earlier, agency hacks had hammered on their doors and broken the news that their relatives were dead; long dead. Relatives that they hadn't seen in fifteen years, more even. In the days after the news broke, the whole thing was about the cards and the letters, the family that didn't realise William and Patricia Wycherley had been murdered and buried. It was an unwritten headline: The family that didn't care.

I pay for my coffee, make smalltalk with the lady on the till for a moment, then purposefully wander over and perch myself at the table next to them.

We sit and make small talk, I tell them who I am and what I do. I tell them that I was there at the start, when they first found the bodies.

"I've read your reports from the trial," she says; and *I* don't know what to say.

She seems haunted, this niece, Hilary Rose. She seems like a private person pulled onto a public stage for the mob to hurl abuse at.

I want to ask her: 'How did you not know? How didn't you suspect?'

But then I think about my own family – about my Welsh relatives on my mother's side who I've not seen since a funeral in the mid 1980s; a great-uncle in Canada I last saw the year I was leaving university; and the army of distant cousins on my father's side from Stoke-on-Trent; some of whom I've met occasionally, most of which I've never met, and never wanted to.

'This is families,' I think. 'This is what we are. We are an inner circle of people we love, and a swirl of names and faces from long ago and far away that our parents mention in passing, for a while; along with the odd letter, faded photographs and cards at Christmas.'

The press benches were full again for the first time in days as Susan Edwards gave evidence in her own defence. It was late in proceedings; the climactic closure of the fourth act. And by the time she got her soliloquy she had already been cast as the villain.

We watched her move from the dock; set free with the jangling of keys and the clunk of a heavy lock.

She made her way past us, just inches away, towards the witness box at the front of the court – looking every bit like a terrified mouse seeking a place to hide.

I could have reached out a hand and touched her sleeve as she walked past – head down, no makeup; shoulders slumped and heavy, dressed in dowdy trousers and a bland cardigan.

Her evidence took most of the day. Sometimes I picked

up on something she said; sometimes I almost drifted off, or cringed at her pain and her anger.

At one point, she admitted she hated her father; not voluntarily, it took an age of Joyce prodding and jabbing away at her until she blew, and she almost screamed her words in her squeaky, nasal voice.

"I hated him. I hated him. I hated him," she shrieked, then covered her face with her hand and wept, her shoulders shaking involuntarily.

After that she was more calm; reasoned, like all the anger had bled out of her.

"I tried to get on with my mother," she said, "but I hated him; I hated him for the abuse and the bullying as well. I tried to get on with mum, and she was never easy, but we were close in a way."

'I hated my father,' I scribbled in my pad.

Then Susan described the hellish weekend when she had been summoned to Mansfield after a six-year gap; summoned by her mother, desperate over the demands that her frail yet obnoxious older husband was putting on her.

It was a drunken few days, full of tension and squabbles, she said; Susan getting out at every opportunity, making desperate and miserable calls to Christopher to discuss her agony.

"They didn't seem to have a relationship," she said. "I never saw her wear a wedding ring and there was nothing between them. There was just that photo of them over the fire from the day they got married.

"When I inherited the money I bought them the house because I wanted us to have a place of our own as a family;

and for a while we were, before I met Chris. Afterwards, my father told me that I'd made their house in London intolerable for him. He said he had terrible memories of his time there and that he needed to get away from London and live out his days back where he grew up. That's why I signed the house over to him, I think; because I felt guilty for making him miserable, and I realised once and for all that I couldn't have both dad and Chris in my life.

"My mother increasingly didn't like him. She didn't want to move to Mansfield, she preferred London. They didn't seem to have a life together and I don't really know why she agreed to go with him, apart from him being such a bully.

"We had a big fall out in 1992 when we went up to see them and dad was horrible to Chris, and he just snapped and walked out. I heard nothing from mum for three years, and then one day I got a letter from her asking me to call her. So I did, just to hear what she'd got to say. It was our secret. Dad didn't know. Chris didn't know. We spoke occasionally and we wrote occasionally.

"Then she called me at her wits' end and she asked me to go up to Mansfield to help her with dad. She said she just didn't feel like she could cope anymore. There wasn't a lot to do when I got there and I went out for some walks by myself to get away from the atmosphere in the house. Mum was drinking and dad was horrible. He said on a few occasions that he didn't want me in the house."

There had been a drunken evening, Susan explained, the night the Wycherleys had died. Susan had been sipping gin, Patricia pouring it down, getting more agitated and more bitter. William had shuffled off to bed with a grunt after half a bottle of scotch, leaving Susan and Patricia alone, drinking at the little dining table. Patricia had got hammered, all sorrow and tears. They decided they would go away together, Susan said, only ever looking at the floor; just to get mum away from dad, just to give her a break.

"She told me to go to the bank on Tuesday and to withdraw cash from the joint account," Susan said. "So we could go away and so mum had some control back. We talked about putting dad in an old folks' home and mum moving in with Chris and I. Mum even wrote the letter to the Halifax to get the accounts sorted."

She described Patricia staggering off to bed and her going up shortly afterwards. She described climbing up to the dingy back bedroom that smelled of old clothes and dust and was full of William's junk. She described turning off the light, climbing into bed and starting to drift into an inebriated yet unsettled sleep.

She described the darkness taking hold of her, the quiet of the room and then oblivion for a moment; shattered by two distinct bangs and the thud of something heavy falling to the floor.

Then she was wide awake again, she said; sitting bolt upright in the night, swinging her legs out of the bed, her feet finding her slippers; then her running blindly for the door, feeling for the handle or the light switch.

In the end Susan isn't believed, we discover as we file back into court surprisingly early on the second day. Her story has been picked to pieces by the scientists and the lawyers, like circling buzzards, and the jury is not with her today.

Susan Edwards has painted a brutal picture of family dysfunction, of hatred and bullying and abuse. She's cast herself as the victim to a monstrous father and an indifferent mother. And in many ways she is.

She has described an awful childhood, an appalling home and then fate finally coming into play; casting her as the villain; knowing how it would look to others and merely covering it up out of desperation; dragging Christopher into the mess because she didn't know what else to do.

Only Susan and Christopher Edwards are both found guilty of the murders of William and Patricia Wycherley. They are then led downstairs to stew on it over the weekend, before they are brought back on Monday to be sentenced.

They can expect a minimum of 15 years. They are both in their mid-to-late 50s now and they will be over 70 before they see the light of day or each other again; if they only get 15 years. And that is the very best they can hope for.

Chapter 12

Neither of the deceased were seen alive after May Day
1998 and the reason for this is plain – on that weekend
they were shot by the defendants and buried in their own
garden – Peter Joyce QC, R v Edwards and Edwards,
Nottingham Crown Court, June 2014.

"Do you remember the story, Susan? Do you remember the lie; the lie that we made up all those years ago, before Bill and Pat were even dead? The story we made up after you first told me what William Wycherley had done to you; the lie we finally agreed when you first found out that your mother had known about it all along?"

Christopher's voice, his calm, soothing voice, speaking out at Susan, huddled against their one working radiator in a darkened room of their borrowed Lille flat.

"We worked it through in our heads, Susan, a joke at first, almost. It was a story of revenge and retribution, or a romance; about our lives going forwards after we'd put Bill and Pat in the ground, if we ever had the nerve to do it."

Susan had looked at Chris as he spoke to her, clutching at her hand, squeezing it; his face emotionless, his eyes cold.

"It had stayed a joke between us until we were in dire straits with money and the bailiffs had come knocking again, and taken away everything we owned from Winnie and Charles – all those treasured words that we'd spent hundreds of evenings poring over; the books, the postcards, the letters, the photographs, the stamps. They were suddenly all gone.

"Was it then that our one sick joke became a plan? Was it me that first came up with it, Susan? Or was it you? Or was it just a silent agreement between us that we had to act, after all of our other choices had been taken away from us?

"In the weeks after, when the money first started rolling in, we didn't really know what to do with it or what to spend it on; when we were forever fearful of a knock on the door or footsteps on the stairs. Do you remember? We rehearsed it and rehearsed it, covering every angle, every detail . . . just in case."

Chris's clipped words had become emotional for a second, like he wanted to cry and shout all at the same time. But Susan couldn't look at him. They had been utterly found out. The game was finally over. They had lived a lie; maintained a lie for fifteen years. They had fled to France and run out of money. Now the only place to go was back to England, where for a long time, it had all been so very different.

As the weeks had become months and the months had become years, keeping Bill and Pat alive and Susan and Christopher out of prison had started to seem like little more than a bit of basic housekeeping, and so slowly the story had faded away from them; left them. But as Christopher talked his soothing and quiet words, it slowly all came back to Susan, knowing that she was going to have to explain herself.

"You had gone to Mansfield to see your parents over the May Bank holiday in 1998. Do you remember that, Susan? You hadn't seen them in six years. It happened after you received a phone call from your mother. She was desperate. She needed some help. Reluctantly you agreed to go. It was dreadful. The atmosphere in the house was appalling and eventually you'd gone to bed and been woken in the early hours by a loud bang. You rushed to your parents' bedroom to find your father lying dead on the floor, your mother standing over his body holding a gun. Do you remember now, Susan? There was a row, Susan. Do you remember? Your mum told you she'd known all along what Bill had done to you when you were a little girl. Perhaps she's gone further – claiming that me and her had previously had an affair. Why not. It's all colour. But it tipped you over, the balance of your mind was temporarily damaged, in that room and faced with those circumstances . . . and you shot her."

"I shot her," Susan had mouthed almost silently. "I remember. It wasn't my fault."

"Then the following weekend you tricked me up there, and you told me what had happened and I agreed to help – because I love you and I need you, and I didn't want you to go to prison. We buried them in the back garden and we took the money because we had to – because it was the only way we could have avoided being discovered. I wasn't there at the time of the killings Susan, you need to remember that. You admit to manslaughter due to diminished responsibility, I admit to burying the bodies and spending the money. I've looked into this. We won't get more than five years each, of which we'd serve half in prison. We might even get let off with suspended sentences."

'But is that what happened?' Susan thought briefly, as a loud knock from the facing door and the call of "All rise" brought her back into the courtroom, and she watched as the Judge, Mrs Justice Kathryn Thirlwall, waltzed to her throne and bowed to the barristers.

Susan sat facing a packed room with Christopher next to her, his carrier bag full of possessions removed from him now; the room rammed full of voyeurs, all come to see the circus freaks; the theatricals almost over.

She spotted a scruffy-haired reporter who needed a shave, nestled into the press bench and looking over at the smartly-dressed young chief inspector, the one who had been Montgomery Clift in her interviews; his tidy hair just starting to fleck with grey, sat further back in the public gallery, holding court with his entourage of detectives, deep in conversation and stifled jokes.

Susan was asked to stand up, as was Chris, and they faced the judge as she prepared to deliver her sentence, waiting for the courtroom to fall silent.

"These were shocking crimes," she said, looking deep into Susan's eyes, "and a great deal has been written about you in recent days. In May of 1998 the two of you planned to shoot and kill William and Patricia Wycherley in their own home, and that is what you did.

"Mr Wycherley was 86, Mrs Wycherley was nearly 64. They were living a quiet, reclusive life in Mansfield. They knew no one. They had as little contact as possible with other people. You knew they wouldn't be missed, if they disappeared . . . and they weren't."

The judge kept speaking but Susan stopped listening. She was back in their dark and dowdy house in London, the council house from when she was a little girl.

She remembered listening to the sound of her father's sombre fingers, tinkering on the keys of the piano that he kept in pride of place in the corner of the lounge – his only possession of note; bought when it fell off the back of a lorry in Edgware and moved dutifully to every new house they ever lived in.

It was his star turn, the piano; William was first to the keys at any party, or in any pub he wandered into. But at home he only ever played it when mum was out, when she went to one of her meetings, and Susan listened to the doleful tinkering with trepidation – as a precursor to what would always follow.

She would sit at the bottom of the stairs, rocking frantically, crying, covering her ears – willing the notes to continue for long enough for mum to get back; only somehow mum never did, not until later when Susan was left curled up in her bed, staring blankly at the darkened wall and praying for sleep.

But the keys would always fall silent, and the only sound would be the quickening of Susan's breathing as she waited, followed by the creak of Williams feet on the floorboards and the screech of the handle; his shadow in the doorway.

"Come on, young lady, you need an early night."

The first time she had gone with him willingly, thinking it was some game he was playing and wanting the affection he'd never given her; only it wasn't a game, at least not the sort she'd ever wanted to play; and the affection he showed had hurt her.

Then each time afterwards she had resisted, fought harder and harder until he would physically pull her up the stairs – her knees bumping up every step and her shoulder retching from his force, leaving her sore and aching for days.

The house was always in darkness to save on the bills and William ignored her screams and protests as he'd dragged her to her room, this ghoulish shadow on the stairs, a cliché from a silent horror film.

And once he'd pulled her inside her bedroom, slammed the door behind them and dumped her on her bed, he would do unspeakable things; things that Susan still forced down to the depths of her mind. He would hurt her, he would make her cry and scream in pain. He would touch her in places where he shouldn't, places that were private, places that were hers. Later he would do more; later he would do much more. He would do things to her and he would make her do things to him, awful things.

But Susan had grown tall and by the age of 11 she was as big as her father, and the incidents slowed as she got stronger and he got weaker; until she'd made it stop.

She had been sat at the bottom of the stairs, pinching at her knuckles and rocking rhythmically to the sound of her father's playing, like she always did; only she had decided that the abuse had come to an end. She had waited for his shuffling feet, the turn of the handle and the sliding of the door over the threadbare carpet. Then, as her father appeared in the doorway – the ghoul on the stairs – and made to clasp her by the wrist, Susan had swung her fist back and punched him hard to his face, sending his reeling backwards.

He'd come at her then, his eyes full of fury and hate, but she had pushed him back hard, sending him tumbling over a hall table and into an undignified heap on the ground.

"If you ever do that again I'll tell mum," Susan had screeched at him. "And I'll tell the police as well."

The abuse stopped then and there, but the shadow on the stairs still came to her when she closed her eyes, still visited her and inflicted brutalities on her, and Susan knew it always would; the demon dragging the screaming little girl to her room, accompanied by the doleful tinkering of piano keys, temporarily silenced by the judge's clipped voice intervening into Susan's thoughts.

"As soon as the banks opened, on the Tuesday after the bank holiday, you were in the building society doing two things, just as you had intended to do – opening a new account in the joint names of yourself and your dead mother, closing two accounts in the joint names of your parents, and taking every penny out of them, about £40,000.

"You say £15,000 went to pay off a credit card.

"What happened to the rest is unclear. You suggested it went on memorabilia. Who knows? Either way, it went to you and Christopher Edwards and you spent it. For 15 years, the two of you took and spent over £175,000 which was payable to Patricia and William Wycherley in private pensions, state pensions, industrial injuries benefits, winter fuel payments and even Christmas bonus payments."

The demon wouldn't relent, it wouldn't leave her, and so Susan had filled her mind with friends – at first Charles and Winnie, standing strong, holding court in the corner of the lounge while Chris was out at work – rough men standing ready to visit violence on those that would do her harm.

But all the money had gone again and Susan and Chris had sold the books and the letters to pay off the bailiffs, and Winnie and Charles had gone away – leaving Susan to empty rooms and dark corridors, and the haunting thump of piano keys swirling in her mind.

She hadn't seen her parents for years – not since the big row in '92 when they'd stormed out, when mum had thrown her out and told her she'd known what her dad had done to her all along – told her she was a bitch, a slut; told her she deserved everything he'd done to her. Then whatever money they had just slipped away to nothing, like it always did. Chris was buying things to make her happy – replacing Winnie and Charles with Gary and Frank and Sammy and the others, filling the flat again, turning it into a gin palace in the days, drowning out her father's subdued keystrokes with tapping feet and jazz-band swing; and booze and cigarettes and flirty talk.

Susan had always suspected that Chris had known about the Ratpack boys – that they came to see her while he was out at the office. Chris wasn't the jealous type, so it didn't matter. He didn't really play Susan's games, but he knew about them all the same; he turned a blind eye to her gin-soaked other life because it kept her happy while he was away at work. He'd given her Winnie and Charles at first, then after the bailiffs had cleaned them out again he'd brought her Gary and the others to brighten up her days. And she much preferred them to dusty old Winston and Charles if the truth be told, who she only ever really liked to please Chris.

And when Susan had reciprocated, when she had given Chris Gerard Depardieu to be his new best friend, he had just played along with it without any real sense of excitement or belief. He'd known. He must have known; because why would Gerard Depardieu want to write letters to Christopher Edwards?

Only over the years Chris had dutifully read all of Gerard's letters, meticulously written back with his own stories and news, passing his scribblings to Susan and asking her to post them for him; knowing they'd go into the fire, or be stored away in a box or a bottom drawer until Susan could work out what to do with them.

So when they decided to kill Bill and Pat, when *Susan* decided to make Chris kill Bill and Pat, it became just another fantasy to add to the long list of make-believes between them.

It was no more real than Gerard Depardieu, or Winnie and Charles, or Gary and the Rat Pack boys. Only it *was* real. It was *all* real. It was all *so* real.

And after they'd done it, after Bill and Pat were in the ground, then the lie became the truth until they really couldn't remember what they had done. And when Bill and

Pat were in the ground the piano stopped in Susan's head and the shadow on the stairs went away.

"I hate him, Chris," she had said, the last time after the bailiffs had been.

"He abused me when I was a child and he robbed me when I was an adult. Can't we kill them, Chris? Can't we kill them both and take my money back?"

"I could kill them," Chris had replied, resting his hand on her knee. "I could kill them with that gun I kept."

Keeping Bill and Pat alive became the next game. Gerard never bothered writing after they shot the Wycherleys.

He didn't need to.

"Having carried out these ruthless killings you got rid of the bodies. I use that phrase deliberately. This was in no sense a burial. There was no dignity, no respect. The point of this was to cover up the killings and move onto the next stage of your plan. You wrapped the bodies in duvet covers, you dragged them down the stairs. You told the neighbours that Mr and Mrs Wycherley had gone on holiday, and then, in due course, that they had decided to sell the house.

"Susan Edwards, you concocted and sent lively and imaginative notes and Christmas cards to relatives to give the impression that your parents were traveling around Ireland, where the air was good. The relatives were completely taken in by your lies – no one asked a single question. You wrote letters to the doctor's surgery when reminders came for vaccinations and the like, refusing them on plausible grounds. But before you began writing letters to maintain the fiction that your parents were still alive, you had first got on with what you were really interested in – getting their money."

Their subdued little flat in Lille, the only light coming through the windows, the only noise coming from the streets – the chatter of voices and the rattle of trams below; and Christopher's calming words in Susan's ear.

"Do you remember the story, Susan? Do you remember the lie? Do you remember how you went up to Mansfield on that May Day bank holiday, after your mum called you in floods of tears, saying she was sick of your dad and that she couldn't cope? She was frantic, Susan, she was desperate; your daughterly instincts kicked in – no matter what had happened in the past, no matter what your father had done to you. It was your mum, and blood was thicker than water.

"Do you remember getting drunk with your mum, and your dad being vile? Do you remember the gunshots in the night and your heavy feet on the hallway carpet; you reaching out blindly into the darkness with your hands?

"Do you remember what you saw in their bedroom – Bill lying dead on the floor, Pat standing over him with her smoking gun? Do you remember the argument that followed? Do you remember picking up the gun from the bed; you frantic, petrified and alone?

"Do you remember your mother's lies and poison and bile? Do you remember her telling you she knew your father had raped you? She told you that very night, Susan, just before you pulled the trigger on her. It wasn't six years earlier; that night in 1992 when they'd thrown us out of the house; the house that you had paid for?

"Do you remember burying the bodies, how we didn't know what to do, so we'd put them in the garden? Do you remember carrying them downstairs in the dead of night and throwing them into that pit I dug in the lawn?

"Detail, Susan. Remember the detail.

"Do you remember fish and chips and watching Dana International win the Eurovision Song Contest? We did do that, but it was back in our flat in London the week after we'd buried your parents. It was just such a lovely detail.

"Do you remember the money, and how we had no choice but to take it, to write the letters and the cards? Do you remember everything, Susan, everything you need to remember?"

And Susan had remembered, standing there in the dock, listening to the judge tearing her story to ribbons; just as she had remembered it as Christopher had led her by the hand from their shabby little Lille flat for the final time, as they'd made their way to the Eurostar terminal. She remembered as he'd closed the door on their brand-new life, which they'd lived for less than a year; leaving the keys in the lock for the landlord to find, looking out for him again in the streets below.

'I remember everything, Chris,' she had thought as they'd walked through the town, munching like beggars on a still-warm baguette.

'I remember everything, Chris,' she thought again as she glanced at Christopher Edwards in the periphery of her vision, standing to the left of her in the dock; just as he'd been as he'd walked her through the streets of France for the final time.

Susan had wanted to tell him about how she'd picked up the bullets from the bedroom floor and put them in a plastic bag with the gun, and thrown them away in a bin somewhere. That was a nice piece of detail, just like the fish and chips. Only that had been Gary's idea and she didn't want Chris to be angry. They held hands; they didn't stop holding hands as they walked through the streets; until they clambered onto the train after the guard waved them through. Susan didn't recall holding Christopher's hand after that, or speaking to him after that; and she knew now that she never would again as the judge's toneless voice brought her back, once again into the light-drenched courtroom.

"You obtained loans and credit cards in Mrs Wycherley's name, and still the spending continued and you decided the house would be sold. You forged the necessary documents and kept the proceeds of sale, just under £67,000. Christopher Edwards, you said you were against the house being sold because it would mean losing control of what you described as the burial site. And so it would. But your concern was only for the two of you – that this loss of control might lead to discovery."

Susan remembered the baking bus in the early summer sun – crawling through London from Victoria up to Golder's Green, her and Chris sitting in silence, not talking, not touching; Susan staring ahead, Chris looking out of the window.

He had watched motionless as they finally broke out beyond the North Circular, out onto the foot of the motorway to start the long drag north – London's outer suburbs finally giving way to fields of green and wheat, scrubland and the occasional commuter town on the sun-drenched horizon.

Chris had stored their bag in the racks above his head. It contained very little – a single change of clothes for them both, toothbrushes, a razor, deodorant, a revolver and a box of bullets.

Occasionally he glanced upwards at it nervously; like he was fearful it may suddenly fall with a jolt, spilling its guilty contents onto the floor; or being taken accidentally by another traveller who had mistaken it for their own.

Chris had handed in everything apart from his Colt Commando. He liked the feel of it too much; he liked its weight and the roughness of its grip in his hand; the fierce kickback it gave when he pulled the trigger. He had been expecting a knock on the door at some point – some police-man or government busybody who'd noticed that he'd owned three guns but had only turned in two. But nobody ever asked; nobody ever came knocking – and so the gun had sat largely forgotten in a bottom drawer, occasionally rediscovered, taken out and handled by cautious hands, giddy to feel its full glory once again.

Milton Keynes had come and gone, Susan and Christopher sitting on the vibrating bus, looking out on the ugly concrete coach station, oblivious to the new faces climbing onboard, looking for a place to sit.

Then it was Leicester, then Nottingham, its own bus station an even uglier underground bunker opposite the courthouse. But they'd sat in silence, Susan and Christopher, appreciating the cool darkness away from the stifling sunshine; knowing there was just one more stop before they could clamber off into the breeze of the early evening.

And eventually Mansfield had arrived, its own bus station nothing more than a potholed concrete square, surrounded by steel railings and littered with beer bottles, pizza boxes, scrunched-up chip wrappers, used condoms and vomit.

A seagull pecked at a forgotten chip while a shirtless teenager kicked a football at a wall, his friends sharing a joint away from the stare of the CCTV cameras.

They wandered through the town, allowing the evening wind to blow at their faces, cooling and chilling the sweat patches under their arms, on their chests; closing their eyes and letting the breeze whip at their flimsy hair.

Susan had called ahead, a few days before. Mum had cried when she'd heard her voice, a sob that soon became an unstoppable stream of joy and grief and giddy excitement, like she had just been contacted by a long-dead loved one.

"I never thought I'd hear your voice again, Susan," she had blurted. "I thought I'd go to my grave regretting what I said to you, saying those things, siding with dad."

The sobs in Patricia's voice raised tears in Susan for an instant, as she remembered her sat on a step at a long-ago party, or singing along to the musicians in the streets of Memphis. But it was merely selfishness, Susan realised. It was just mum wanting to be loved, not wanting to be lonely anymore, or alone anymore. And it was too late.

"You must come and see us, you must bring Christopher,"

302

she had gabbled in her excitement. "Come for the bank holiday weekend. The neighbours will be away. We can all have a drink and raise the roof and we won't upset anybody."

"And dad? What about dad?"

"Don't you worry about him. He's a pussycat these days. He's old and doddery. He's had his sting pulled out."

They had both laughed at that, although Susan's smile hadn't spread to her eyes.

As they'd neared the house, they stopped at the corner shop; a bottle of gin for mum and a bottle of Scotch for dad, just to show there were no hard feelings. Then finally they'd walked around the corner into Blenheim Close, where Susan knocked on the door.

Patricia opened it immediately, folding her arms around her daughter and weeping uncontrollably. Susan cried too, throwing her own arms around her; but Susan's were tears of sorrow. As they stepped over the threshold Christopher rubbed his hand down the side of his bag, feeling through the canvas for the shape of the revolver and the box of shells. Then he closed the door.

"Susan Edwards, 30 years ago you told your husband that you had been sexually abused by your father when you were a little girl. You told the police the same thing, and repeated it to the jury in your trial.

"Because you are an accomplished liar and a fantasist I have hesitated before accepting this. However there is evidence, wholly independent of the two of you, that when you were married, William Wycherley was irrationally jealous. On reflection and balance therefore I accept that your father had sexually assaulted you when you were young. The abuse stopped when you were 11. You left home in your early 20s."

Susan broke down suddenly, her face cracking and her shoulders rolling.

Christopher reached out to touch her hand, unreciprocated; only the judge hadn't finished.

"That background may well explain why you hated him, which you did, and why you have no remorse about killing him. But given that you left home in the early 1980s, some 15 years before the murders, I cannot accept that his conduct, wholly wrong as it was, explains your decision to kill him in 1998.

"There was, however, something that you held against both your parents for many years. When you were 21 you were left £10,000. Some of it you spent on holidays for yourself and your mother, and the rest was used in the purchase of your parents' home in Edgware. Your name was on the deeds. You say that your parents emotionally blackmailed you into signing over your interest in the house to them. That was in 1983 and it is plain from your interviews and from your evidence in the trial that you considered then and still consider that your parents had deprived you of what you thought was rightfully yours. They sold that house at a profit, and bought a cheaper house in Mansfield. They kept all of the proceeds. You never forgave them. Your resentment festered for years and at the same time you were getting yourself into debt."

Susan's ears closed off again and she was remembering the end of an evening of whisky and gin; mum slurring her words, dad sleepy on Scotch, even Chris unsteady on his feet, breaking his sobriety for a dose of Dutch courage.

They were all sleepy and a little bit drunk, all putting off their beds for reasons of their own.

Patricia was still gushing, joyful and grateful; an elderly lady who'd received a surprise visit from a neglectful grandson she thought had forgotten about her. William was pensive and cautious, but affable almost; the past six years and the spinning of the earth had taken away what remained of his poison. He was weak and spent, looking for restitution somehow. Chris was slumped on the corner of the sofa, not watching the telly; rather staring out of the window at the lights in the houses opposite, while Susan sat passively, sipping on gin, quiet and waiting.

"Right, I'm going up," William Wycherley had said finally, struggling to his feet.

Susan watched him make his way unsteadily to the door, relying on his stick to keep him upright. They all listened to his shuffling feet down the hallway, his delicate soles on the stairs, creaking lightly on every step; the thump on his feet on the landing upstairs, followed by the sound of his bedroom door gliding closed with a thud and the clicking of a light being switched on.

Pat had carried on talking but she was making less and less sense; just laughing and crying in equal measures, occasionally rising to her feet, staggering to Susan and giving her another tearful hug.

Eventually she had gone up too, aiming for the door on her own now-unsteady feet.

Then Susan and Christopher had sat in silence, enduring the awkward weight of the living room and the creaks of the house settling into sleep. They had sat for a long time.

"Are you coming up?" Susan had asked eventually, rising to her feet.

There was no answer for a moment.

"Chris?"

"No," he replied, vacantly. "No, I think I'll stay down here for a bit. You go up though. I might watch the end of Eurovision."

"That's next weekend."

Susan made her way heavily up the stairs, feeling her way down the corridor to the back bedroom, finding the door and fumbling her way to the bed.

The gin went to work and she drifted, finding temporary sleep and flashing dreams; flickering back to consciousness every now and then, listening out for the noises in the night. She laid on top of the bed in all of her clothes, listening; the hiss of passing cars, a barking dog, a drunken couple arguing on their way home from a night out on the town.

Then finally, eventually, she had fallen down into the deep pit of sleep where she found nothing but oblivion. She didn't hear the footsteps on the stairs, or the sliding of the door. She didn't hear the light clicking on, the first bang of the gun, the scream in the night, the thump to the floor, or the outraged shout that was suddenly cut short.

But she did hear the second.

Then she was flying across the room, her hands outstretched – finding the door with her fingers, finding the landing with her feet, all the time reaching out to the thin strip of light that marked the entrance to her parents' bedroom.

"Chris?"

No answer.

"Chris?" she screamed.

"Don't come in."

But her hands had found the doorknob and she pushed against it heavily.

"Don't come in, Susan."

But she was in. Mum was dead. Dad was dying; and Chris was standing over them both, lowering his revolver and looking around like he'd just concluded a duel.

Christopher had killed them. Susan had made him. The judge had said so.

"You are both in your late 50s and you are going to spend most, if not all, of the rest of your lives in prison. I accept that prison has been very difficult for both of you. Susan Edwards, I accept that you are particularly isolated and will remain so throughout your sentence.

"Christopher Edwards, Susan Edwards, the sentence I impose upon each of you is the same. On each count of murder, life imprisonment with a minimum term to be served before you are considered for parole of 25 years."

Then Mrs Justice Thirlwall nodded to the guards.

"Take them down," she said.

Keys rattled and chains clinked, as an iron door swung open with a heavy, metallic whine.

Susan looked out at the sea of condemning faces for a final time and picked out the features of the young detective who had questioned her; the one that was Montgomery Clift. He looked straight at her – no emotion, no compassion or condemnation that she could detect; just relief, like he was closing a chapter. Then he rose to his feet, pulled a phone out of his pocket and went to the door without a backwards glance.

As Susan was led firmly down the stairs, her hands behind her and cuffed so tightly it pinched, it felt a little like she was descending into Hell, almost willingly. Her guard drove her heavily down the stone steps to the corridor below, his heavy boots thudding on the tiles. Over her shoulder Christopher took out what was left of the light, which vanished entirely when the iron door was slammed behind them.

It was no dungeon they were in, more a bunker; all straight lines and square concrete walls and floors, neat strip-lighting, vents and the steady buzz of electricity through the walls.

Susan was forced further down the corridor, back to the tiny cell where she would wait for her prison transport and the apologetic handshake from her barrister.

All around her there was the noise of laughter and shouting and screaming; the slamming of doors, and weeping and wailing.

Do you remember the story, Susan? Do you remember the lie?

'It wasn't a lie,' Susan thought. 'It wasn't a lie.'

Then she heard the tinker of piano keys, along with the slap of her flat shoes on the concrete floor; Chris behind her, his footsteps behind her, suddenly out of step, then falling silent with the slamming of a cell door.

Piano keys.

Gary Cooper greeted her half way down the strip; all slick-haired, strong-jawed and smart, wearing a guard's uniform.

"Hello, Gary", she said and smiled, but he didn't reciprocate.

"This way please, Mrs Edwards."

He led her to a room right down at the far end, his frame casting a pitch shadow along the soulless walls.

There was light coming from inside her cell, and the sound of a tinkering piano. Susan hoped it was Sammy and Frank and the gang, hanging out and having a ball, waiting for her to join the party. She hoped that Gary would come in as well, spark up a cigarette and sip on a whisky.

But the playing in there was too sullen and morose, Susan realised as she was forced ever closer to the cell door. The playing was too sombre to be Sammy on the keys; too operatic and dark. It was an old man that Susan could hear playing; a dead man's fingers soullessly hammering at the ivories, hitting at the keys mechanically, like there was no joy left to be found in them.

Epilogue

*Fourteen people went to the Wycherleys' funeral on 11
July. None of them could say they knew the couple they
were mourning. Bill's nieces came, as did several victim
support officers, Sue Bramley and her daughter, who now
live at 2 Blenheim Close, and a reporter from the local
paper – Jenny Kleeman, The Guardian, Saturday, October
25, 2014.*

It's grey and muggy with tepid heat and overcast skies – a
gloom in the air that can't be explained; disappointment
perhaps over a promising early Summer that has turned to
rain and heavy skies from the first day of July.

I'm due a holiday; a few weeks away from my desk
where I can fly out to the sunshine, stick my head in a
book, drink too much and not care what's happening in
the news. Only it's still a month away and I'm treading
water in the office, back in the grind of charity bike rides,
and muckraking over what the council might be up to.

I've been bored, to be fair; until today. Today is different.

I stand outside the crematorium with a small huddle of
people; none of us really talking, none of us really knowing
each other, apart from a small smattering of relatives.

I stand outside the small chapel while my photographer, Anne, loiters on the corner, waiting for the cortege to slide into view.

Then, with the rustle of tyres on gravel, the sudden clicking stutter of Anne's camera firing into life, and the hushing of voices from those assembled, two pristinely silver hearses pulled around the corner and came to a halt, almost like an apology.

Two coffins made from a faded ash emerge and are carried inside by a team of undertakers who almost outnumber the mourners. There is one dignified bouquet on each of them; one says 'Bill', the other 'Pat'. We fall in behind them, all fourteen of us following William and Patricia Wycherley; their defiled bones hidden away in off-white caskets.

I'd been asked to attend by the relatives, by William's nieces Hilary Rose and Christine Harford. I'm the only journalist there; sworn to secrecy to avoid another media scrum at the cemetery gates. Apart from Christine and Hilary and their families, there are a couple of police family liaison officers; there's no sign of Griffin or his sidekick. Griffin has moved back into uniform temporarily to get a superintendent's stripe on his seldom-worn uniform.

Then there is me, a humanist preacher and Sue Bramley, who lives at 2 Blenheim Close now, along with her daughter. Sue loves the house and doesn't want to move.

There is no sign of Vivian Steenson.

The humanist preacher gives a sanitised and clinical account of William's early life; little is known of Patricia. He recounts chapel meetings in clapped-out halls, music played on Sunday nights, and temperance; miners down the pit six days a week and William's desire for escape and adventure.

The preacher mentions William's time in Canada, but not why he went there, or why he waited so long after the war to return. There is no mention of child abuse and conflict and family feuds. There is no mention of William bullying his daughter out of her inheritance, or trying to force her out of her marriage. There is no mention of Susan at all. There are just miners and terraced houses, clapped out meeting halls, and poverty, almost stolen from a Lawrence novel. He talks about William's musical talents as a young man; his desire to live a quiet life in older age; and little else. And so it comes to an end and slowly, deliberately, people begin to file out, getting heavily to their feet before heading to the door and the drab daylight beyond.

But I remain in my seat. I wait until they have all departed, all the assembled, tucking in my knees to let them pass, nodding sympathy at those who file out from the benches in front of me. There are tears. I spot Hilary Rose sobbing at one point, her husband reaching out and clasping a hand to her knee; the other folding around her.

Finally the room contains me and two coffins and I rise to my feet and walk slowly, warily to the front of the chapel; placing myself between them. On top of each box is a wreath with a solitary card pinned to its centre. A hand-scribbled note on both reads, 'Finally at rest'. I linger for a moment, then I walk to the door and head out into the early afternoon gloom. Hilary Rose comes to join me.

"We're going for lunch," she says. "Will you come?"

"I'd love to," I say, "but I can't. I've got to get this written up then head out to a council meeting."

She nods a sad smile and takes my hand.

"We're going to take the wreaths back to Blenheim Close," she says, "after we've eaten. We're going to fill the house with flowers."

I drive back to the office and write my story. Then I head to my council meeting and sit through it; bored and disinterested, before returning to the office again to churn out more words; telling myself that I'm too old now to still be working at ten at night when I've been here since eight in the morning, wondering whether one day I'll listen.

I turn off the lights and I head down the stairs; set the alarm, lock the front doors and fumble for my car keys. I look at the now-darkened sky and the abandoned car park. I imagine my story about the Wycherleys' funeral already whizzing around in the ether above my head; already being read by people in Manhattan, Milan or Malibu, and suddenly I feel old.

I look up at our luridly-green newspaper masthead hanging precariously above the front door to the office – no longer open to the public since they laid off the counter staff; the office situated on an out-of-town business park, nestled between the new pub, the car showroom and the mental hospital.

It will be almost a week from now before the Wycherleys' funeral appears in print. It will be almost a week from now before the old people of Mansfield will remember that weird murder that happened over in Forest Town the year before, and be reminded of it by the front page on the newsstands as they shuffle past. I lean against the boot of my battered old Saab, I put my hands in my pockets and I look up again at the ugly green sign.

"Your days are numbered, old son" I tell it, like I'm putting a dying relative to bed. "Your days are numbered . . . and so are mine."

It starts to rain and I clamber into the driver's seat and gun the engine. I hook a right, and then another, onto the dual carriageway that skirts the town; the one that takes traffic away from Mansfield towards the dying Lincolnshire seaside towns for weekends away; the one where people get killed all the time.

I turn on my wipers and I rub at my eyes, squinting at the night and the drizzle on the windscreen, as the blades flick away the downpour; me, staring into the darkness and ignoring the blinding lights that keep coming towards me.

Afterword

I wrote this book after I was contacted by a couple of true crime production companies wanting me to participate in documentaries about the Wycherley Murders, and the BBC who, at the time, were considering commissioning a drama about the case. I did take part – I'm probably too vain not to have done. But it did get me thinking, and it made me feel like the story that I knew better than anyone else, the story that I was in from the start and saw through to the bitter end, was slowly being taken from me. I had to set it down, how I saw it and lived it . . . and so here it is, my version of events.

Despite what I wrote early in Chapter 1, DI Tony Rawlins is a fictional character, or perhaps more a mishmash of a number of serving police officers that I spoke to about the case, both during the investigation and the subsequent trial, as well as afterwards while I was preparing this book. As a necessity, Rawlins had to be created because the identities of these people needed to be protected. But he is fictional all the same, and any opinions he expresses throughout the narrative; any memory he shares with the reader are my own or my invention. Estelle, the police press officer, is a combination of any number of different people

I dealt with from the Nottinghamshire Police press office regarding the murders. She is not based on any of them, and is effectively an invention – again a necessity. Adamson is also a creation, along with Christopher Edward's boss at the office.

Rob Griffin is real, as is Stuart Hamilton, Khaldoun Kabbani, Martin Hall and all the lawyers who took part in the trial, and I have made every effort to only place them in the narrative in accordance with the record, where they were and what they did. I have also endeavoured not to put words into their mouths – what they say in the book, they said at the time, or as near as I could recreate. What they did in the book, they did at the time. Ash, Nick Frame, Phil, Helen and Issy are all real people, and I have attempted to capture their personalities, hopefully without causing offense.

In truth, this book would never have made it out there without the help, support and assistance of many other people, and I am indebted to Gayle Whelan for her initial feedback on what would become the penultimate draft, and to Kate Belcher for her endless support and encouragement, for spotting my typos and correcting my tenses. Kate, you invested in this, and I will be forever grateful. And thank you to Jenny Kleeman, for reading various drafts, and for offering your support, and for kicking me up the backside to get it written, without ever realising it. I am also indebted to the relatives of the Wycherleys for inviting me in. I truly know how painful this must have been for you all.

I am indebted to all those current and former police officers and other officials who spoke to me during my investigations, to all those friends who chipped in in numerous ways, to Rachel and Ollie, for turning me loose to spend endless evenings alone over several years to write this book. I am grateful to you most of all.

I am indebted to Andrew Tennant and Liam Relph for their talent, patience and understanding in all things design, to Sheila for helping me over the final hurdle, to Helen Faccio and Mark Taylor Batty for their last-minute input, and to a lady who I shall only refer to as Edna, who told me her story and would only talk to me.

Andy Done-Johnson, February, 2020.

Printed in Great Britain
by Amazon